OUTSIDER

A RYKER RETURNS THRILLER

ROB SINCLAIR

Print ISBN 978-1-914614-59-0

ALSO BY ROB SINCLAIR

Imposter 13

1

PRAGUE, CZECHIA

Sunrise remained over an hour away, though the glow of street lights, seeping in through a gap between the thin curtains, softly lit the bedroom in the cramped apartment. James Ryker's eyes were open, his gaze resting on the slender shape of the figure next to him. She was asleep, breathing lightly, her loose dark hair draped over her bare shoulders.

Ryker rose from the mattress, being careful not to pull the tussled duvet from her naked body. No need to rouse her.

In the grip of winter, the heating in the apartment was adequate but the space was hardly toasty. Away from the warmth of the bed, Ryker's skin prickled as he edged over to the window. He pulled the curtains a little further apart and peered to the street below. On the second floor of the five-storey building, he hardly had a glorious view of the city here – simply the walls and windows of the other blocks that surrounded this one. It wasn't a scenic view Ryker was interested in. He was interested in the street. The people in it. The vehicles. A near subconscious habit.

He studied the few pedestrians and parked cars. Nothing to worry about there.

As quietly as he could, Ryker pulled on his clothes. He went to the bathroom, closed the door, then turned on the light. He glanced at himself in the mirror. No doubt he looked as fresh this morning as he had done most mornings these last few weeks. He'd enjoyed his time here. With her. He was sure he'd enjoy many more mornings, afternoons, evenings here – if he stayed.

He wouldn't.

He turned off the bathroom light then stepped back into the bedroom. He moved over to the bed. She hadn't stirred. Her eyes remained closed. He picked up his bag and turned for the door.

'You'd really leave without saying goodbye?'

He paused. Closed his eyes for a beat, then opened them again as he turned to face her. She shuffled up a little in the bed and pulled the duvet higher, above her chest, clutching the soft, warm fabric like a comforter.

'You were sleeping,' he said.

They held each other's gaze for a few moments and the silence grew increasingly taut and uncomfortable. For Ryker at least. The look on her face, in the poorly lit room, was hard to gauge. Disappointment? Anger? A little bit of both, he thought, and both were understandable.

'Is this really it?' she asked.

'You knew I wouldn't stay forever.'

'You don't have anywhere else to go.'

'That's not really the point.'

'Then what is the point?'

He couldn't explain. Not even to himself, so certainly not to her.

The easiest explanation was that he was leaving in order to protect her – not an untruth, exactly – but stating his reasons so simply would only open up far too many further questions. Questions he wouldn't give her an answer to. She wasn't the first person he'd left under such circumstances. Likely she wouldn't be the last.

The problem? Ryker's past. For nearly twenty years, carrying out his government's dirty work, travelling the globe, fulfilling their secretive and shady orders, Ryker had built far more enemies than friends. Enemies who remained a threat as long as he still breathed.

He was sure he'd left that life behind him for good now, but he'd never truly settle. He'd initially started this nomadic life to protect his good friend, Sam Moreno, after heat from his past had nearly seen her killed. Before her lay a string of similarly fateful ends, the painful memories of which clawed at his troubled mind daily.

If he stayed in Prague, how long before Simona, too, became embroiled in his dark past?

Yet that wasn't the full or only explanation for him needing to leave. Another factor was that the longer he stayed, the more he'd fall for her. Even after his troubled life, Ryker was more than capable of love, but he'd do all that he could to avoid it.

'I'll miss you,' she said.

He moved over to her and sat down on the edge of the bed and put his hand on hers. He leaned over and kissed her on the forehead.

'I'll miss you too.'

As he pulled back he held her eye again. But not for long. He had nothing left to say. No point in prolonging the difficult moment.

Ryker got up from the bed, and headed for the door.

2

BLODSTEIN, NORWAY

The blasting wind pelted Sigurd Berg's already weathered face with sleety rain. His cheeks stung. His lips were chafed raw. His nose streamed. He was sure he'd look like some fucking dumb caricature of Rudolph.

Of all the nights to be doing this...

With a constant grating, scraping noise, he scrabbled and heaved the barrel across the tarmac. Not rolled. He couldn't afford to put the thing on its side and risk the lid popping open and the contents spilling out. The edge of the dock was ten yards away. Beyond it, the inky salt water rippled under the dim light of the moon that was throttled by dark clouds. Berg shivered as he looked out.

Lifeless.

He heaved again and the barrel moved all of a few inches. He was out of breath, his heart pounded his ribs. But this would all be over with soon enough. The first barrel was already on board.

Berg took a breath and grit his teeth and pushed with more effort still. Finally some momentum. In a single burst of strength and energy and endeavour the barrel shifted a few feet, then a few more. Finally the end was in sight.

He froze when he heard a car engine. Nearby. The fact the sound had cut through the howling wind confirmed it was close. He whipped his head around. He'd left on a single light in the factory, in the office area. From out here the inner illumination was only faintly visible through the sporadic, grimy translucent panels in the warehouse roof.

Berg glanced from beyond the factory to the road. Sure enough, two bright headlight beams bounced into view as the vehicle came over the hump toward the entrance to the yard.

He groaned, took his hands from the barrel and strode away. At least the wind was behind him now, pushing him forward with vigour.

He reached the side door to the warehouse area as the car came to a pause at the closed gates. With the glare of the headlights he had no clue who was behind the wheel. He slipped inside and closed the door behind him then stared across the space. The office was in the opposite corner. Why hadn't he turned the light off after he'd pushed the last barrel outside?

He heard a car door open then close. A clunk as the outer gates opened. Berg rushed over and into the office, and slid in behind his desk.

Shit. Hat. Gloves. Coat. Berg stripped them all off quickly and stuffed them under the desk then fired up his computer and stared at the screen just as the figure came into view in the open doorway.

He jumped theatrically.

'Marius! What the hell?'

Marius was one of two warehouse managers. Berg's employee, technically.

'What's going on?' Marius said, his suspicion clear, even if he was speaking to his boss.

Berg got to his feet, narrowed his eyes. 'What are you doing here? At this time of night?'

That was the way to do it. Push back. Make *him* feel uncomfortable.

Marius looked a little taken aback. 'I was... I was passing by. I thought I saw a light on. I did warn you about security. You know–'

'Yes, I know. Rosen Tech's factory was broken into last month. Thank you.'

Rosen Tech's sleek new factory was a little over half a mile from here. A huge, space-age structure that had cost hundreds of millions of kroner. Berg remained dubious as to how his lifelong peer – essentially competitor – Erik Rosen had found the investment for that. He would be lying if he said he hadn't smiled broadly when he'd heard the place had been ransacked one night. Vandals, who'd destroyed millions' worth of equipment.

Why? Who knew.

Berg didn't want to know.

'Yeah, well, I just wanted to make sure everything was okay,' Marius said.

'It is. I'm just getting some details ready for the audit.'

Berg glanced at his watch. Quarter past two. He wanted to ask Marius where the hell he'd been until this time of night, but mostly he just wanted the guy to get lost.

'You're sure everything is okay?' Marius asked. 'You look...'

For some reason he didn't finish the sentence.

'I'm nearly done,' Berg said. 'You should get home. Doesn't your shift start at eight?'

Marius said nothing as he continued to stare. Then he nodded and looked back over to the main warehouse area.

'See you tomorrow then?' he said as he briefly glanced back.

'Yeah.'

He moved away. Berg craned his neck to follow his movement. Marius paused as he looked across the warehouse floor. What had he seen?

Berg's heart thudded in his chest even more quickly now than when he'd been outside. Had he made a mistake? He'd tried his best to clean up, but...

He looked across the office space. Weapon... weapon... there must be something.

Just outside the office. A wrench.

He got to his feet. Marius looked back over to him again. Seriously unimpressed about something...

But then he simply turned and walked for the exit.

Berg remained where he was. Didn't move a muscle. Not until he heard the car door. Then the engine. Then the gates. Open. Close. Engine fading.

Seconds later all he could hear was the wind and rain outside, and his erratic heartbeat.

He exhaled then took a few seconds to get his breathing under control before he strode out to the warehouse floor. He looked left, right, up, down.

No. Nothing there. Nothing suspicious at least.

But time was getting away from him. He had to get this done.

He grabbed his hat, gloves and coat, put them all back on, then moved out into the bitter night once more. He glanced toward the gates. No one there now.

Unless Marius had sneaked around the corner or something? But why would he do that?

Berg put those silly thoughts to the side. Back to work. He fought against the wind and rain to reach the barrel. The weather seemed even worse now than before.

With renewed strength, he shoved the barrel the rest of the way, then as delicately as he could – which wasn't very delicate at all – he pushed the barrel over the edge and onto the deck of the boat. A thunderous thud echoed as the barrel smacked down, and the ship wobbled side to side. He jumped down beside the barrel and made sure it stayed upright. It did. Not a very delicate way to get the barrels on board, but the boat would be fine – it'd seen worse treatment than this out in the beastly North Sea.

He sighed in relief. Now that he, the barrels and their contents were all on board, tonight's journey would be a cinch.

Minutes later the engine chugged as the boat pushed away from the dock, and out into the infinite blackness. He didn't need to go far. Just far enough for the barrels to be well under, and out of sight forever.

He was less than two miles from shore when he turned off the engine and the boat slowed, rocking up and down on the choppy waves. Not the stormiest of nights, but still it would make the task of hauling the barrels over the edge that little bit more difficult.

Berg got to work. The first barrel went over the edge with relative ease. The second was harder – after all, its contents were that bit more weighty than the first. As he shoved and heaved and lifted, Berg imagined the top of the barrel peeling away. The contents spilling all over him and the ship's deck. The thought was enough to cause his stomach to turn over. Not helped by the constantly swaying craft he was standing on.

Finally, with a huge splash that sent a rush of freezing salt water all over him, the second barrel was in the sea, glugging out of sight, and on its way to the bottom.

Berg didn't move from the spot for a couple of minutes as he stared at the water. Quite why, he wasn't sure. Partly because he was waiting to see if either of the barrels would resurface. But how could they, with the weight inside? The other reason was because his mind was racing with calamitous thoughts, not least his imaginings of what other horrors lay down there at the bottom of the sea. This surely wasn't the first time someone had made a trip out here like this.

It was *his* first. He prayed it'd be the last.

Morose thoughts taking over, he slunk back inside the cabin and got the boat moving back to shore.

———

Four am had come and gone by the time Berg arrived home. He'd be up again at seven. In the bedroom, he stripped off and slipped into bed. His skin was ice cold all over. He didn't move over to Isabell. She was sleeping soundly and his coldness would surely disturb her.

No luck. He'd already managed to do that somehow. She groaned and sighed and turned over to face him.

'Where have you been?' she asked with her eyes still closed.

'Sorry,' was all he said to that.

He reached out and took her hand. She flinched a little but then wrapped her fingers around his.

'Is everything okay?'

'Yes,' he said. 'Yes. Of course.'

His voice had sounded sincere enough. He just hoped the darkness in the room helped to mask the lie.

3
_____

Rain battered down on the ferry as it made its approach to Norway. Few passengers were outside on the front deck. Ryker was. Even on a grim and grey winter's morning, the view of the mountains as they closed in on Trondheim was spectacular. Sweeping up from the sloshing grey salt water, the pine-covered mountains were draped in a blanket of snow, just wisps of green and brown here and there, the mountaintops obscured by a thick layer of mist that hung in place like a halo.

Water – equal measure of rain and sea spray – cascaded off Ryker's overcoat and trousers, but at least he was dressed for it with heavy-duty weatherproof gear. No point in coming to one of the wettest places on earth otherwise.

Despite the incredible scenery, memories of Prague and Simona burned in Ryker's mind as the ferry jostled over the rough sea.

Should he have stayed longer? Should he go back?

'It looks better on a clear day,' came a voice next to him.

Ryker turned to face the woman. A foot shorter than his tall frame, she wore a thick red windbreaker, the fur-edged hood pulled over her head, hiding part of her face. Her English was good, though it carried an obvious Scandinavian twang.

'It looks pretty good to me,' Ryker said.

She laughed. 'You don't mind the weather?'

'I've seen worse.'

She pulled the hood back a little to reveal more of her face. A nice face. He guessed she was late thirties, early forties. Her skin was soft and smooth-looking but held the finest of lines around the edges of her smile, and around her eyes which were a dazzling green – an attractive complement to her flowing red hair that was bunched around her face by her thick hood.

'At least it's not too cold,' she said.

It'd been far colder in Prague. Here, the oceanic climate meant relatively mild winters, although every season was wet, and the further north he chose to venture, the colder and snowier it would become.

'You're here for a holiday?' she asked.

Ryker paused a little before answering that one. 'Yeah. How did you know I was English?'

She looked a little taken aback by the accusatory tone, but his mind was naturally whirring with thoughts. It wasn't at all unlike his past to creep up on him wherever he went. Had this woman approached him with an ulterior motive?

'Just a good guess,' she said.

Ryker wasn't so sure about that.

'You're staying in Trondheim?' she asked.

'I haven't decided yet.'

She laughed and brushed the water off the front of her coat. A pointless exercise really. More a gesture to emphasise whatever point she was about to make.

'I'm soaked. I think I'll go back inside. You can... come and tell me all about your trip.'

Ryker held her eye for a few moments. An image of Simona flashed in his mind. But what was he supposed to do? For all he knew he'd never be back in that city again, never mind in her bed.

'Yeah, why not,' he said.

An hour later and the ramps were down and the cars emptied out of the wide open jaws of the hull one after the other. Ryker was one of only four foot passengers. Heidi wasn't. She was in her car somewhere within the mess of other vehicles behind him. A marine biologist, she lived a half hour's drive from the ferry terminal in the centre of Trondheim. She'd offered to give Ryker a lift to wherever he was staying. He declined. Primarily because he didn't yet know where he was staying, but also because he hadn't even set foot on Norwegian soil yet and didn't want to have any ties to this place so soon. Instead, they'd exchanged numbers, though her ability to contact him was dependent on him keeping his burner phone. Which was likely only in the immediate short term.

Still, the chat he'd had with her had been relaxed and natural and made him relish what was to come from this new land all the more.

Ryker made his way out over the ramp, and onto the pavement of the dock. The rain had lightened, the scene in front of him more clear. The city's buildings rose into the mountains that closeted around them. The peaks of the mountains, way up high in the distance, had nothing but snow on them, covering the rocks and trees.

Beyond the expansive dock area, where two other large ferries were unloading, the water's edge was dotted with quaint buildings with pointed roofs, and timber-clad walls that were painted a variety of vibrant colours. Pretty. But Ryker had already decided on his approach here that he wasn't going to stay in the city. Not yet anyway. His appetite had been whetted by those spectacular views of the mountains and fjords. And after Prague he wanted to escape urban life for a while.

As he strode across the tarmac, the car next to him slowed. Heidi, of course. She wound down the window of her green BMW and beamed him a smile.

'You sure you don't want a ride?'

'I'm good.'

She looked disappointed. 'See you around then.'

Was that a parting comment, or a hopeful question? Ryker wasn't sure.

'Yeah,' he said, before her window glided up and her car grumbled off toward the road.

Time for Ryker to find his own transportation.

Another hour and a half later and he was in a rented Volvo – he was in Scandinavia after all – travelling further north, away from civilisation, and into the snow and cold. The twisting road he found himself on was a good hundred feet from the rippling water of the fjord to his left. To the other side of him the pine-covered mountain rose tall, no end in sight, such was the steepness of the elevation. Even after travelling for only a few miles from the city, he saw little sign of life, few cars on the road. A shame, in a way, that more people hadn't experienced such a dramatic landscape.

Ryker's distraction got the better of him. As he rounded a slight bend in the road, he only spotted the moped at the last second. The road was hardly wide, but it was certainly wide enough for two cars to pass, but the driver of the tiny moped came way over the central line. Ryker pumped the brake pedal, honked his horn. The moped swerved and missed the front of Ryker's car by all of a few inches before shooting off past him. Ryker, his car slowed right down, glanced in his rear-view mirror to follow the moped as it whizzed away. Except despite avoiding the crash, the driver wobbled about all over. The back and forth worsened, the brake light came on... the next second the moped flipped to the side and the driver skidded off onto the greasy road as the bike smacked up against the rocky verge.

Ryker slammed the brake and was out of the car a second later, rushing over to the fallen figure.

'Hey!' Ryker shouted out. 'You okay?'

The figure groaned – a man, or a boy? – and rolled over, then propped himself up. He was slight. Dressed in jeans and a thin jacket, both of which were now sopping wet. Hardly adequate attire for riding a two-wheeler. The low-speed fall had at least saved him from serious injury. Ryker kneeled down as the guy pulled the helmet from his head. Not a man at all. A teenager. All of fourteen, fifteen. His youthful face was creased in pain. He blurted something angrily at Ryker.

'Sorry? My Norwegian isn't too good.'

'Asshole,' he said to Ryker, shrugging him off.

Ryker was about to bite back at that, but didn't. The kid had been on his side of the road. What had Ryker done wrong?

'Are you okay?' Ryker asked again. The kid groggily stood up. He seemed fine. Probably a few bruises, a few scrapes where he'd rattled across the tarmac, but his clothes had no obvious bloody tears.

The boy said nothing. How much English did he have? He was scrawny. His skin pale. He was a bag of bones. He went to walk away.

'Hey, wait a minute,' Ryker said as he grabbed his arm.

'Fuck off,' the kid said, whipping his arm away. Ryker noted the graze down the left side of his face. His eye was swollen up.

Those weren't from the crash.

'What happened to you?' Ryker asked as the boy stormed toward his crumpled motor.

A blast of a siren from behind Ryker. He turned to see a police car coming past his Volvo. Its lights weren't on. The siren had been to get their attention. Ryker remained in position as the car came to a stop. A few yards away the boy had reached his moped and hastily tried to pull it up and to untwist the front end.

A portly policeman got out of the car, popped a hat over his head.

He rattled off something in Norwegian. It wasn't clear if he was speaking to Ryker or the kid.

'It's okay,' Ryker said. 'He fell off, but he's fine.'

The policeman glared at Ryker for a second before turning to the boy.

'Henrik,' he shouted out.

The boy took no notice. He was on the moped now. He tried to start it up. The motor chugged away but to no avail. What was the kid doing?

A pickup truck approached at speed from the opposite direction. Had they not seen? Ryker waved his arms about and at the last moment the black Nissan Navara came to a sudden, rocking stop. Ryker peered beyond the glass. Two men up front. The diesel engine remained grumbling. Both men remained in their seats. He didn't like the looks on their faces.

Henrik groaned in frustration and kicked the moped before stepping off and tossing it to the ground. He looked from the pickup, to Ryker, to the policeman. Desperation in his eyes.

The policeman spoke to him again, a little more conciliatory this time. Henrik didn't budge.

'What's going on?' Ryker asked the policeman.

'It's fine,' the policeman said. 'I know him. I'll take him back to his home.'

Except the kid didn't seem too interested in that.

The policeman walked toward Ryker.

'What's your name?' he said.

'Carl.'

'Carl what?'

'Carl Logan.'

He seemed to contemplate something.

'Okay, Carl. You don't need to worry about this. It was an accident. Where were you going anyway?'

'North.'

An odd look from the policeman. 'Well, you keep on going then. Let me sort this out.'

Ryker didn't budge from the spot. The policeman huffed then moved over to Henrik who was standing, jittery, like a rabbit surrounded by a hungry skulk of foxes.

'You good?' Ryker shouted over to him.

The boy held Ryker's eye but didn't answer. The policeman said something to Henrik before taking his arm and ushering him toward the police car.

'Are you okay?' Ryker asked Henrik as they approached. Henrik held Ryker's eye but didn't say a word.

Moments later he was stuffed into the back of the police car.

'What about his moped?' Ryker shouted to the policeman.

'I'll sort it. You carry on with your day.'

Behind him the two men stepped from the pickup truck. One was big and bulky. Or maybe the bulk was just his clothing. The other was more wiry. He was the one who glared over to Ryker and mumbled something under his breath. Ryker glared back as the two of them grabbed the moped and hauled it into the back of the pickup truck. A brief shouted exchange followed between the wiry man and the police officer.

Moments later the police car swung around and headed off out of sight, the same way it'd come.

Ryker remained out in the cold as the pickup rumbled by him. The wiry man did his best to keep his eyes facing forward, paying no attention to Ryker at all.

When they were out of sight, Ryker moved back to his Volvo.

Then he set off after them.

4

It didn't take long for Ryker to catch up with the Nissan – there'd hardly been a high-speed getaway. The police car was about fifty yards further ahead, both vehicles travelling a sensible speed on the twisty and icy road. Ryker kept his distance from the Nissan, not so far as to keep out of sight from them, but simply far enough to drive safely. His brain continued to rumble with thoughts about the boy, Henrik. Where'd he been going? How had the policeman and the pickup come across him so quickly? Pure coincidence? It certainly seemed everyone knew each other, though Ryker guessed perhaps that was simply the way of life out here where so few people lived.

Still, the look on the boy's face...

Five miles later and they hadn't passed even a semblance of civilisation. No villages or towns, no petrol station, not even any turns from the road. Nowhere *to* turn. Simply the water one side and the steep incline of the mountain the other. Though Ryker did notice they were slowly heading higher. A few miles earlier the road had been all of ten yards above water level. Now they were halfway up the mountain it seemed, the drop to the left, down to the fjord, steep and rocky and deadly. For some reason

Ryker's mind envisaged a car slipping off the road and right through the not exactly sturdy-looking barrier, the wreckage tumbling down the cliff edge to a watery fate.

How many times had that happened?

He shook the thought away and glanced to the satnav screen. Barely anything to see except for the green of forest and the blue of water. No. As he looked again, just coming into view right at the top of the screen was a name. Blodstein. A village, he presumed. He'd seen the name before on the few road signs he'd passed, though it was surely a tiny place given the green and blue all around it.

The flick of red brake lights ahead grabbed Ryker's attention. He swung his focus out front and got ready to slam the pedal. He held back his foot when he realised the Nissan was only slowing. No emergency stop needed. He slowed too, the distance between the two vehicles closed. He was close enough to see the eyes of the driver in his rear-view mirror, if it weren't for the blackened glass at the back of the pickup.

Was the driver looking at him?

The police car remained directly in front of the Nissan. Beyond that a hulking lorry, almost as wide as the road, its bulky carriage piled high with huge tree trunks. Twenty, possibly thirty. Weighty. Which explained why, as they continued to head up the incline, the speed had dropped to below twenty miles per hour.

They rounded a bend and the police car abruptly pulled out and accelerated past the lorry. The sound of the revved engine filtered into Ryker's cabin and within seconds the police car was out of sight somewhere beyond. The pickup took a chance, on a blind bend, and did the same. That, too, was soon out of view.

Ryker waited a few seconds. Stayed patient. As before, it wasn't as though this was a high-speed chase. Still...

Thirty seconds later and there remained no end in sight to

the continuous bend. Ryker glanced at the satnav screen again. The land snaked around tightly – a good half mile before the road straightened out again.

He decided to go for it. He pulled out. No sooner had he done so, he spotted the van heading right for him. The horn blared. Ryker braked and swung back behind the lorry as the van blasted past.

He growled in frustration. At himself as much as anything else. What was he doing?

Then he noticed a turning on the right. The first he'd seen in miles. No signpost for what lay down the narrow road. Had the other cars gone down there?

Not long after he passed by another road. And another. Finally signs of life?

They hit a straight. Ryker didn't hesitate. He pulled out and slammed the accelerator and the Volvo whined as it picked up speed. Ryker held his breath. The width of the lorry gave him only inches to spare either side.

Nothing to worry about. Before long the lorry faded into the distance behind him. Ryker kept the pace on, the car gliding around corner after corner, his speed well over the limit but easily within his capability. With the road having previously snaked upward, now he headed down as the land levelled out. Not a mountain anymore. More a gentle hill. In the distance, by the water's edge, a small cluster of buildings became visible.

Blodstein.

He passed by a grotty-looking road sign – indicating the town boundary – that looked like it was from the 1950s. Ryker slowed as he reached the first of the buildings at the edge of the town. A warehouse of some sorts, rather than a home, followed by various other commercial buildings, a couple of shops, before he hit the main strip of the town. A bit bigger than he'd imagined it would be. Perhaps a hundred or more homes, tightly clustered around the water and rising into the forest to his right.

No sign of the Nissan or the police car.

Ryker came to a stop at the red light of a crossroad. The layout of the land here was surprisingly flat. Surprisingly uniform too, with a long straight road ahead, and one similarly intersecting it left to right. Low-rise buildings were dotted along both roads. The cluster immediately by the crossroads were all businesses. A convenience store. A hardware shop. A bank. A café. Plus a church. A quaint town hall. A much more functional building: police station.

A single police car outside it. Not the one Ryker had followed.

Ryker jumped in his seat when the thunderous blast of a horn shuddered through him. The log-carrying lorry filled his mirrors. He realised the lights were on green.

Ryker turned left and pulled into a small but empty car park that seemed to service both the café and the convenience store.

He shut off the engine then took a moment to gather his thoughts before he stepped out. No rain now, but it was much colder here than in Trondheim, even despite the fact that the clouds above were parting, slivers of blue poking through, though little that the winter sun's rays could do to elevate the temperature.

Ryker closed the car door and looked about the place. The roads were quiet. So, too, the pockmarked pavements. It was the middle of the working day but Blodstein felt like a ghost town, and what he saw reminded him of some of the far-flung small towns he'd passed through many a time in the American West – low, flat, barren. Not as sandy.

The café was open. Despite there being no other cars near his, he could see – through the tall windows – at least three patrons inside. Two servers.

He hadn't eaten for hours.

He moved toward the door. In among the pictures of food on the windows, mostly labelled in native Norwegian, were plenty of recognisable words too. Diner. Burgers. Fries. In fact the name of the place was Wendy's. It all seemed a little surreal.

Ryker opened the door and received a tinkle from the bell above in response. A couple of heads turned his way, but for the patrons it was nothing more than a cursory glance. The young waitress, however – mid-twenties, he guessed, with long, wavy brown hair – beamed him a smile and tootled over with a notepad in hand. She greeted him in Norwegian. He did his best to respond in kind.

'You're English,' she deduced with ease. It would never cease to amaze him how adept the Scandinavians were with language. Even despite his ability to speak more than half a dozen tongues fluently, he always felt a step behind these people.

'I am,' he said.

'We don't get so many tourists here,' she said. Her voice was soft and her accent strong, but her English was good. The broad smile that remained on her face suggested either she was happy to have someone new for once, or just happy to be able to try out her English.

'You don't?' Ryker said. 'I can't understand why. It's beautiful here.' He turned around to look outside as the words passed his lips, though then felt a bit foolish when he realised the view from the diner consisted of nothing except for the run-down buildings across the street.

When he faced her again she gave him a dubious look, as though she had no idea what he'd meant.

'Yeah,' she said. 'I guess everyone has their own taste. Are you eating?'

'Please.'

'This way.'

She showed him to a table by the window, away from the other customers: two middle-aged men together at the far end, a teenage boy with his face in his phone. Two women – mother and daughter? – closer by him. Two more men at stools at the bar. One was watching the grainy TV. The other was in conversation with the waiter behind the bar who was making coffee from an impressive-looking machine.

Busier than he'd thought.

'Would you like a drink?' the waitress asked him.

'A coffee, please.'

'Americano? I mean, I know you're not American, but...'

'Short and black please.'

She smiled again then headed off. Ryker perused the menu. An eclectic mix that ranged from burger and fries, to any manner of eggs, to schnitzels, wursts, stews, fish. When the waitress returned he settled for a selection of Smørrebrød – typically Scandinavian open-faced sandwiches topped with various cold meats, cheeses and fish.

'Good choice,' she said to him with a wink.

As he sat and waited for the food, Ryker kept his eyes mostly on the outside, looking for any sign of the police car or the Nissan he'd followed earlier. Or for any of the occupants, the boy – Henrik – included. He saw nothing. Had they all simply passed through this town?

Why did he even care?

The food soon arrived.

'Where are you staying?' the waitress asked him.

Ryker stared at her, unsure the intent behind the question.

'Sorry, it's just that...'

'You don't get many tourists around here.'

'We don't. And there aren't really many choices for hotels. Just two actually. Sorry. If you didn't know that.'

'I didn't. But it's not a problem.'

'The one near here, it's not really very good. The nicer one is down by the water. A bit more modern. For business people, really.' She looked unsure, like she didn't know what else to say. 'If there's anything more you need, just yell.'

'Shout,' Ryker said.

'Sorry?'

'I don't know why, but we'd say, *just shout.* Not yell.'

She looked confused. Then turned for the door when the bell tinkled. Ryker had seen the approach of the woman who stepped inside – hard not to given she wore a thick, bright yellow overcoat. An emblazoned overcoat.

Ryker kept one eye on the policewoman as she continued inside, and the waitress rushed over to her. A flurry of fast-paced, light-hearted conversation between the two followed – they clearly knew one another – before the policewoman was shown to a booth in Ryker's direction.

Ryker didn't stare but he kept his eyes flitting back and forth to the copper as she walked toward him and into the booth. She sat down facing him. Three tables away. Suspicion in her eyes every time she glanced his way.

Yes, this place was definitely like his experience of those remote towns in the American West. Ryker was clearly the outsider here. Everyone in this place knew it, even if he felt little by way of threat.

At least so far.

Yet he was only halfway through his sandwiches, chewing through a mouthful of cold salmon, when a vehicle outside the window caught his eye. A police car. *The* police car. He recognised the number plate. And the face of the driver, a glimpse of which Ryker caught when the car pulled off the road and into the car park.

Ryker looked over to the policewoman. She stared outside to her colleagues, her hands wrapped around a mug of coffee.

Then she caught Ryker's eye. Suspicion still. He looked away first. Seconds later the tinkle of the bell once more as not one, but two uniformed officers stepped into the café. No Henrik.

The officers didn't wait to be shown to their colleague. She turned and smiled to greet them. The portly officer did a double take when he spotted Ryker, glared before he turned to sit facing away. His partner joined him that side of the booth. Between the two of them their backs shielded the policewoman from Ryker's view.

The three began a muted conversation, none of them paying Ryker any attention.

He could just finish his food and leave. Leave the café. Leave this town.

Instead:

'Is he okay?' Ryker called out.

The two policemen swivelled to face him. The policewoman craned her neck. All three had their eyes on Ryker. The portly officer, though, was the only one with a seething glare.

'Who?' he said.

'The boy. Henrik, I think? Is he okay?'

'Oh, him.' The officer waved the question away with a flap of his chunky hand. 'Yes, he's fine.'

He went to turn back around.

'You took him home then?' Ryker asked. 'I mean, I assume he's not been arrested or anything?'

'Why are you so interested?'

'Just wanted to make sure he was okay.'

'You feel bad for nearly killing him?'

Ryker paused before he answered that one.

'He wasn't badly hurt, was he?'

'Nothing that a couple of bandages and some rest won't make better.'

'I'm glad to hear that.'

His colleague next to him seemed bored by the conversation and turned back. But Mr Portly continued to glare at Ryker.

'Carl Logan, you said your name was?'

'I did. And you are?'

The glare deepened, if that was possible.

'Politiførstebetjent Wold,' he said. 'That's Inspector Wold for you.'

Ryker was glad for the clarification as he'd struggled with the tongue-twister that had preceded it.

'You're here on business?' Wold asked.

'Not really.'

'Holiday?'

'I guess so.'

'Where are you staying?'

'I don't know yet.'

A sniff of disapproval. 'Well, there's not much choice here–'

'Just the two. I heard.'

Wold humphed. 'And not much to see. Not much to do around here at all really. Trondheim is nicer. I think that's where you came from.'

Ryker raised an eyebrow at the statement.

'Your car. It's rented from a shop in Trondheim.'

Nothing on the outside of the car showed that, which meant Wold had searched the licence plate. Interesting.

'Thanks for the advice,' Ryker said.

Wold's eyes narrowed before he turned back to his colleagues. Ryker realised the waitress – over by the bar – was staring. He glanced to her and she nervously looked away.

Odd little place, to say the least.

Ryker finished his food but he didn't move. He ordered another coffee and kept his eyes busy and his ears strained, but even the little he could hear of the conversations around him meant nothing.

Eventually Wold and his colleagues got up from their booth. A now customary glower was sent in Ryker's direction before the three of them headed on out. Wold and his male colleague went back to their car. The policewoman moved off on foot in the other direction. All were out of sight as Ryker sipped the last of his coffee.

Another? No, he'd had enough. He left cash on the table then headed for the door.

Outside, the sun now beamed down, barely a wisp of cloud in the blue sky above. The snow-tipped buildings of the town and the tarmac road and pavement all glistened in the sunlight, the whole scene looking serene and almost fabricated.

Ryker's Volvo was once again the only car parked up. Across the other side of the street, at the minuscule police station, he saw no sign of Wold's car. So where'd they gone to?

Ryker moved over to his car. Movement to his left. He looked over to see a bright yellow shape peel away from the shadows by the side of the café.

The policewoman.

'Officer,' Ryker said.

'Pettersen,' she said. 'I heard you say something to the inspector about a boy.'

Her English was smooth, far less of a foreign accent than the waitress, or Wold's. The slight lilt to it suggested she'd spent time in the West Midlands in England, or perhaps her English teacher had been from there. It was a refreshing though slightly odd difference to the generally Americanised accent of many of her fellow Norwegians.

'Henrik,' Ryker said. 'You know him?'

A twinge in her eye. 'No. I don't think so. But I was interested in what you said.'

'Because?'

'Because you're not from here. I wasn't sure what this was about.'

'You didn't ask your colleague?'

'Didn't I?'

A strange silence followed as both held the other's eye.

'There was a boy on a moped,' Ryker said. 'A few miles from here. He was on the wrong side of the road. He swerved to avoid me and fell off. He wasn't badly hurt. But he did seem... agitated.'

'Agitated?'

Did she not understand? 'Unhappy about something.'

'Probably you knocking him off his moped.' She smiled at her own apparent quip.

'Your colleague, Wold, turned up. He took Henrik.'

'Took him?'

'In his police car.'

She looked really dubious now. About which part, Ryker wasn't sure.

'The boy said his name was Henrik?' she asked.

Ryker thought about that for a second. 'No. The boy didn't say that. But Henrik is what Wold called him.'

'So Wold knew him?'

'Seemed to.'

She nodded.

'Is this something–'

'You should go,' she said.

'Go?'

'You weren't planning on staying here, were you?'

'I wasn't?'

'There's not really anything to see here. No good places to stay.'

'So I keep getting told.'

Another silence.

'It was... strange meeting you, Mr Logan.'

'Likewise.'

He put his hand to his door, opened it, and sank down into the seat.

Pettersen remained standing by the side of the car. He fired up the engine, put the gearstick into reverse and checked the mirrors before swinging out into the road. He selected first then rolled forward to the red lights. In his mirror, Pettersen continued to stand on the pavement, her eyes fixed on him. Ryker looked back to the road.

Left to head further north. Right to go back to Trondheim. Ahead?

Another glance in the mirror. Pettersen remained, clearly intent on seeing him off.

The lights flicked to green. Ryker flicked the left indicator on and headed that way. Pettersen was out of sight.

What would she do now?

He had no clue.

But he did know that, one way or another – hotel or no hotel – he wasn't finished in this strange little town.

5

Berg was still sleeping when Isabell woke him. She was sitting on the edge of the bed, already dressed, staring at him. *That* look in her eye. The unimpressed look. The disapproving look. The disappointed look.

'You were late last night.'

He shuffled up in the bed. 'I've got a lot going on.'

'Don't you always?'

With that she stood up and walked out of the room. Moments later he heard a clunk then a bang as the front door opened and closed.

Berg rolled his eyes and stood from the bed. Within twenty minutes he was fed, watered, and in his car on the way to work. Though he didn't head straight to the factory. For some reason he couldn't face it. Not after last night. Not with the thoughts of those barrels, the contents, what he'd done, still rattling through his mind.

This was all for the best. All part of the bigger plan. He had to keep telling himself that.

He parked up in the town and grabbed a takeaway coffee

and pastry before heading back to his car. He nearly jumped out of his skin when he heard his named being hissed.

'Sigurd!'

He spun and looked over to the dumpster at the side of the café.

Berg grit his teeth when he saw who it was. Nyland.

'What the hell are–'

'She's here,' he said, barely a whisper. 'Right over the road.'

Berg knew what Nyland meant. 'Shit. Where?' he said, as he for some reason ducked and rushed to Nyland's side.

Nyland pointed across the street. A few buildings further down. A house.

'They're inside.'

'Right here?' That sneaky bitch. 'Who is he?'

'I can tell you... but, perhaps not here. Just in case they see us. And I thought you wanted me watching?'

Berg gazed over to the other side of the street again. He half expected to see his wife appear at the window, her naked breasts bouncing as that piece of filth ravaged her from behind.

'Get in the car,' he hissed through gritted teeth.

'But–'

'Just get in the damn car.'

They both did so and Berg sped off in the direction of the factory, though within a hundred yards he pulled up by the side of the road, right on the edge of town.

'Who is he?'

His heart thudded, his brain was on fire. Rage consumed him. He needed to rein it in but how was he supposed to do that?

Nyland shuffled as he pulled his hand from his pocket. 'The file is in my car,' he said. Apologetically? Or was he irritated by the fact he'd been whisked away? 'But I have these photos on my phone.'

He handed the device over and Berg stared at the screen. His wife, a bigger smile on her face than he'd seen in years, walked side by side with a man he didn't recognise. A tall, well-dressed, handsome man, even to Berg's eyes.

Various shots of them. Walking, smiling. But that was all really. Hardly anything scandalous, much less conclusive.

'His name's Stefan Tronstad,' Nyland said. 'Forty-one years old. From Oslo originally. He's a lawyer.'

'What kind of lawyer?'

He looked to Nyland who seemed a little confused. The PI shrugged.

'Just a lawyer. He's based in Trondheim. Or was before.'

'Before? Before what?'

'If it matters to you I can look into it?'

Berg didn't answer that. Wasn't the answer obvious?

'What about the house?' he asked.

'I don't know yet. It's not Tronstad's home address. I was following her from your home this morning. It's the first time I've seen them go into that house.'

What the hell was going on?

Well, he had a pretty good idea. Yet these pictures... Was there a reasonable explanation?

'Tell me exactly what you've seen. Of the two of them together. Of him on his own.'

'I haven't followed him on his own before.'

'Why not?'

'Because... look, Mr Berg, I'm just one man. I'm doing my best to get information for you. If you want me–'

Berg stared at the pictures on the screen once more. Inside, his blood continued to boil. Not just at his wife and this Tronstad, but at the man sitting next to him.

'There's nothing here,' Berg said, his voice surprisingly calm. For a moment at least. 'There's nothing here!' he boomed, tossing the phone at Nyland who reeled back. 'You know what I want? Find out what she's doing with him. I want everything you can get. Emails, text messages, pictures. Pictures of them fucking. Not the two of them walking side by side on the street.'

'Mr... Mr Berg.'

Berg glared at him.

'Will you calm down?'

Berg said nothing. Nyland looked like he'd shat his pants. What kind of a PI was he? Available. Local. That's what kind.

'I-I explained to you before,' Nyland stammered. 'There are limits to what I can do. Legally. You're asking for me to obtain private infor–'

'Are you telling me you can't do it, or you won't?'

'Is... is there a difference?'

Berg didn't answer. He continued to hold Nyland's eye. Willing the younger man to concede.

'I have to ask, Mr Berg, what is the endgame here? For you?'

Good question. And Berg didn't yet know the answer. The answer, of course, depended on exactly what Nyland found.

One thing Berg did know: plenty of space remained at the bottom of the North Sea.

Nyland sighed. 'I'll do what I can. But... to cross this line, you know you'll have to–'

'Just tell me how much. Money isn't the issue. I'll have it in your account today.'

Nyland opened his mouth as though to say something else, but nothing came out except a strange sigh. Almost a whimper. To think this man was once a real-life detective in Trondheim. A catcher of rapists and murderers. Berg guessed there were reasons why seasoned detectives became PIs. Burnouts. Alcoholics. Those who couldn't deal with the stresses of major crimes. Those on the opposite side of the spectrum who were loose cannons who couldn't stick to the police's many rules.

Where did Nyland sit on that line of morality, ethics, mental health and aptitude? Certainly not the loose cannon type, who was nothing more than a sadist with a badge. Nyland was far too strait-laced. Most likely he'd wet his pants at the first bad thing he'd seen so had turned to this watered-down version of a PI as some sort of recovery mechanism.

Berg would persist with him. For now. To get another chump in he'd have to look further afield, probably to Oslo, and that would cost him both time and money, and he wasn't going to sit around and wait while some bastard screwed his bitch of a wife behind his back, probably both laughing at him while they did so.

'So we're agreed?' Berg said.

Nyland nodded.

'Good. Now get out of my car.'

Nyland didn't hesitate. He opened the door and stepped out without another word. Berg had half expected the PI to grumble and ask for a lift back to town.

Berg floored it and the tyres screeched and skidded, kicking up snow and dirt before the car bombed down the road, away from Nyland.

Berg looked at his watch. Quarter to ten. People would be wondering where he was. A passing thought rushed through his mind. Not for the first time. Had he cleared up properly last night? He'd been so tired, so mentally out of it with the grim task at hand, he was sure he'd done his best at the time. But in the cold light of day... had he? Even despite the lack of sleep, shouldn't he have made an effort to get up early and get to the factory before anyone else to make sure everything was in order? To make sure he'd cleaned up every last drop of blood. Inside and out. Out? Well, hopefully the early morning sleet had cleared up anything there, but he couldn't be sure, and the more and more he thought about it now, the more worried he became.

At least the thoughts were enough to take his mind off his wife.

Yet, what would await him as he drove through the gates? A bunch of burly workers standing debating what had taken place? A gaggle of police officers, lights on their cars flashing, cuffs at the ready as they waited for him to arrive?

No. None of that. When he arrived, everything was quiet and... exactly as it should be.

He parked his car in his spot, shut down the engine, stepped out and shivered as a blast of icy cold wind from the sea hit his skin. Pleasantly refreshing. He'd never not enjoy the sea air. It had a way of bringing clarity of thought.

Walking a little taller, Berg headed on inside. Machinery whirred. The forklift rattled back and forth. Men and women shouted and talked and joked. Berg nodded greetings to the people who looked over as he headed to his office. He didn't quite make it.

Marius.

'Sigurd, finally. Where've you been?'

'Is there a problem?'

'I don't know. You tell me?'

The men stared at each other, as though each was waiting for the other to cave.

'Two men are here to see you,' Marius said.

Berg glanced over and through his office window. Sure enough he could just make out the tops of two heads.

'Who?'

Visitors? He thought about the cars outside in the car park. He hadn't spotted any that caught his eye. Certainly not a police car out there. An unmarked detective's car perhaps?

'Who is it?' Berg asked again. 'I don't have any appointments.'

'I know. I saw that from your diary. They wouldn't even tell me their names. They simply insisted they speak to you, and you only.'

'And you showed them in?'

Marius rubbed the back of his neck. 'They were very insistent.'

'Insistent how?'

'You'll see for yourself, I mean, I don't know them, but... well, I'm pretty sure they're Russian.'

Berg's heart faltered.

6

Berg stepped into the room. *His* office. Four eyes were on him in an instant. Two bloodshot ones that belonged to a face that could only be described as having been carved from rock – hard, mottled, pointed. The man's head was sunken into his shoulders. In his seat, he didn't look tall, but he certainly looked like the kind of brute anyone would do well to avoid. The other man... a stark contrast. His green eyes sparkled. His face was fresh, even if it was lined with age – late forties? – further given away by his silver hair. As he stood, Berg saw that he was tall and lean and smartly dressed.

'*God morgen, mine herrer,*' Berg said, as pleasantly and relaxed as he could as he shut the door, then moved over to the tall man and shook his hand.

The man spoke a greeting in return which Berg couldn't decipher a single word of. He had no need to understand such a vulgar tongue as Russian.

He moved to his desk and was halfway to sitting down...

A knock on the door. It opened a few inches. 'Do you need me at all?' Marius said, poking his head through the gap.

'No. You get on with your day,' Berg said.

Marius had no way of knowing the pretext behind the Russians being here – did he? – yet the edge of suspicion in his tone, in his features, was poorly conceived. Would the Russians themselves realise?

Although more clued in than his employee, Berg had never met these two men before, even if he did know why they were in his office. Kind of.

'Please close the door,' Berg said to Marius.

Marius said nothing more but did as instructed.

Berg returned his gaze to his unwelcome guests. The tall man was seated once more.

'Can we continue in English?' the tall man asked. Despite the sparkle in his bright eyes, his stare was intense and uncomfortable.

'My English is better than my Russian,' Berg said.

A forced-looking smile from the tall man. 'My name is–'

'I don't need to know your name.'

The tall man closed his mouth and the relaxed look on his face faltered. Berg's stomach churned horribly but he tried his best to remain confident on the outside.

'My name is Valeri Sychev,' the tall man said. 'This is my partner, Andrey.'

No second name for him apparently.

'We work for Mr Jesper.'

'I figured that. How is the rare creature?'

Sychev's face twisted. Perhaps Berg's choice of English hadn't been interpreted correctly. Or perhaps it had.

'What I mean is, Mr Jesper is a man I hear a lot of, but I have never met him. Did you know that?'

Sychev nodded. Andrey glared. Had he even blinked yet?

'He only meets people who need to see him,' Sychev said.

Andrey muttered something in Russian with a snide grin on his pockmarked face.

'What was that?' Berg said, holding the brute's eye. Quite why he felt the need to challenge, he wasn't sure. Other than he was certain that to show weakness to these men was the absolute worst thing he could do.

'Please, gentlemen,' Sychev said, 'let us not begin something.'

'Why are you here?' Berg said. 'I have a very busy day ahead of me.'

'I can imagine,' Sychev said. 'You've been working very hard recently, I hear.'

Berg held his tongue now. A knowing smile slowly crept up the sides of Sychev's mouth.

'A very late night for you, last night?'

No. Sychev couldn't know about that. How?

'I think we are more alike than you might know,' Sychev added.

'I find that hard to believe. Please, can you explain why you are here. Like I said, I'm very busy.'

'We're here to talk business.'

'My business? What do you know about turbines?'

Sychev laughed, as though the question was a dumb one. 'Not as much as you, my friend. But that's why you're in charge of your company. I'm a businessman, not a scientist.'

Berg said nothing to that.

'But turbines?' Sychev said with a shrug. 'I do like machines. I like to think how men invent them. It's fascinating. To understand how a machine works, to think of all the thousands of pieces that fit together for success. It's like thinking about how a person's mind works.'

Berg wasn't so sure he saw the link.

'You could tell me some more about what you do here, if you like?' Sychev said.

A strange proposition. Given what he'd just said, did he

really care? Particularly given the whole pretext of him being here.

Berg kept his mouth shut.

'You started this business yourself?'

Berg nodded.

'A long time ago?'

'Nearly twenty years.'

'You were young.'

'Younger than I am now.'

'How could you even afford to do that at such an age? It would be one thing to start something small from nothing. A shop. An internet business, I suppose that's not too hard? But making turbines. How much is each one?'

'We make more than one type. For many different applications.'

'But probably millions.'

'Dollars? Kroner?' Berg shrugged again. 'Yes, it could be millions.'

Probably easier just to state that than to try to explain all the ins and outs.

'A young man in his twenties, you must have had money from somewhere?'

Berg assumed given the direction of the conversation, that Sychev knew exactly how the business had started.

'Nice to have a father with deep pockets,' Sychev said. 'Am I right?'

'Did you really come all this way to talk about my father?'

'Not exactly. He's dead, isn't he?'

'He's been dead for fifteen years.'

'So he never got to see this business rise?'

'Unfortunately not.'

'But it was his seed which allowed it to sprout from the earth.'

'A nice way of putting it.'

Sychev smiled again, as though pleased with his own eloquence. Or wisdom. Perhaps both.

'A seed to make this business sprout from the earth,' Sychev said. 'But you're still nothing more than a stem with a single flower.'

'I am?' Berg said with a raised eyebrow. What nonsense was this?

'You need something else to turn your little flower into a blossoming tree.'

Berg rolled his eyes. 'A tree. How about a fucking forest? A thousand trees.'

Sychev said nothing to that.

'Okay, I think I'm done with the stupid comparisons now,' Berg said.

Sychev squirmed, obviously offended, but what did he want? A damn poetry award?

'We visited your friend recently,' Sychev said.

'My friend?'

'Erik Rosen.'

Berg clamped his teeth. His eyes flicked from Sychev to the windows behind him, checking to the warehouse beyond as though worried someone out there was watching and listening.

'Erik Rosen is not my friend.'

'No? Acquaintances then? But you heard what happened to him?'

'I heard there was a problem at his factory.'

Sychev laughed now. Hearty, deliberately over the top. A caricature of whatever kind of bad guy he was trying to be.

'Yes. Quite a big problem for him,' Sychev said. 'I can tell you, we're a long way to resolving those problems for him now. It's always good to overcome hurdles that are put before us.'

Berg had suspected the Russians were likely behind the

sabotage at Rosen Tech. But why? It didn't make sense to him. Blackmail? Or had Rosen simply pissed them off, or tried to go against them?

'I'll ask the same question to you, Mr Berg, as I asked to Mr Rosen.'

But then Sychev didn't ask a question at all. Simply stared at Berg as though waiting for an answer.

'A question?' Berg prompted eventually.

'Wouldn't you like to be rich? *Really* rich?'

The question rumbled in Berg's mind. For a moment he imagined the men sitting before him had sprouted horns. Their skin deep red. Fire leaping up from the floor. Demons, sent from the devil himself, asking him to sell his soul.

Wasn't that the best comparison for this meeting?

Except Berg didn't have a soul to sell. Not after what he'd already done.

'Mr Berg?'

'However you try to word it, you're not here to help me,' Berg said.

'But of course we are. We like your business. You've done so well to raise it to where it is. But you must see there are limits to what *you* can do. With us, there are no limits.'

'Is that right?'

'It is. I've already done my research, and I have here, in my satchel, tender documents which will explain to you exactly how we can start. *Legitimate* contracts, there for the taking, from your very own government. And others too, across Europe, Central Asia. Thousands of turbines. Green energy. It's what everyone wants. And this is just a starter. This isn't just Norway, every country is doing the same.'

'I know all this. Why me?'

'There are many reasons why. Most are not important. What's important is that you could see Berg Industries reach levels you couldn't even have dreamed about before. Hundreds of millions of dollars for this work alone. *Billions* of your kroner.' He said the last sentence with a mocking laugh, as though the currency was unworthy of him.

Sychev brought the satchel to his lap, but he didn't open it. One hand rested on the clasp.

The room fell silent. The four eyes remained on Berg.

'Would you like me to go further?' Sychev asked. He tapped the clasp with his fingers.

Pandora's box. That was what that satchel represented.

'Get out,' Berg said.

Sychev looked genuinely puzzled. Andrey grinned as though this was his favoured outcome. The thought of what that meant made Berg's insides curdle even more.

'I said, get out,' Berg said, his voice raised, the words hissing through clenched teeth.

He rose to his feet. Fists on table.

'Get out! And don't ever come back here.'

The two Russians glanced at each other. Then Sychev stood.

'I won't take offence,' Sychev said. 'Andrey... well, you'd have to ask him. But I appreciate maybe I moved too fast for you. Perhaps some time to think?'

Andrey was on his feet now too. Yes, he was short. But what he lacked in height he certainly made up for in brawn. Still, in that moment, Berg no longer felt intimidated. He was seething. If these men knew the lengths he'd go to, in order to protect his business, his life, they'd surely show him more respect.

Perhaps he'd have to show them.

Sychev picked his thick coat from the back of his chair and slipped it over his shoulders.

'It was a pleasure to meet you in person,' Sychev said.

'Just go,' Berg said. 'I don't want to see either of you here again.'

Sychev had a hand on the doorknob. He twisted his neck to face Berg.

'I'm sorry, Mr Berg, but I'm afraid that simply won't be an option.'

Sychev opened the door and stepped out. Andrey followed him. Berg stayed where he was. The Russians could make their own way out. He wasn't sure he could move, his brain was so consumed with grim thoughts of what the hell he'd just done.

7

Ryker didn't leave Blodstein for long. A further forty-minute drive north revealed nothing but twisting road and snow and ice, with no indication of where the next town lay, or what it would contain. His brain whirred with conflicting ideas for what he should do next. One of the most compelling options was to simply keep driving. Don't return to Blodstein. Ever. He had no business there. He hadn't come to Northern Europe to ingratiate himself into other people's lives and problems.

Yet he wouldn't be true to himself if he walked away knowing that he could have helped. Could have helped people who *needed* help.

And it wasn't as though he was pressed for time. He sacrificed nothing of his own plans by staying in the area longer than originally intended.

So he drove back to Blodstein. He scoped out the two hotels. One was a new and sleek aluminium and glass structure, operated by a chain name that Ryker recognised and which, given its proximity to the waterfront factories and warehouses, was surely catered toward corporate use, on the odd chance that

Blodstein ever received out of town business people. The other was a much more traditional-looking affair, comprising a slightly grimy-looking and blocky four-storey brick structure just off the main shopping street. Drab-looking, it had shoddy signage and a car park at its side with space for only six cars, with much of the space taken up by ugly-looking steel vents and bins.

He chose the latter – the unimaginatively named Blodstein Gjestehus. He was no corporate type.

He parked up in one of the available spaces and moved inside. Gloomy, a smell of old wood and grease. The ageing bespectacled man sitting behind the scratched-up reception counter wore a waist jacket and shirt with bow tie, though managed to make the look scruffy and unkempt.

'*God morgen,*' Ryker said.

A raised eyebrow as the man looked up from his newspaper.

'You want a room?' the man asked, switching to English. Once again, sound instincts, and a decent grasp of the language, even if it was heavily accented.

'Your cheapest will do,' Ryker said.

'That's all we do. You have credit card?'

'I'll pay cash.'

'How many nights.'

'One at a time.'

The man sighed. 'A thousand kroner a night.'

Ryker whistled. The man looked unimpressed. Ryker palmed the notes onto the countertop while the receptionist chose a bulky-looking key from the pigeonholes behind him.

'Room three,' he said, placing the key next to the money.

The man took the notes, stuffed them into a drawer, then picked up his newspaper again.

'That's it?' Ryker asked. 'You don't need any details or–'

'What details would I need? You're the only person staying.'

'Do I get any food? Breakfast?'

The receptionist glanced up from the paper and glared at Ryker like a patriarch would at a disappointing son.

'Breakfast? You want me to do you a buffet? Freshly squeezed juice. Eggs, bacon?'

Was he actually offering that?

'This isn't the Hilton,' he added before Ryker responded. 'The kitchen's closed for the winter. Sorry. We don't get many visitors.'

'Glad to be doing my part then,' Ryker said.

The receptionist gave a quizzical look, but said nothing more.

'Any recommendations then for food around here? Things to do?'

'Have you really come here for a holiday?' the man asked, in a way which suggested Ryker was crazy if the answer was yes.

Ryker's smile seemed to soften the man a little.

'There's an Italian along the street. I can't promise it's as good as Rome, but it serves pizza, which is probably the most exciting food we can offer here. Things to do?' He sighed and shrugged. 'Do you like fishing?'

'Not really.'

He shook his head. 'You came here, not my fault.'

Ryker held his smile. The man took no notice and got back to his reading before Ryker walked away.

———

Half an hour later Ryker was on the move again. The hotel room was basic, a little worn, but perfectly useable. Together with its own mini bathroom the space was a huge step above many places Ryker had stayed over the years, even if he'd also on occasion been afforded the chance to stay in ultra-luxury. All he needed here was somewhere warm and dry. Though he wouldn't want to spend hours on end inside there either. And so he headed out.

Through the morning he'd become more and more curious about the attitudes of the locals in this far-flung region. Not unfriendly, exactly, but certainly very wary and questioning of outsiders. Not hostility, but more surprise and almost shame.

In a strange way, Ryker's affinity toward the place, and its people, was slowly growing. As though he found solace and meaning in this closed-off, lost cause of a place.

Ryker didn't return to his car on leaving the hotel. The town was hardly sprawling so he decided to explore on foot, the slower pace allowing him to take more in.

He headed to the waterfront first. Industrial was the key word to describe the area. He found no shops or bars or outdoor dining options, simply a run of businesses, stretching along the water in both directions, way past the residential hub of the town. Some were small, little more than simple warehouses with berths onto the water, fishing nets and crates stacked high on the grounds. Others were much larger, comprising multiple units on sprawling manufacturing sites. Many were basic-looking and a little downtrodden, like much of the town, but one or two were more modern and sleek and quite clearly had seen recent investment. Clues were given here and there as to the purpose of the businesses from their names, which, as far as Ryker could gather, largely centred around the exploitation of everything the North Sea had to offer: fish, hydropower, solar and wind, and, of course, oil and gas.

Ryker paid a brief visit to the local library, which provided free internet, as well as a records room that held access to reams of old documents, and microfiche records, detailing the area's history. It had been years since Ryker had seen something so antiquated, though in many ways he relished the chance to sit himself down in there and see what he could find.

Not today.

Having completed his self-guided tour of Blodstein by early afternoon, Ryker decided to get on the move again. He got into his car and headed south, out of the town, retracing his route from earlier in the day when he'd been stuck behind the log-carrying lorry. He'd lost both the police car and the pickup truck then, but he wasn't sure either had headed into Blodstein. At least not to stop. He surely would have seen them there. Even though Wold had later turned up at the café, where had he been in the interim?

Ryker recalled the few turnings he'd seen from the main road, heading into the forests. It was those roads he would explore. He'd figured from an earlier perusal of a map of the area on his phone that a factory of some sort was located out there. Nothing that was labelled on the map, but satellite images clearly showed a cluster of buildings a few miles from the town, deep in the pine forest.

Even as he approached where he believed those buildings to be, he saw no indication on his satnav screen as to what lay ahead, no signage on the roads to indicate a town, village, or even a business in the forest.

What he did see, after travelling along the first of the tracks outside of Blodstein for just over two miles, was the first signs of logging. Piles of huge pine trunks, several trees high and wide, stacked in the forest. Stumps jutted out of the ground here, there and everywhere like a giant-sized whack-a-mole.

The whir of machinery drifted. The grind of chainsaws. The sickly, sharp smell of sap.

Ryker glanced off to his right where a hydraulic crane arm hoisted up a pile of trunks from the forest floor with the ease of a man picking up toothpicks. The crane arm opened and unceremoniously dumped the huge trunks onto the trailer of a waiting lorry with a calamitous boom. A little further along came the mammoth machinery of the fellers – tracked beasts with cutting arms that clasped around tree trunks like shackles.

Men in bright orange coats were dotted about. Hard hats, boots, all of them looked big and bulky, stereotypical lumberjacks, even if all of the hard work was being carried out by machine rather than man. At least as far as Ryker could see.

A few of the workers looked over at Ryker's Volvo as he slowly passed, though he didn't spot anything or anyone that piqued his interest. He soon reached what he was sure was the cluster of buildings he'd spotted on the satellite images earlier. Not a factory at all. The buildings were all timber and corrugated steel structures. Temporary-looking, perhaps used only as long as this area of forest was being cleared, and which consisted of little more than shells to house machinery and trunks that were waiting to be transported to cutting shops. Ryker pulled over on the road, fifty yards away from the cluster of buildings, and watched the operation with interest for a few moments.

He heard it before he saw it. A tractor, its huge wheels rumbling across rough ground, its diesel engine churning. It came out from Ryker's blind spot, from the trees behind him. The driver slowed as he passed and Ryker looked up to see the guy gesticulating and mouthing off, though he couldn't translate any of the angry Norwegian above the din of the motor.

The tractor, lifting arm attached to the front, rattled away, into the forecourt area and over to a pile of logs where it came to a rocking stop with the lifting arms inches from the wood. The cab door opened and the driver jumped down, still shouting and gesticulating as he marched toward Ryker. He was mid-height but plump with a rounded face. Glasses, stubble, bright red cheeks. Ryker could tell from his shouting that he was out of breath as he strode.

Ryker stood from his car and hung on the open door.

He caught a few of the words from the man. Mostly centred around 'get out of the way' and the like, interspersed with a few choice swear words.

'Actually my mother's dead,' Ryker shouted in retort.

The man stopped walking, stopped talking too. Then started up again.

'I thought you were the new guy,' he said, English now, voice still raised, as he moved within a few yards of Ryker. Hardly such a distance to require him to shout. Perhaps his hearing was screwed because of the constant din of machinery which echoed around them even with none of the beasts in sight. 'I was about to send you back where you came from.'

'I'm not your new guy,' Ryker said.

The man checked his watch. Whoever the new guy was, he was in trouble all right.

'You're English?' the man said.

Ryker nodded.

'You shouldn't be out here.'

'I was passing through.'

A dubious look now. 'Going where? There's nothing out here but us.'

'There's no road through here?'

'Does it look like there is? I need you to move. We have trucks coming through all the time. If you cause an accident–'

'I'll move. But perhaps you can help me?'

'With what?'

'You're in charge here?'

'Not really.'

'Then who is?'

'He's not here. I guess... yeah, today I guess I am in charge.'

'I'm looking for someone.'

'Who?'

The doubt in his eyes grew. He looked seriously uncomfortable now. Behind him, two other figures, it looked like a man and a woman, over by the largest of the buildings, had stopped what they were doing and were looking over.

'I don't know that yet,' Ryker said. 'They drive a Nissan pickup.' Ryker rattled off the licence plate. 'I'm sure they're local.'

The man's face twitched. His eyes flicked off to his left, as though searching for someone there. Ryker glanced, too, but could see nothing but trees.

'Do you know who owns that car?' Ryker asked.

'Why do you want to know?'

Ryker held his hands up. The man's defensiveness was clear.

'It's nothing bad. I was just in the café in Blodstein. You know the one?'

'There's only one.'

'The two guys were in there. One of them dropped some money outside.'

The man said nothing now.

'Can you help me?'

'You drove out here just for this?'

Ryker shrugged. 'I'm sure they came in this direction.'

'You could have left the money with the café.'

'Or I could keep it. I just thought I'd be nice.'

Ryker went to get back into his car.

'How much?' the man asked.

Behind him the man and woman edged forward. Smoke billowed out around the woman's face from a cigarette. The man next to her shouted over. *Are you okay?* Ryker thought the words meant.

'Ja,' was the simple response from Mr Red Cheeks.

'How much?' he asked Ryker again.

'How much did they drop?'

'What else would I be asking?'

'Ten thousand.'

An even more dubious look now.

'That's quite a lot where I come from,' Ryker said. 'Would probably only buy me a few beers around here.'

He laughed at his own quip. The man didn't. The two others joined him, one either side. The woman, on the left, was the youngest of them but had a hard look in her eyes. Tattoos covered her bare arms. The choice of body warmer and high-vis jacket rather than full overcoat was obviously designed to show the tats off. The man on the opposite side was huge – a good two or three inches over Ryker's six foot four frame, and bulkier too – with a long beard like a Viking warrior. He spat on the ground and mumbled something under his breath.

'What about you two?' Ryker said. 'I'm looking for–'

'We don't know anything about it,' the boss said. 'So can you please go back the way you came so we can get on with our jobs.'

Behind the three workers the rumble of machinery grew as one of the beasts approached from the forest beyond. Ryker spotted a flash of yellow behind the warehouse before an almighty boom and crash sounded out. Logs falling, it sounded like. The thumping noise pulsed through Ryker, and echoed into the distance. Birds screeched and flew from the pines into the sky. Silence for a few moments before all manner of shouting from the warehouse.

The boss turned to the Viking and rattled off an angry tirade. Perhaps telling the two of them that they should have been over there helping.

The man turned back to Ryker.

'Sorry, but you can see what it's like here. It's dangerous, even for us. You need to leave.'

Ryker remained where he was.

'I can't help you. Now go.'

With that the man finally turned away and stomped off. His two wing-persons remained but no further words were exchanged. Ryker sat down in his car seat and shut the door. He turned the engine back on, swung around in the road then slowly drove away. He kept his eyes flitting to his mirrors as he went. The boss had already reached the warehouse, ready to scold whoever had caused the mess, or perhaps to call the ambulance to save whoever had been injured. His two workers remained, watching Ryker. When they were just about out of sight, the Viking took his phone out of his pocket and placed it up to his ear.

Ryker was sure at that point that his trip into the forest hadn't been a waste after all.

8

Ryker reached the main road and turned left, his mind busy. Of course, he was taking a leap, but he was sure the red-cheeked boss at the logging site had known exactly which car Ryker was referring to, and knew exactly who it belonged to. It was already starkly apparent that in this small corner of the world, everyone knew everyone else. He also believed – certainly *wanted* to believe – that the Viking had pulled his phone to his ear, as Ryker left, in order to call whoever needed to know about the intrusive outsider.

Good.

The more feathers he ruffled, the sooner he'd find some answers, one way or another.

Back on the main road, he went past the next turning on the left – it was too close to the logging site. For some reason, it felt like moving a little further afield was a better bet. He took the next turning instead. Earlier in the day, on his ride from Trondheim to here, this had been the first he'd passed, when he'd been stuck behind the lorry. It was the least well laid of each of the turns. A narrow road, tarmac for the first hundred yards, heavily pounded dirt after that, with pine trees just beyond his wing mirrors each side, and needles from the trees scattered across the track. The road didn't even appear on his satnav so he had no clue how far it'd go, or what it would connect to, if anything.

After nearly two miles he finally had an answer. A home. Of sorts. A wide, single-storey structure. A little dilapidated in its appearance with moss-covered roof tiles and grimy windows, in some places boarded up. A large area around the house was cleared of trees but it was hardly manicured. Among the dirt and pine needles lay all manner of clutter, from unused outdoor tables and chairs to a rusting trailer, quad bike, push bikes, piles of logs. A car. Not the Nissan. But was someone home?

A moped. Propped up against the side of the house. The same one Henrik had fallen from? Ryker couldn't be sure. It was certainly the same colour. Looked like it had seen better days.

Ryker pulled the car to a stop.

He thought for only a couple of seconds before he turned back around and left.

––––––––

Fifteen minutes later, his face ice cold, Ryker carefully stepped through the forest. He had some simple provisions in the backpack over his shoulders. He'd left his car in the forest, two hundred yards behind him, the vehicle twenty yards from the road that ran parallel between the logging site and the run-down home he once again headed for.

Much better to arrive inconspicuously on foot, through the trees, than on the road where his car was so obvious.

The plan?

Get close enough to the building to see who was home. Get inside if he could. If it was empty? Wait.

If he'd made a mistake, he'd be on his way soon enough.

If his hunch was right...

He moved over a rise in the forest and the house came into view below, fifty yards away. Ryker stopped and crouched down as he stared toward the building. He was approaching from the side now, and could see around the back of the house, too, where a raised deck – cleared of snow, but green and damp – wrapped around. The same car remained parked up. No signs or sounds of anyone as Ryker waited.

He moved again, more slowly, more carefully now. Step by step, tree to tree, he tried to keep the noise of his feet on the forest floor as quiet as possible. The only sounds he heard, over his steady breathing, was the gentle rustle of the trees, and the ever-so-distant hum of machinery from the logging site.

At least that's what Ryker thought the hum was, but in the quiet, he realised the sound was slowly getting louder.

He pulled up against a thick trunk, all of twenty yards from the clearing. He saw movement between the trees off to his right. A car. He pulled as far around the tree trunk as he could. Seconds later the car came into the clearing.

A pickup truck, but not the Nissan. Shame.

Ryker spied as the vehicle came to a stop. Two figures got out of the driver's side, facing Ryker. Another joined from the passenger side. Three people. Ryker recognised two of them. The Viking and the tattooed woman. Okay, not such a shame after all.

The third passenger – another man – Ryker didn't know. The Viking glanced across the forest, right past where Ryker lay hidden, as the three of them talked. Ryker was too far, his Norwegian too poor for him to understand the conversation, but it wasn't jovial.

As the other two remained standing by the pickup's bonnet, the Viking sauntered across to the front door of the house. At least what passed as a front door. He knocked. Waited. No answer.

He turned back to the other two and mouthed off something. Not anger, but he wasn't happy. On his instruction, Ryker assumed, the woman took her phone out and she turned to face the forest as she spoke. Her voice, her manner became more frustrated. The Viking, irate, stomped over to her, grabbed the phone from her ear and started blasting down the line. All the while he stared across the forest.

His eyes settled.

Had he seen?

He finished the conversation. Handed the phone back to the woman without taking his eyes from the spot where Ryker remained hunched. He muttered something. Then he walked forward. The other two followed. They spread out, each step slow and careful.

No, they hadn't spotted him. If they had they would have moved more quickly. But something had spooked them. With the three edging forward, Ryker made the call to fall back, even though a large part of him wanted to stand his ground. To fight? He didn't even know what he was fighting for yet.

He soon moved back over the rise in the forest and behind him the three were momentarily out of sight on the other side. He took the chance and quickened his pace. Pumped his arms and legs to move as quickly as he could back to his car. What he made up for in speed, he lost in stealth.

The inevitable happened. Likely as they came over the top of the hill. The angry shouting from behind told Ryker they'd spotted him. Nothing he could do about it now. He didn't look back, but continued to take long, fast strides to his car. He reached it. Dived in. Fired the engine up. Hit reverse. The tyres skidded on the loose ground, finding just enough traction to pull the car backward, through the gaps in the trees, toward the road. Ryker had his eyes flitting between his mirrors and the three figures in front of him, closing in all the time. They were too far to worry him now he was in his car. No sign of any weapons by their sides – he was in no danger of potshots.

But they'd seen him. They'd seen his car.

He reached tarmac and swung around and sped off toward the main road. He checked his mirrors a couple of times but saw no sign of the three heading into the road.

Would they head back to their car to follow him? Try to run him out of Blodstein for good? Ryker was torn between driving slow, waiting to see if they caught up, or speeding out of there and back to the relative safety of the town.

He never quite decided which, instead driving a steady speed until he reached Blodstein, no sign of the pickup. He pulled left at the junction and into the café car park. He glanced to the windows. Spotted the same waitress as earlier in the day, dutifully seeing to a couple sitting by the window.

The engine of Ryker's car rumbled away. He looked over to the junction as he considered his next move.

Sure enough the pickup truck pulled up to the lights. They'd given chase after all.

From a close distance Ryker could see the eyes of the driver. He looked over to Ryker. Then the pickup swung a hard left, through the red light, cutting the corner, right over the pedestrian pavement. The vehicle bobbed on its suspension as it raced over the kerb and toward Ryker's car.

Undeterred, Ryker shut his engine down and stepped out into the cold.

Tyres screeched. The pickup came to a rocking stop a couple of yards from Ryker's Volvo. The three jumped down onto the tarmac. Ryker held his ground as the Viking shouted over, moving into stride.

A short-lived stride.

The blip from the police car siren stopped him and his companions in their tracks. All three, Ryker too, looked over to the road, to the squad car that pulled up. Ryker had spotted it approaching already. One key reason why he'd chosen to stand and face the onrushing crew in the first place.

The driver's window wound down. Wold. Of course. He shouted over to Viking and his chums. Viking muttered back, then turned to Ryker, and, like before at the logging site, gobbed a mouthful of phlegm onto the floor. The spit landed a couple of feet from Ryker's shoes. Ryker didn't react. The Viking fumed – looked seriously pissed off, as though Ryker had violated his sister or worse.

'Nice,' Ryker said with a mocking grin. To egg the Viking on? Maybe.

Ryker could see in the guy's eyes that he really wanted to bound forward and smash his fist into Ryker's face. Perhaps the only reason he didn't was because Wold stepped from his car and moved over.

The Viking – somewhat reluctantly – backed down. He signalled to his chums and the three of them retreated to the pickup and were on their way, the Viking holding Ryker's eye with an evil glare as long as he could until they were out of sight.

'You can take that smile from your face,' Wold said as he approached Ryker.

He didn't look happy.

'Right place, right time?' Ryker said.

'Is that how you see it?'

'Is there another explanation for you being here?'

Wold didn't answer that. He came to a stop a couple of steps from Ryker. Apparently he was on his own now. No sign of Pettersen or the other officer who'd been with him in the café earlier.

'You know those chumps?' Ryker asked.

'Chumps? I don't know what that means. Do I know those people? Yes, I do. I think I know everyone in this town.'

'The guy with the beard–'

'Erling.'

'I don't think he likes me much.'

'I'm not sure anyone around here likes you. A lot of people are talking about you.'

'They are? Why?'

'Why are you still here, Carl Logan?'

'I'm on vacation.'

'I find that hard to believe.'

'Because?'

Wold sighed.

'I'm staying at the Blodstein guesthouse,' Ryker said. 'You can check with the guy there if you like.'

'I already know that,' Wold said.

Ryker would have looked surprised if he was. He wasn't.

'I also know you visited Erling and the others at work.'

'The loggers?'

'Sorry?'

'Who runs that operation exactly?'

'I don't understand you.'

'Is there a company name or something? I didn't spot anything. Just seemed odd, all those men out there in the forest like that.'

Wold huffed, like he was getting fed up with Ryker. Well, yeah, that much was abundantly clear.

'You went to that logging site, asking questions?'

'Asking questions isn't allowed around here?'

'It's private property.'

'I didn't see a sign.'

'Then later you were seen roaming in the woods of another property.'

'I went for a walk. Must have got lost. My mistake.'

Wold glared. 'Road accident, and trespassing twice in the same day. Ask me, shouldn't I arrest you by now?'

Ryker said nothing to that.

'I looked you up.'

'Okay?'

'Carl Logan. Very hard to find much information.'

Ryker shrugged.

'You have ID?'

'I do.'

'Can I see it?'

'You don't believe I am who I say I am?'

'I don't know yet.'

'My ID is in the hotel.'

Wold seemed to chew on that one.

'I'd much prefer it if you were to leave this town now,' Wold said.

'I figured that.'

'I can sense that the longer you stay, the more chance there is of trouble. For you.'

Ryker once again kept his mouth shut.

'I'd rather you leave, but I'm thinking you won't.'

Ryker shrugged again.

'I can only say, if you do stay, know that I'm going to be watching you very, very closely, Carl Logan.'

A silent stand-off. Neither man blinked. The clunk as the café door opened stole the attention of them both. Just the couple from the window coming out. They both looked over, a little disapprovingly, then walked away in the opposite direction.

'So?' Wold said, grabbing Ryker's attention once more.

'So I'm hungry. See you around, Inspector.'

Ryker brushed past him, and toward the café door.

9

After eating and refreshing, Ryker headed back to his hotel room. He was a little surprised to make it there without any further sight of either the Viking – Erling? – or Wold, or Pettersen or any of the other people he'd already encountered through the day. He'd expected at least one of them to be watching him, following him. Perhaps that was unnecessary. It already appeared Wold had a clear idea of Ryker's movements through the day. Was the entire area hooked up to surveilling for outsiders?

Once again he didn't spend long in his hotel room. Boredom came easily to him, and overall he felt frustrated and dissatisfied from the day. He wanted to keep prowling, because doing so was the only way he could delve deeper into the lives of the town's inhabitants, which was the only way he was going to scratch the surface to determine what lay beneath.

Something bad. He couldn't escape that feeling.

Was that because his ominous feelings held truth, or simply because of the way he viewed the world after so many years of seeing and dealing with the worst that societies had to offer?

Darkness had descended. It came early this far north in the

winter. The Italian restaurant was open and looked inviting, but it wasn't that long since he'd last eaten. It was also a little... too nice. That wasn't the place Ryker would find anything of interest. He spotted what looked like a bar, a little further down the street. A simple swinging sign and frosted windows were the only indication of the establishment which lay beyond. That, and the two men standing smoking cigarettes outside in the cold and dark.

Ryker headed in and found the inside as he'd expected. Basic, with wood everywhere. A smell of stale sweat and beer. A bigger space than he'd imagined, perhaps, close to a dozen people inside, though they were eaten up by the mostly empty space. The clientele, like the decor, was like stepping back a few decades: all but two of the people inside were male. One of the females was the barmaid. The other was Miss Tattoos. She was sitting with a group of five men in the far corner – by far the biggest and loudest group in the place, though hardly rowdy. The yellow-and-orange coats on the backs of the chairs suggested they'd all come drinking straight from work. All from the logging site, or from the factories too?

Miss Tattoo was the first of them to look over. Soon each of them had taken at least a cursory glance in Ryker's direction. Not outright hostility, but certainly wariness. No sign of Erling now, or anyone else Ryker had seen before.

He ordered a beer and parted company with way too much money for the drink. It did taste good though. He took a seat at a table for two at the far side of the bar to the group, facing them so he could keep an eye on them.

He received a few more glances, mostly from the woman, though it wasn't until the door opened that events took a more interesting turn. Viking, aka Erling. With the other man from the pickup. Plus a man that caused Ryker to initially double take.

The wiry man from the Nissan. The one who'd spoken to Wold earlier in the day when he and his friend had hauled Henrik's moped into their pickup.

Ryker sat back in his chair and waited. There it was. Erling looked over first. He looked seriously surprised to see Ryker. Perhaps in part because of the nonchalance in Ryker's pose. Ryker could tell the guy clenched his jaw. The new arrivals carried on to the group at the back without a word in Ryker's direction. Moments later Erling was at the bar, stealing a glance in Ryker's direction every now and then. He took a tray full of beers over to his friends. They made way for him and a couple of minutes of happy but boisterous chatting and drinking followed before Viking leaned over to Miss Tattoo and whispered something in her ear, holding Ryker's eye the whole time.

The next moment she rose to her feet, beer in hand, and wandered over to Ryker with a confident swagger and a glint in her dark eyes.

'You want some company?' she said, her accented English all the more difficult to understand because of the slur. Alcohol, Ryker assumed, but perhaps she always spoke like that.

'Not really.'

Her eyes narrowed but she didn't say anything. After a few moments of silence she pulled out the chair opposite Ryker and took the seat without further comment. Without her high-vis vest on, Ryker saw that her arm-displaying tank top was a severely low-cut affair that revealed yet more tattoos on her overspilling cleavage. Revealing. The way she used her arms and elbows to squeeze her chest together as she sat suggested the look was deliberately aimed to draw the attention of others. She was confident all right. Probably very popular among her overly masculine group.

Both of them took a mouthful of beer as the silence extended.

'A lot of people are talking about you,' she said.

'I'm a popular guy.'

She laughed.

'What's your name?' she asked.

'You don't know?'

She shrugged.

'James,' Ryker said.

She looked a little confused by that. So clearly she'd already heard the name Carl Logan, one way or another. She didn't question the discrepancy.

'I'm Sonja.'

'Pleased to meet you, Sonja.'

'Why are you here?' she asked.

'Is there another bar I should be in?'

'There's one in the hotel.'

'The guesthouse?'

She laughed. 'No. Not that one. The one by the water. That's where most visitors stay. This bar is... more local. But I meant, why are you here, in our town, at all?'

'I've been asked that a lot of times today.'

'You were spying on us earlier.'

'I was?'

'You shouldn't.'

'Because?'

'Because it's not very nice. And because next time you do, it won't be me who comes to talk to you.'

Ryker flicked his gaze over her shoulder and, as if on cue, Erling glanced.

'You know,' Ryker said, 'the more people around here who talk to me like this, the more determined I am to stick around and find out what's going on. So thanks.'

He lifted his glass in toast to that. She didn't reciprocate.

'You could come and join us,' Sonja said. 'Tell us all about you.'

'You really want me to?'

'I think if we got enough beer in you...'

'I'm not a big drinker.'

'Even better,' she said with a wink.

'I think I'm happier over here. But you're welcome to stay and keep me company.'

'Yeah? And why am *I* so welcome.' A sneaky smile on her face now. 'Would you be so keen if Erling was sitting here instead?'

She looked over her shoulder again.

'Actually, he looks like an interesting chap.'

A questioning flicker on her face. Perhaps she hadn't understood the colloquial term.

The look was gone in a flash and replaced with something altogether more sultry. At least that was what Ryker thought she'd intended, though honestly, he couldn't have been less interested in her.

She opened her mouth to say something else, but then stopped when the door to the bar opened. Both she and Ryker glanced over. Two men walked in. In the space of a couple of seconds the room went noticeably quieter. A far greater reaction than when Ryker had arrived.

One of the new arrivals was tall and slim with silver hair. The other was a bulldog of a man, all muscle and mottled skin and a face that looked like it had seen several hundred rounds in the ring. Locals? Ryker didn't think so. But he also didn't feel they were unknowns. Something about the amplified tension in the room suggested otherwise.

Without saying a word, Sonja grabbed her drink, got to her feet, and scuttled back to Erling and their comrades.

The newcomers moved over to the bar. Neither took a seat as they ordered a drink. Two neat whiskies, Ryker noted. Slowly the silence turned to a muted hush. Erling got to his feet. Did everything to avoid Ryker's eye now as he moved over to the bar. Silver Fox paid him no attention at all as Erling leaned over and spoke quietly to Bulldog. Then Bulldog turned and spoke – relayed? – to Silver Fox, who in turn responded to Bulldog. All very odd. Clearly Erling wasn't worthy of the tall man's attention. Finally, the message was passed back to Erling whose face turned sour before he retreated back to his seat.

Moments later the two new arrivals had downed their drinks and were heading to the exit. Ryker received the quickest flash of a look from the deadpan Bulldog as the two men left. No sooner had they gone and Sonja was back standing over Ryker's table. No drink now. Her coat was in her hand.

'You need to come with us,' she said.

'I do?'

Behind her four of the other men, Erling included, were on their feet putting their coats on. Only a couple of men remained sitting, faces glum as they shook their heads and grumbled to each other.

'Come on,' she said, her tone hardly inviting.

'To where?'

'Just get off your ass and come with me.'

Ryker sat back in his seat.

Erling stormed over.

'You're pissing off the wrong people,' he snarled. 'Outside. Now.'

With that he and his friends stormed out, leaving Sonja hanging over Ryker, her arms folded in defiance. He picked up his drink and drained the glass dry.

'Please. You don't really have an option. There are some people you just don't say no to.'

He guessed she was right about that. And honestly? He was intrigued as to exactly what was about to happen.

One thing he knew for sure: as always, his instincts for finding trouble were second to none.

He grabbed his coat and got to his feet.

10

Sonja walked behind Ryker as he moved for the exit. He was braced and ready. He stepped out into the dark night. One, two, three men, standing in the road outside, an arc around the bar entrance.

'This way.'

A gravelly voice off to Ryker's side. Erling.

Ryker turned. Erling was a couple of yards away. Standing tall, but not looking like he was about to make a move. The other three men remained motionless. Ryker had expected an ambush the second he'd stepped over the threshold. He'd been ready for it. Kind of wanted it.

So what was this?

Erling turned and walked. Ryker hesitated for a second before he moved in tow behind him.

He glanced to the other men. Caught sight of movement directly behind, from the bar.

Sonja.

WHACK.

Ryker stumbled from the blow to the back of the head. A hard strike. Club? Stone? His vision blurred but he managed to stay on his feet. Yet the hit he'd taken was enough to have the desired effect. Erling faced Ryker, a grin on his face now. Finally, the other men rushed him. A short tussle followed as Ryker's arms were secured behind him and his legs kicked out from underneath.

They dragged Ryker along, down a side street – an alley? – that was near pitch black, so dark Ryker, through his blurred vision, couldn't tell if it was a dead end or not.

They tossed him to the ground. He had enough focus to bring his arms out to prevent his face from smacking into the hard surface. But no time for respite. Feet crowded around him. A boot crushed his hand and ground it down into the tarmac. Ryker grimaced in pain.

He craned his neck to look up, and found himself staring into the dark eyes of the Bulldog. Around him, in the blackness, all he could make out of the others was the glimmer of the whites of their eyes – like a pack of wolves circling its prey in the bleak wilderness.

A voice from the dark.

'Who are you?'

English, but the accent...? Not a local.

Ryker tried to see where the voice came from but the angle was too acute and Bulldog ground his foot down harder as if warning him not to look. To who? Silver Fox?

Ryker said nothing.

'I asked you a question.'

'I didn't like how you asked it.'

WHACK.

Ryker grimaced again as pain shot through his back. Who'd hit him? He had no clue. Erling? Sonja? One of the others? He could hear them breathing. Hear them shuffling around him.

'Don't think this situation isn't real,' said the voice from the dark. 'I can make you suffer like you wouldn't believe.'

'If you believe that, then you really don't know me at all.'

WHACK.

Another strike across the back, and Bulldog ground his foot down harder still. Ryker's hand was wet and sticky and he imagined the skin was already torn.

'Why are you here?'

A short pause as Ryker thought of a suitable response.

'Let... me up. I'll tell you.'

A short pause on the other side of the stilted conversation this time. Then an instruction. Not English. Not Norwegian. Not Russian – Ryker could speak that language fluently – but something close to it. Balachka, possibly. A fluid dialect, commonly a blend of Ukrainian and Russian, spoken by the Cossacks of the North Caucasus.

The Bulldog lifted his foot and a wave of pain shot through Ryker's arm as he pulled his mangled hand close to his side. He was grabbed under the armpits by unseen figures and hauled upright.

He couldn't see them. But he could feel them. Could sense them.

He'd held back. He'd wanted to see what was at play. Now was the time to move.

Ryker summoned his inner focus and spun low. Kicked out. Next, elbow out, arced up, he made solid connection with the pointed joint and received a howl of pain in response. He spun again, opposite elbow pounding down like a hammer this time. He shimmied. Reached out and grabbed. Shouted out in pain. He'd grabbed with his injured hand. He fought through it. Twisted the arm around. Carried on twisting until the figure it belonged to crumpled to his knees, groaning as his arm was pushed to bursting point.

'No,' came the simple command from behind Ryker. He winced when he felt pressure on his side. An arm – vice-like –

wormed around his neck. He barely resisted. The risk wasn't worth it. Not with the knife pushed right up against his kidney. A nasty blow if the threat was followed through. Even with his clothes and coat on, a long enough, sharp enough blade would slip through the layers and his flesh with ease. A potentially fatal blow.

'Let him go.' The same voice. The same accent as the Silver Fox. Bulldog. The local hardmen were one thing, but Ryker was already far more wary of these two. After all, it was clear they were calling the shots.

Ryker released the arm and kicked the man beneath him to the ground. Just enough light seeped in from the road, onto the man's pain-filled face, to show it wasn't Erling, but one of his friends. The other lump that Ryker had felled rose back to his feet, nursing his skull where Ryker had hammered with his elbow. Erling and the others remained somewhere in the darkness.

Ryker's biggest problem, though, was Bulldog, and the knife he held to Ryker's side. The arm around his neck remained firm but not choking. He imagined Bulldog had plenty more effort to give if he wished.

'No games now,' said Silver Fox. 'Who are you, why are you here?'

Ryker didn't answer. He only thought about how he could fight back. Except every option he pondered had the prospect of fatality. For him.

Then came a police car siren behind him. He hadn't heard the approach. Lights flashed, blue and red, the beams illuminating the space around him in strobe. Bulldog whipped Ryker around so they were facing the new arrivals.

Doors opened. Shouting. A man. Woman.

Bulldog released Ryker's neck. A stampede ensued as Erling and crew sought to escape.

Ryker spun on his heel, looked down the alley. No one there in the darkness. The two Russians – or whatever they were – had vanished.

'Stop!'

Pettersen.

Ryker turned to face her. The boot of the police car was open. She stood by it, shotgun in her hands. She flicked the barrel from Ryker, to the man to his left. Then to the one to his right. The two he'd fought with, both of whom had been too slow to leg it. Everyone else had already scarpered.

'What the hell have you done?' Pettersen questioned, glaring at Ryker as her colleague edged forward.

'Self-defence,' Ryker said.

'Huh,' was all she said to that, clearly not convinced.

Ryker held up his mangled hand. In the flashes of blue and red he could see the damage for the first time. The skin was dark and glistened with blood and was torn, flesh gaping in places. Bad, but perhaps not as bad as he'd at first feared. It'd heal.

Ryker glanced to the two men beside him in turn. One looked like he needed a lie down. The other, who'd nearly had his arm snapped in two, looked a little too smug for Ryker's liking.

'Seven on one,' Ryker said. 'At least I think it was.'

'Seven?' the policeman said. 'I don't see seven.'

'That's because you let them get away,' Ryker said, turning his gaze to him. The officer had his hand on his hip, though nothing but a baton and handcuffs in his belt. The shotgun had come from the car. These officers weren't otherwise armed.

'We have to bring you to the station,' Pettersen said. 'All of you.'

'Fine with me,' Ryker said, not really feeling it. 'But on one condition.'

'You don't give us orders,' the policeman said.

'What condition?' Pettersen asked.

'The bar. They have two security cameras inside. One on the outside. There's also one on the outside of that office building over the road. You check all of those recordings. They'll back up what happened here.'

Pettersen and the policeman glanced to one another. So, too, did the two chumps either side of Ryker.

'You two. Go home,' Pettersen said, looking to the two men. 'I know where to find you.'

They didn't question her instruction. Ryker wanted to but decided against it. Pettersen pulled the gun down and placed it back into the boot.

'Now, get in the car,' she said to Ryker.

He did as he was told.

11

Berg's day had been long and tiring. Not least because he'd barely slept the night before. Not least because of all the shit he was still having to deal with on top of his *actual* work: thoughts of his wife with that lawyer, Tronstad, thoughts of how to get Nyland moving more quickly, and, perhaps most pertinently, thoughts of how he was going to deal with the Russians.

The time edged past ten pm as he stepped inside his home. A lot earlier than the previous night, at least.

No lights on downstairs, but he'd spotted Isabell's car on the drive, so she must be home. No sign of Nyland anywhere outside, staking out. Perhaps because he was so good at remaining unseen. Most likely because he wasn't there and hadn't been for hours. But then was it reasonable to expect him to be watching twenty-four hours a day?

Yes, given the money Nyland was now asking for, it was reasonable. Hopefully he was at least following up on Tronstad right now.

Berg messaged Nyland to check that very point. He idled about in the dark downstairs while he waited for a response.

A text message came through. A long, rambling message. He imagined the verbal diarrhoea spewing from Nyland's lips. Excuses. Nothing more.

No. Nyland wasn't staking out Tronstad, though he insisted he was doing everything he could.

Did he even believe that himself?

'Sigurd, is that you?' came the soft and slightly worried voice of Isabell from the top of the stairs.

Berg put his phone in his pocket and moved into the hallway. He'd deal with Nyland in the morning.

'Yes, dear,' he called up the stairs.

'Are you coming to bed?'

'I'll be there shortly.'

He listened to the soft patter of her footsteps as she returned to their bedroom. He let out a long and contemplative sigh as he stared through to the kitchen at the back of the house, and the windows to the outside – nothing visible in the darkness beyond. He shivered unexpectedly. Nothing visible. But was that the truth? Flashing thoughts pulsed in his mind once more. The Russians. How closely were they watching him?

Did they *know*? About the barrels at the bottom of the North Sea?

Did anyone?

Sometimes he wondered what he'd done wrong to be tested like this. Every time he tried to solve one of life's problems, another two sprang up from the dead, rotting roots of the first. A vicious propagation that if he didn't stamp out would eventually swallow him alive.

He couldn't let it.

He turned and moved for the stairs.

The only light on upstairs was the lamp on his bedside table. Isabell often left it like that when she went to bed first. As though she couldn't face the dark alone. As though his light being left on was a signal drawing him back home and to bed.

Last night it hadn't been on though, when he'd arrived home after his trip on the sea. Why? Had she simply got tired of waiting? Or...

'Come on,' she said, not looking at him as she shuffled under the covers. 'It's getting late. I have to be up early again.'

He said nothing as he moved to the en suite. Minutes later he flicked off his light and crawled under the covers. His side of the bed was ice cold. He shuffled toward her, and her warmth. She was facing away from him but he knew she wasn't yet asleep.

'Did you have a good day?' he asked, his voice quiet and soft.

She squirmed and moaned as though his question had roused her. 'Very,' she said in a sleepy tone.

'You worked all day?' he asked.

Work. Not work. She was a freelance event planner. She *worked* from home. How many events were there to plan in this part of the world at this time of the year?

'Yes. There's a conference to plan in Molde.'

'I thought that wasn't until March.'

'But it's a big one.'

'You were out most of the day then?'

'Not all day.'

'You do anything interesting?'

She turned over now. The room was dark enough but he could see her face, her eyes, and a look somewhere between irritation and discomfort.

'Not really. This is a lot of questions. For you.'

He huffed. He leaned in and planted a soft kiss on her lips. She smelled of roses and juniper. Or something like that. She smelled sweet. Good. She didn't react to the kiss, so he tried again. This time she kissed back, until he pulled away. He gazed at her, their faces only inches apart. He was aroused. He pushed himself closer, pressing up against her body.

'It's really late,' she said.

'Not really.' He moved in for another kiss but this time she moved back.

'This isn't like you,' she said.

'I can't kiss my wife?'

'You can. But usually you don't.'

He said nothing to that. Isabell was his wife. He loved her. They'd been married seventeen years and he'd never stopped loving her, even through all of their troubles and heartache. He'd always love her.

He also hated her. Hated so much about her. From the way she withheld herself – her body – from him like this, almost for the sole purpose of exerting power, to the way she brushed her hair noisily when he was trying to sleep in the morning, to the way she crunched her toast with her breakfast.

Petty grievances, really. But most of all he hated the thought of her with another man.

He leaned in for a kiss again. Ran his hand under her pyjama top. She kissed him back this time. Let him play with her breast. She didn't try to touch him though. Tease.

He slowly pulsed his hips forward and back, rubbing up against her, determined that she'd get the idea and cave eventually. She murmured contentedly. Images of her luscious naked body stuck in his mind. Her luscious body from years gone by, at least. She looked good naked, for her age, but the passage of time told on both of them.

Unwelcome thoughts crept into his head. Her naked body. But not him with her. Tronstad. Tall. Athletic. Toned muscle. An expert in the bed. No competition versus Sigurd.

His body tensed in anger. Though only for a few moments.

Somehow, the longer the thoughts lingered, the more it added to his arousal.

What the hell was that?

Was it the knowledge that he knew what she was doing? He knew her deception and was himself deceiving *her* by not revealing it?

Knowledge is power, as the saying goes.

He pushed the thought away. He slid his hand down. Past her belly button, under the elastic waist of her pyjama bottoms and knickers and onto her warm and moist crotch.

'Sigurd, no,' she said, reeling back and yanking his hand out. 'Not tonight. I'm sorry. Just... cuddle me.'

She turned over.

He thought for a moment as anger and frustration consumed him.

He imagined a hammer in his hand. Imagined bludgeoning her, there and then, in the bed. The noise. The smell. The sight of blood-soaked sheets underneath pounded flesh.

He shook the thoughts away. What was wrong with him?

'I need a drink.'

He grabbed his phone from the bedside table, and got out of bed.

12

One am had come and gone as Pettersen pulled the police car to the side of the road outside Blodstein Gjestehus. It was late. Ryker was tired. His now bandaged hand throbbed away, hurt like hell, despite the painkillers he'd been given. Still, the night could have ended far worse – either outside in that alley where he'd been so outnumbered, or in the police station, where he may well have spent more than a few hours in a cell. If it weren't for Pettersen.

Luckily Wold wasn't working the night, otherwise Ryker was sure he wouldn't have been granted such an early release, nor a release without charge.

Pettersen had worked quickly to gather the video evidence that Ryker had insisted on. She'd even shown him some of the clips in an interview room when she'd been trying to understand the sequence of events, and exactly who was and wasn't involved in the altercation. The were no clips of the main fracas, in the alley, but at least enough to back up Ryker's story.

The fact she hadn't charged Ryker with any crime suggested she did, ultimately, believe him.

What irked, at least a little, was that she seemingly had no intention of hauling in any of the locals for questioning. As though the whole thing, once Ryker's side of the story was confirmed, was an awkward spat where each party was as bad as the other.

Ryker could have insisted on further action against the gang, but what would be the point? The most important thing from his position was that he wasn't cooped up in a cell. He hated cells.

'I really don't know why you came here,' Pettersen said, looking over to Ryker. The engine remained rumbling away. Other than the police car, the street outside was deserted. 'But don't you think it would be better for everyone if you left now?'

'You sound just like the others,' Ryker said, holding her gaze. He saw the flash of insult in her eyes.

She looked away.

'That doesn't really answer the point,' she said.

'The more times I hear that question, the less I want to give an answer.'

'That's just silly.'

He guessed she had a point.

She broke out in a smile and seemed to relax a little. 'You want to hear a joke?' she said.

Ryker was a bit bemused by the proposition, by the turn in mood, but... 'Yeah, go on then.'

'A police officer is on patrol when he comes across a woman, standing in the road at a busy junction. He approaches her and shouts from the pavement to ask if she's okay. She replies, *Yes, but how do I get to the hospital from here?* The officer says, *Just keep standing there a little longer.*'

Ryker shook his head and smiled. But he also quickly realised perhaps her joke had been well chosen.

'You're saying I'm the woman in the road?' he asked. 'I stay here long enough and I'll get hurt?'

Pettersen shrugged. 'Am I?'

'I'm here because of the boy. Henrik. I don't know why, but I don't trust that he's okay.'

Ryker caught her eye. She looked uncomfortable now.

'Do you know who I'm talking about?' Ryker asked.

'I've only ever known two Henriks around here. One is the manager in there.' She indicated to the hotel. 'The other was a boy who lived here. But he hasn't been around for years.'

'Hasn't been around? That's a strange way of saying it.'

'What I mean is... he was... an orphan, I guess. He moved away years ago, to a new family.'

'You think that's the same Henrik I saw today?'

'I really don't know. I don't understand why he'd be back. But I also don't understand why it'd be a problem if he is.'

'Did you ask Wold about him?'

She didn't answer that. Ryker wasn't sure why, but he didn't push it.

'How did you even hear about what happened tonight?' he asked instead. 'You showed up just at the right time. Not for the first time today the police have been on hand, right on cue.'

Once again she didn't answer. It was natural for a police officer to keep elements of their work close, but was that the only reason for her silence?

'You believed me tonight,' Ryker said. 'I think your colleagues wouldn't have listened to a word I said. They would have assumed the outsider was in the wrong and banged me up.'

'I do my job. I do it properly.'

'I sense that. That's what I like about you.'

She caught his eye again, her face a little softer from the flattery. She shut the engine down and a strange silence followed for a few seconds.

'I get why people don't like me,' Ryker said. 'I'm not from here. I turn up, asking hard questions–'

'Sticking your nose in–'

'Only where I see something I don't like. I'm not trying to invade people's privacy. But I know something isn't right here.'

'You would make a terrible policeman. We use evidence. We don't just move around, invading lives until we find dirt.'

That was a fair point. And she was right, he would make a terrible policeman. On the other hand he'd made a very good agent for the Joint Intelligence Agency – the JIA, a secretive organisation previously run by the UK and US governments, until it had imploded in part due to his actions. He'd made a very good agent for the JIA for the very reason that he willingly flouted traditional rules, laws, regulations in order to get answers. In his time he'd worked with many of the more official government agencies and organisations, too, the police included, but had always hated it. Hated the constraints they were placed under, as necessary as he knew they were in the grander scheme of law and order.

'What you should be asking yourself,' Ryker said, 'is how, in the space of one day, did I nearly get myself killed here, in this town. That's not normal. That tells you I've hit too close to home on something.'

Her eyes narrowed. 'Sometimes your words don't make full sense to me.'

'But I think you know exactly what I'm talking about.'

She sighed and looked out the front again. 'Do you know the best thing about living in a small place like this?'

Ryker shrugged.

'We have so little crime. Honestly. The numbers are amazing. Violent crime in the area we cover is a tenth of that in the cities. Why?'

Ryker smirked. She looked offended by his response.

'It's not because the police are useless,' she said, clearly agitated by his reaction. 'It's because we really do know one another. We know almost everything about each other's lives. How can you commit crime when you know people so well? When you know that everything you do will be known by everyone else. Of course, we do still get some bad things, but it's much less than other places.'

'Perhaps you're right,' Ryker said. 'Most of the time at least. But, and I'm just saying maybe, and this is no reflection on you... but perhaps there's something bigger happening here, something worse than you've seen before.'

She sighed.

'My father was in the police too,' she said.

She left the statement hanging. Ryker waited for her to carry on.

'When I was much younger, just a child, there was a murder. It was a really big thing. There hadn't been a murder here for years. A housewife was strangled. Her body dumped in the water. The tides brought her to shore, otherwise we may never have found her.'

She paused from the story, looking out of her window again. Ryker sensed a certain pain in her body language. From the story, or something else, he wasn't sure.

'My father, he was so... determined. He was a good inspector, but... he never gave up on anything. Had to know everything.'

She flicked an accusatory look to Ryker now.

'Very much like you,' she said.

Ryker said nothing to that.

'He dug, and he dug. Caused problems for lots of people trying to get answers. What happened? The murderer was the woman's husband. Of course, he'd always been one of the suspects, partners are always most likely. The problem was... he'd killed her because she found out he was abusing their girls. But as my father closed in, the man chose the worst possible way out. One night, he killed those girls as they slept. Then he killed himself. Four deaths.'

She went quiet. She looked disturbed. Ryker worked the story over in his head.

'You're saying your father blamed himself for the girls' deaths?'

'Maybe not my father, like I said, he was very much like you. But lots of other people blamed him.'

'What else could he have done? If he hadn't investigated the first murder, the husband would have remained free. Would have continued to abuse his daughters and who knows what else?'

'I know that,' she said, the anger in her tone clear.

'Then what are you saying?'

'That there are different ways to get to the truth. Maximum destruction isn't always necessary.'

Fair point. Though Ryker didn't let on.

'What happened to your father?'

'He's dead.'

Her words carried a certain finality, and Ryker chose not to delve deeper. Instead...

'Those two Russians–'

'What Russians?' Pettersen interrupted, exasperation in her tone now.

'The two men.'

'You told me they *weren't* Russian.'

'They're probably from a border country. Possibly Ukraine. I don't know for sure.'

She rolled her eyes. 'We didn't even see their faces on the cameras.'

'Not on the cameras, no. But *I* saw their faces.'

Bulldog and Silver Fox had been especially covert. Heads down, hats and hoods covering their heads when they approached the bar. Inside, even with their faces revealed, they'd held their heads at angles, away from the cameras, so that nothing more than passing glimpses from the sides had been captured of their features. Not coincidence, but absolute deliberate action on their part. They were clever, well rehearsed. Careful. Dangerous.

Pettersen didn't buy any of that. She'd claimed back at the station that it was pure luck – or lack of it – that they had no clear images of them.

'I told you already–'

'You would know if there were two foreign troublemakers in town,' Ryker said.

She looked even more pissed off that he'd tried to finish the sentence for her.

'That's not what I was going to say. I was going to say, I would know if there were two foreign troublemakers who our locals are in a gang with. The men you were fighting with tonight? There's nothing special about them. They're not gangsters. Yes they're rough, but they're just normal men. There's no mafia boss here.'

'I'm not saying there is.'

'Then what are you saying?'

'That maybe you don't know everything about these people, even if you think you do.'

'You can get out now.'

He held her eye for a moment longer. Something in her look... he liked her. He didn't want to piss her off, even if he could tell he had. But was that down to his attitude with her, or because he was opening her eyes to uncomfortable truths?

'Goodnight, Inspector Pettersen.'

He put his hand to the door.

'You paid for only one night here,' she said.

He paused. He wasn't sure if her words were a statement or a question.

'Yeah,' he said.

'Don't pay for another. Please.'

He said nothing.

'See you in the morning,' she added.

He didn't question what she meant by that.

He got out of the car, stretching as he did so, then closed the door. The engine remained off. He moved to the hotel. Locked up. Of course. He could hardly have expected the manager or receptionist or whatever he was to have stayed up waiting...

Clunk.

Well, apparently...

Locks released, the door was opened and two bleary eyes peered to Ryker from behind a pair of glasses.

'Finally,' the receptionist – the other Henrik? – said. 'What a night.'

Ryker couldn't have agreed more.

He moved inside. Glanced over his shoulder and caught Pettersen's eye before the front door was closed and locked up.

Ryker apologised, more than once, then headed to his room. He didn't turn the light on. He moved to the window, curtains open, and peered down below.

Pettersen remained. Would she really be there all night?

Ryker checked his watch. The face was badly scratched from the earlier scuffle. A shame. He liked this piece.

Regardless, he'd had enough adventure for one day. He'd restart tomorrow, whether or not Pettersen was still there. He set the alarm on his phone for seven am, then got ready for some much needed sleep.

13

Konstantin looked up from the shimmering blade of the knife in his hand, and to his form in the grotty mirror of the men's toilet. At least, what had once been a toilet, many years ago when this place had last seen real use.

The patchwork lines of raised flesh across his tattooed chest glowed in the thin light. The newest of the scars, a three-inch long gash just above his left nipple, remained deeply red and swollen, the edges wet where the skin continually pulled apart anytime he exerted effort. He didn't need stitches. It would heal over soon enough.

He muttered under his breath. Incoherent to anyone who could have overheard, but the words were deliberate, methodical. Prayer-like.

Penance. Atonement. Is that how others would describe this ritual? All Konstantin knew was that it was necessary, and that he couldn't operate without this.

He held the knife higher. Focused hard on the reflection of the blade in the mirror. He touched the point of the knife onto his skin, the opposite side to the rawest of the scars. His skin tingled with the sensation, pimples forming around the knife point as though inviting what was to come.

With his teeth gritted he pulled the blade down and across. Skin and flesh parted.

This was a deep one. It needed to be. He slashed the knife again, a line parallel to the first, equally as deep.

Yes, he felt pain, but Konstantin didn't murmur. Didn't make a sound other than his constant, calm breathing. With the knife down by his side, he watched as blood oozed from the open wound. He focused on the sight, on the pain that pulsed. He didn't like pain. He was no masochist. He didn't thrive off it. That wasn't why he did this.

He did this to remind himself of who he was. What he did.

Splat.

Just a faint noise – the sound of a drop of blood falling from the knife and into the puddle of water on the cracked tile floor. Somehow the sound snapped him from his thoughts. He looked down. Past his naked torso, past his dirtied jeans, past his black boots, to the floor. For a few moments he watched the ripples in the dirty liquid as the blood diffused into the water.

Soon all was still and quiet once more.

It was time.

He turned away from the mirror, pulled open the door. He strode across the concrete floor. Swathes of sunlight burst into the grotty structure from the holes in the walls and the tall gabled roof way up high. An expansive room of what used to be a... he had no clue. He didn't care.

The two figures in front of him gently swung back and forth, the ropes around their ankles suspending them from the rafters above. Both figures were naked, both gagged. They faced him, and had moaned as soon as he'd opened the door. As he closed in on them the noise grew louder and more frantic. The man, on the left of the two, bucked from side to side, forward and back, as though swinging more forcibly was somehow going to help him now. Somehow prevent what was to come.

It was the man Konstantin moved over to. In his late forties, the man was big, muscled – good genes – though he'd enjoyed his lavish life that little bit too much given the pouch around his gut, and the way, hanging upside down, his chest sagged toward his neck.

Konstantin squatted down and looked into the man's eyes.

'You know why you're here,' Konstantin said. 'You may even know who I am.'

A strong but muffled response.

'It will help if you know who I am. Help to persuade you there is only one correct choice for you here.'

Konstantin reached forward. The man froze now. Konstantin brought his motion to a stop and reached a finger underneath the cloth gag, by the side of the man's head, well away from his jaw in case he had the stupid thought of trying to bite.

'When I take this off, you can scream if you want. Scream until your lungs burn and your throat bleeds. But it won't help. Or you can listen to what I have to say, and tell me what I need to know.'

No response from the man. His wife, next to him, sobbed.

Konstantin whipped the knife up and sliced through the gag. A little knick on the man's skin too, which was perhaps why he squirmed and moaned in pain, but it was nothing, a scratch really.

'Now. Tell me who tried to kill Jesper.'

'What? No. I don't–'

Konstanin growled with effort as he threw a fist into the man's bouncy gut. The captive hadn't been prepared for the shot and air burst from his lips and Konstantin saw the fight in his eyes as he struggled to keep his oxygen-starved brain from drifting. Five seconds. Ten seconds. Enough.

'I'll only ask the question one more time. After that, I'll move to your wife. She won't get a question. I'll simply take her apart. Skin. Flesh. Bones. Piece by piece. I won't stop. Not until she's lying in bits by your feet. Then I'll do the same to you.'

Both of them sobbed and begged.

'Who tried to kill Jesper?'

'I... I don't know!' the man screamed.

Konstantin sighed and hung his head. So be it. He'd earned his stripes for today after all.

He shuffled over to the woman. Her feminine smell tickled his nose. He wasn't aroused as he looked over her svelte, naked body, though he did think it was such a waste. Such a waste that her husband would protect his own honour – was that it? – over this beauty.

So be it. His choice.

Konstantin lifted the knife, and sank it into her flesh.

Thirty minutes later, Konstantin returned to the sink, out of breath. His hands, arms, chest, face, everything on him, glistened with a mix of perspiration and blood and crimson-soaked sinew.

He filled the bucket with water from the tap then tipped the contents over his head, using a scrubbing brush to get rid of a good portion of the red stuff from his skin. His chest stung like crazy as he rubbed over the fresh wounds.

Yes, he'd certainly earned those today.

He moved back out. As he grabbed his bag from beside the door, he took nothing more than a cursory glance at the lumps of butchered flesh across the way that used to be two human beings. He was midway through towelling himself dry when a buzzing came from the front pocket of the bag. His phone. Only one person had this number.

'Yes,' he said.

'Did he tell you?'

'No.'

'So they're both dead?'

Konstantin stared across the bloodstained floor to the corpses.

'Both of them.'

Silence on the other end. Was this not what Jesper wanted?

'Maybe he didn't know after all,' Jesper said.

If Konstantin had to give an opinion, he'd say the same. Surely no man could bear witness to their wife being savaged like that otherwise. Not that their fate hadn't already been sealed, either way.

Konstantin didn't care. He'd only done what had been asked.

'Leave the bodies,' Jesper said. 'I want them found.'

'Okay.'

He'd have preferred to burn the place down. Destroy the evidence of his presence here, even if he didn't really care much for such things. Did it really matter if he left DNA here for a forensics team to try and trace? If the law ever found him, and if he couldn't escape, he'd only ever get what he deserved.

'And I have something else for you. Details to follow.'

The call ended. Konstantin pulled the phone from his ear and looked to the screen. After a few seconds a text message popped up. A simple message. Just two pieces of information: a name, a place. The name he didn't recognise. The place, he did.

Trondheim, Norway.

14

Ryker awoke five minutes before his alarm went off. Before anything else he rose from the bed and edged over to the window. Daylight wouldn't arrive for some time, and the dark street outside was quiet and serene.

His eyes rested on the police car, right outside the entrance. From the angle he couldn't tell whether it was Pettersen's car or some other colleague who'd taken over in the intervening small hours of the night. Either way, Ryker was less than impressed. He showered and dressed and packed his things and headed down. No sign of Henrik, the manager, on the ground floor. No sign of anyone at all. Ryker let himself out.

He walked over to the police car. Sure enough, it was Pettersen. She was behind the wheel, although her chair was reclined and her head was laid back, her eyes closed.

He could just walk away...

He knocked on the glass. She jumped to attention. Looked more than a little embarrassed. She wiped at her mouth then fumbled with the buttons to eventually wind the window down.

'You could have just slept in your bed,' Ryker said.

She glanced to the dashboard.

'You're up early,' she said.

'Seemed a shame to wake you.'

'Why did you?'

'I thought it was unfair to slink off when you've put so much effort in to keep an eye on me.'

She glanced to his shoulder. His bag.

'You told me not to stay another night,' he explained, as if an explanation was needed.

'I didn't think you'd listen.'

'Made all the more clear by you still being here.'

'So you're really leaving?'

He sensed a slight disappointment in her manner and tone.

'Any tips on where I should go next?' Ryker asked.

'North or south?'

'Either.'

She squirmed in her seat – her best attempt at stretching in the confined space.

'I'm off shift at eight. You want breakfast? I'll tell you everything I know about my country.'

An interesting proposition. And he rarely turned down an invitation for food, but...

'Another time,' he said, straightening up. 'See you around, Inspector.'

He walked over to his Volvo. No doubt she'd follow him out of town, to make sure he really was leaving. Fine by him.

After all, it was early. He'd be back soon enough.

———

Midday had come and gone as Ryker once again approached Blodstein from the south. Hours of driving had taken its toll. More than anything he was bored. Had it all been a waste of time? Possibly. But at least, for now, he should be able to travel a little more freely given his departure from town, and his emergence in a different car. The newly rented Ford was a step up from the Volvo he'd handed back in Trondheim. Bigger, roomier, and more of a fit with the other cars he'd seen around the remote area – plus, the car had no insignia anywhere on its body showing it was a rental. Of course, the simple deception likely wouldn't last long, but he had no tail on him now, and if he kept his trail clean, he could start to find some real answers without worrying about being banged up in a cell.

He didn't go straight into Blodstein, even if he could have used the rest. Instead, he took the penultimate turning on the right before he hit the town, carried on down the track, and pulled into the same spot in the forest as the previous day. All was quiet, at least from what he could see and hear from inside the cabin.

He shivered as he got out of the car. With a miserable overcast sky above, and sleety, wispy snow filling the air, the temperature was several degrees below freezing. Ryker hunched down in his coat and headed off into the forest, trudging across the soggy undergrowth toward the house. He moved over the rise, and paused – as he had done the previous day – to look down to the house.

All quiet. A virtually identical scene to the day before. Except for one big difference. The Nissan pickup truck was parked in the clearing.

Ryker had a balaclava in his pocket. He thought about putting it on. But was there really any point? He hated the things, always felt suffocated by them – not least because they reminded him of the sacks and other garments that had been forcibly pulled over his head on the many occasions he'd suffered torture – but he had to admit that the prospect of the extra warmth appealed.

He didn't bother. He was happy to stand face to face with whoever was down there.

He moved with caution, heading a little deeper into the forest than the last time to approach the house from the back. Other than the Nissan, he saw no sign of life at the house at all. From this angle he could see a steel vent rising from the roof, most likely from a boiler, though no visible gases plumed out of the top.

He reached the final tree before the clearing and stopped. Looked around for a couple of minutes. Spotted one, two, security cameras, though they were each facing near side-on to the building, to capture the immediate perimeter, and he was sure he wasn't in view of either. If he was to get any closer, though, he would be.

But then, was there really someone inside, sat at a little monitor watching security footage in real time all day? Highly unlikely, and if there was, that only made Ryker all the more determined to find out why.

Time to move.

He slipped out from behind the tree, and as softly as he could he padded across the sloppy mud of the clearing to the back corner of the property where the large decking area stretched out.

The building had a window a few yards either side of the corner, a back door. Ryker edged left first, across the side of the house, to the window there. He sneaked a peek. Then took a longer look. The glass was so grimy – green sludge from years of weathering covered the outside – that he could barely make out a thing of what lay beyond. Whatever it was, it was a small, closed-off room, he decided, with no other natural light coming into there.

He moved around the corner, onto the decking, to the next window. Boarded up from the inside. Not helpful at all.

But as he held his breath for a moment he did hear something beyond the thin wood-clad walls. Light thudding... someone walking. Getting louder...

The back door, only yards from Ryker, swung open. He rushed back as quickly as he could, around the corner. He pressed himself up against the wall. He'd been quick, but he couldn't be sure if he'd been seen or not. Perhaps someone had seen him on the camera feed after all?

Footsteps on the deck. Just one person. They stopped moving. Still no indication that they'd been alerted by Ryker's presence.

He waited, his breathing calm and slow and silent. The person – a man – mumbled, but he was only talking to himself. Ryker heard a fizzle and then the man let out a long exhale. Smoking?

More mumbling, then a few footsteps before the door banged shut once more.

Ryker waited a moment in the silence before he leaned forward to steal a glance around the corner...

'Asshole.'

A calm and confident insult delivered by the man standing right there at the corner. The wiry man from the Nissan. A snarl on his face. A bat in his hand. The bat arced toward Ryker's head.

He ducked, stepped left. The bat smashed into the side of the house. Ryker bunched his fist and pounded it into the man's side. The guy groaned in pain. Ryker grabbed the end of the bat with his good hand, used the elbow of his other arm to swipe down against the man's wrist to prise his grip from the wood.

Ryker lifted the bat and pulled it up against the man's windpipe. He pulled tight. The man coughed and spluttered and Ryker squeezed harder still to force him to the ground, himself taking a knee in the process. The man clawed at the wood.

Clawed at Ryker's hands and arms as he rasped and gasped. Ryker let go of the bat and tossed it, immediately snaking an arm around the man's neck. Just as much grip, one less hand needed, which was good for two reasons. One, it meant he didn't have to strain with his still bandaged hand. Two, it freed that hand up to check the man's pockets. Keys. Phone. E-cig. No weapons.

The back door opened again. Another man stepped out. Another man Ryker recognised. The second, bulkier man from the Nissan. Ryker removed his arm, rose, and raced forward. The man spotted him. Shock was the first expression to register on his face. Ryker dove forward, feet first, slid across the greasy deck, right into the man's legs. He caved. Ryker bounced up, both men righted themselves, moved together at the far end of the deck, squaring up for a further attack.

'We don't have to do this,' Ryker said, looking from the men to the open doorway he was standing by.

A dark corridor. It was difficult to make out much more inside. Who else was in there?

The two men muttered in their native language.

Movement inside. Ryker could hear the soft padding of feet, but could still see nothing in the gloomy interior.

'Who's in there?' Ryker asked. No answer. 'The boy? Henrik?'

The two men looked at one another. One remained glaring, but the other, the bigger and nastier-looking of the two, broke out into a smile.

'Is he in there?' Ryker asked.

The smiling man didn't answer Ryker, but shouted out, looking at the house as he did so. Ryker didn't understand a word of what he said. But the sound of movement inside ramped up. Ryker instinctively stepped back from the doorway, giving himself extra room to move. The two men remained on the far side of the deck, both at the ready. Ryker could quite easily fell them, though he was much more interested in what was about to come out from the inside, which was where his eyes rested.

Movement to his right. Ryker whipped his eyes that way. It was the smiling man, crouching to pick up the fallen bat. His friend half-stepped forward to protect him while he was prone on the ground. Ryker left them. A bat didn't worry him too much.

When he looked back to the doorway his heart bounced in his chest when he saw the tall silhouetted figured moving forward. Ryker tensed, another half step back, away from the door. A man's shout from within.

'He says to keep calm,' Smiler said, off to Ryker's left. 'No one will be hurt.'

Ryker said nothing. Slowly, the figure moved closer to the door. As the dim natural light finally hit his form, Ryker inhaled sharply. It wasn't just a third man – Erling, no less – but the boy. Walking in front of Erling, his eyes, his every movement, were nervous and jittery.

'You again?' Erling said when he and the boy were standing on the deck. Henrik was close to him, hands by his sides. Erling's arms were down by his sides too, his hands out of sight behind the boy's back. Was he holding a weapon there?

'Henrik?' Ryker asked, holding his eyes on the boy, and the boy only.

A short pause before the boy nodded.

'He's my son,' Erling said. 'You're scaring him.'

Ryker flicked his gaze to Erling and back to Henrik. No reaction to the man's words on the boy's face.

'You're scaring him,' Erling said again. 'He doesn't know why you're here to hurt us.'

'Hurt you?' Ryker said, his focus on Henrik still. 'I'm not going to hurt you.'

'Then you should go,' Erling said. 'The police are already coming.'

Ryker looked over each of the men now, a sliver of doubt creeping in. Could the explanation really be so simple? And what of the threat of the police? Ryker had already had more than one let-off with them. So, too, had these men, that was for sure, after the stunt that Erling had pulled the previous day at the bar. The conversation with Pettersen from the night rattled in Ryker's mind, about his 'style' of investigation. Was Ryker really in the wrong here?

'You want me to go?' Ryker asked Henrik.

Henrik didn't answer at first. Instead, he glanced over to the two men.

'Henrik. Look at me, not them,' Ryker said. 'Do you want me to go?'

His youthful face quivered, like he couldn't choose the answer. Surely if anything Erling had said was true, then the answer would have been simple.

The uncertainty on Henrik's face turned to a nod.

'See,' Erling said.

Ryker wasn't sure he did.

'How about I call Inspector Pettersen,' Ryker said. He reached to his pocket. The man with the bat jumped forward a step then stopped – a warning, nothing more.

'I'm just going for my phone,' Ryker assured him. 'I'm not armed. But I'm sure Pettersen would be interested to know Henrik is safe and well. She was concerned when I told her about the accident yesterday.'

Erling's face remained screwed in anger – his resting face, perhaps. Ryker had certainly seen that look on him more than any other. Henrik looked more petrified than ever. He breathed heavily as though he could sense a fight looming.

Ryker's fingers reached inside his pocket. He grasped the phone. Had nearly pulled it out...

'Don't.' The man with the bat. 'Put it down and take your hand out. Now.'

Ryker paused. 'You don't want me to call the police?'

No answer.

'Now why would that be?'

'Put the phone down.'

Ryker pulled his hand free. Still holding on to the phone.

'Oops,' he said.

The two men charged him. Henrik screamed when Erling grabbed a handful of his hair and yanked his head back. Erling's other hand came into view. Knife. Erling dragged Henrik back toward the house as the boy squirmed and moaned. Ryker wanted to go after him...

He could do nothing but duck and bring up his arm to protect himself from the swinging bat. The wood crashed into his forearm, sending a shudder of pain through his bones. He lashed out with his fist, catching the now not-so-smiley man in his groin. A cheap shot. Ryker couldn't care less. He leaped up, forearm pulled back, his injured hand close to his chin, the elbow pointed out and upward. A horrific crack sounded as the elbow connected under the man's jaw. His head jerked back and he tumbled to the deck. Ryker drove forward with a knee to the groin of Bat-man. Another. Another. He grabbed the man by the shoulders, thrust him up against the wall of the house and delivered one last ferocious blow with his knee, grinding the joint into the man's already pounded flesh.

Ryker let go and the guy crumpled to the deck, face screwed, tears streaming as he clutched at whatever was left of his manhood.

A scream – Henrik – and a shout – Erling – from inside the

house. Ryker raced over just as Henrik bounded out of the open door. Blood dripped down his chin.

'Henrik!'

Ryker reached out for him, but Henrik shrugged him off and the next second the huge Erling bulldozed him to the ground, the force of the hit like a juggernaut. Ryker crashed to the decking, the air pushed from his lungs. Erling landed on top. Thumped his fists into Ryker's sides.

Ryker twisted his neck to see Henrik rushing toward the trees.

'Henrik, no!'

Ryker winced when a fist caught him in the jaw. Blood dribbled down his chin. But when he saw the balled fist coming his way again, he realised the blood was from Erling's hand. Henrik had bitten him?

Ryker blocked the fist, but took another to the side. Erling was big, in all likelihood stronger, but Ryker wasn't going to lie and take the blows. With Erling acting with fury, and intent on punishing, Ryker reached up and sank his jaws into Erling's upper arm – a sweet spot of nerves between the biceps and triceps. Erling squirmed and squealed like a pig. Ryker held on until the big man's strength faded, then he let go and shoved Erling away and slid out from underneath.

Ryker jumped to his feet, fighting through the fog in his head and the aches in his body as much as he could. A heel to the back of Erling's head kept him down on the ground. The other two men were fighting through their own pain. For now the ruckus was over, but before long all three would be up and fighting.

'Henrik!' Ryker shouted out, looking to the spot in the forest where Henrik had gone – the opposite direction to where Ryker's car was parked. No sign of the boy now.

Ryker set off for the trees.

'Henrik!' he shouted once more, but by the time the house had faded into the distance behind him, he decided to keep his mouth shut. No point in drawing the others in.

Ryker moved as quickly as he could, looking back every other step to check for a chasing pack. Where had the boy gone? He knew from looking at satellite images that there was nothing out in this direction for miles around.

After moving for several minutes, Ryker stopped. He spun around on the spot, eyes darting. Nothing around him but trees and ice-cold air.

SNAP.

Off to his left. Ryker crouched and spun again.

A squirrel was four yards away, perched on its hind legs, staring at Ryker as though curious at the imposter.

SNAP.

Ryker spun again. Not a squirrel this time, but... what was it? He could see nothing.

'Henrik?' Ryker asked, quietly, hopefully.

No response.

Ryker looked back the way he'd come. At least the way he thought he'd come. He could see nothing but dense trees in every direction, and with the overcast sky hiding the sun, it was near impossible to determine direction.

He shivered. How long would the teenager last out here on his own? Ryker, well-trained in the past for surviving such inhospitable climates, was positive he could make it several days, far longer if he could source – forage or scavenge – food, but a youngster on his own?

Memories swam in Ryker's mind. Some of his worst. Of being alone, abandoned in the cold. He felt for Henrik... but if he didn't want to be found, what was Ryker supposed to do?

The sound of a not-too-distant siren hung in the air. Coming from behind him.

Police. They were after Ryker, no doubt. Most likely Wold, if Erling and his men had made the call.

What about Pettersen? In theory, alerting the police, having a rescue party, was the best bet of anyone finding Henrik, though Ryker had no clue who he could trust.

One thing he did know, he saw little point in traipsing aimlessly through the cold, particularly when he had Erling and his gang, plus the police, on his tail and all wanting his blood.

Ryker hung his head. Then, from out of the trees in front of him...

'Mister,' Henrik said, slinking into view. His cheeks were red from exertion, but without a coat on he shivered violently, his arms cradled to his chest. 'Mister, you'll help me?'

Ryker nodded. 'Yes. I will.'

15

R yker gave his coat to Henrik. The kid needed it more than he did. Still, within a few minutes it was Ryker whose body shook with cold. They'd barely made any progress in moving back to his car. Down below, they could hear the search party, talking, calling to one another as they moved through the forest.

Ryker and Henrik huddled down by the thick trunk of a tree. Henrik, having initially looked petrified when he'd come out into the open in front of Ryker, now seemed far more relaxed, though he'd hardly spoken a word since.

'We need to get to my car,' Ryker said, not taking his eyes from the trees in front of them. 'It's north of the house. Probably over a mile from here. But to get there we'll have to move further inland to avoid them.'

Did Henrik even understand all of what Ryker was saying? He nodded as though he did. Ryker had so many questions. For now, the one and only aim, though, was to get to the car and get away.

'I hear something,' Henrik said, flicking his gaze off to the left. He shuffled closer to Ryker at the same time, as though seeking comfort.

Ryker looked to the same spot. He'd heard it too. It was why he'd stopped here in the first place. He couldn't be sure how many people were out there searching. The men from the house – if they were up to it. Police? Any other locals who were part of whatever plot this was, or who had at least been tricked into helping against the 'outsider'? Ryker was sure to be painted the bad guy here, whatever the hell was going on.

The one thing he was most wary of? Dogs. He was content that, given enough time, he and Henrik could bypass all of the search party, if they moved far enough away. But if the search party had dogs... that was a different game altogether. Plus, the longer he and Henrik stayed out in the cold, the greater the risk from exposure for both of them.

As they waited, Ryker had no sight of the men, but after a long period of silence he was sure whoever they'd heard had passed by.

He rose, slowly, carefully. A further shiver ran through him with his elongated body more exposed. Henrik followed and Ryker put a hand behind his back to guide him off to the right, heading east – at least what Ryker thought was east – further inland and away from the house. A necessary step before they could circle north and to his car.

'No,' Henrik said, not moving from the spot. 'Not that way.'

Ryker looked to him, trying to read his face, his mood.

'More men,' Henrik said.

'Another house?' Ryker asked.

Henrik shook his head. 'The trees. Tree men.'

'Loggers? Chopping the trees?'

Ryker motioned the action, his hand an axe, in case Henrik hadn't otherwise understood. Henrik smirked and nodded.

Ryker guessed it made some sense that there would be logging out to the east of them too. The buildings at the logging site he'd been to the previous day were only a few miles north. It wasn't unthinkable that the same operation covered multiple square miles around here. Or even that more than one company operated out here in the vast woodlands. Either way, Henrik's apprehension was clear, and whether or not that apprehension was built on solid foundation or not, Ryker had to give it attention.

'We have to get to the car,' Ryker said. 'Then a town. We'll freeze out here.'

'We go to the road this way. It's quicker.'

Ryker didn't like that idea at all. The main road, even if it was potentially the shortest route back to ultimate safety, would leave them in the open, far too exposed to whatever threat they faced from the people hunting them.

'No,' Ryker said, shaking his head. 'It's too dangerous.'

But Henrik wasn't listening. The next second he'd shrugged away from Ryker's arm and moved at speed in the opposite direction. Ryker growled and set off after him.

'Henrik!'

The boy took no notice. And he was surprisingly nimble on his feet when he wanted to be. Putting paid to all caution, he was more or less at a run, weaving left and right through the trees, darting over fallen branches and trunks.

'Henrik, stop!' Ryker hissed, trying to be quiet, discreet, but not really succeeding. It was one thing to move quickly, but to move recklessly would only give away their position. But what could Ryker do except follow closely? He couldn't let Henrik get away.

After less than a minute, though, Henrik suddenly pulled up. He panted from exertion. Ryker too.

'What is it?' Ryker said.

No sooner had the words passed his lips, he heard it.

Dogs.

Henrik's panicked eyes found Ryker's.

'Come on,' Henrik said.

Ryker didn't question him this time. The dogs were somewhere behind them. To the north and east of their position. Getting back to the car in that direction was out of the question.

They both moved into a sprint. Or as close to a sprint as they could manage. At full pelt on a flat surface Ryker was sure he could have outrun the youngster, but across the obstacles of the frozen forest, the lighter and more gainly youth had the advantage. Ryker, certainly fit, but far heavier and three decades older, was soon seriously out of breath. His legs ached from lactate build-up. His lungs ached from constant heavy breaths. His head pounded from the fight he'd already been involved in...

Henrik looked like he could go on all day.

At least the cold wasn't bothering Ryker so much now.

But the dogs were. Their frantic barking became louder with every stride Ryker took. Were they leashed?

Did it matter?

'Henrik, be careful!'

Ryker saw it before the boy. Or at least had decided on caution first. He slowed up as they approached the ridge. Henrik did too, but only at the last second. Too late. He lost his footing – ice? Wet branch? He fell back onto his rear and with a panicked shriek slid out of Ryker's view.

'Henrik!'

In a moment of panic Ryker raced forward, fearing the worst.

Not quite. But it wasn't good either. A long, icy, snowy slope. Ryker threw himself to the ground and slid down the bank after Henrik, at least a hundred feet of clear space in front of them; snow and ice, just a few sparse trees. At the end... a sheer drop.

'Henrik!' Ryker shouted out again. A pretty useless instruction really, he realised.

But then Henrik hit something unseen. A branch under the snow perhaps?

Ryker hurtled past him, his speedier momentum aided further by his much heavier frame. Snow blasted up into his face making it near impossible to see clearly, but he was sure the cliff edge was only yards away. He flipped his body over so he was on his belly. He squinted hard, fighting to see what was coming up. There. A stump.

He battled against gravity to shift his body weight across. Reached out with both arms. Tried his best to wrap them around the stump...

He managed it... for all of a second before the pendulum momentum of his body caused his grip to fail and his body twisted around so he was moving head first.

Five yards to the edge. Four. Three.

He reached out and grabbed what looked like nothing more than a thin branch sticking up from the snow. Somehow it held.

Ryker dug in. Feet. Knees. Fingers. Finally he was at a stop.

'Help!' Henrik screamed as his flailing body raced toward Ryker.

Ryker reached out to try and grab Henrik's arm. No good. Henrik slid by...

Got him. By the ankle. Ryker was nearly pulled away, too, but somehow had dug himself into the ice enough to hold firm.

Henrik's scream heightened. When Ryker looked down, he could see why. The kid's torso was out of sight, dangling over the edge of the cliff.

Ryker strained and grimaced. 'Hold on!'

He doubled his grip by grabbing Henrik's ankle with his bandaged hand. Well, it had been bandaged. Now the cloth was torn and bloodied and flapping freely. Ryker ignored the pain. He growled in effort as he hauled Henrik back over the edge.

Both of them rolled onto their backs, heavy breaths spilling into the cold air above them.

'Close,' Ryker said.

Henrik laughed. Ryker already liked him.

But they were far from in the clear. As Ryker looked back up the slope, he spotted the gathering crowd. One, two, three, four men at the top. Two dogs. On leads. Jumping against their restraints, barking and yelping with excitement and anticipation.

The next second, the dogs were unleashed.

'Oh shit,' Ryker said.

16

The dogs – Alsatians – half slid, half galloped down the slope, barking excitedly, frantically. Ryker tried to get to his feet but slipped and decided he was better off closer to the ground. As carefully as he could, he slid his body to the edge. Peered down below. A big drop. Easily as big as the slope they'd just slid down, but sheer, jagged rock. The empty, twisting road to Blodstein was right there at the bottom. If they'd fallen over the edge, they almost certainly wouldn't have survived.

'Over there,' Henrik said, pointing to the north side. 'We can climb.'

Ryker thought he knew which part Henrik was referring to. Twenty steps in front of them, the rock face split in two creating a ridge about halfway down its face. Under any other circumstances, Ryker would have said Henrik was crazy to even suggest they attempt it.

'Come on!' Henrik said. He moved onto his feet, but looked shaky. He remained hunched, knees bent, so his hands were inches from the snow. He looked more like a monkey than a human as he jostled forward. Ryker glanced to the dogs. They were nearly halfway down already.

What choice did they have?

He shuffled along behind Henrik, teetering on the edge of the cliff, one slip away from a fall that was surely fatal.

Henrik paused. Ryker pulled up by his side. They were directly above the ridge which protruded all of two yards from the main rock face. But with it were numerous other smaller indentations and shards sticking out. Perfect for a rock climbing enthusiast. Not so perfect in the ice cold, with one injured hand, no gear, and dogs chasing.

Ryker moved first. He turned to face up the slope then eased his body down. Down. One step and one painful handhold at a time. He'd barely begun when his foot slipped. He tried his best to regain traction but his frozen digits simply had too little strength.

Ryker fell.

'No!' Henrik screamed.

He'd barely finished the one word call when Ryker's back smacked down onto rock. The ridge. It was nothing more than pure luck that his body didn't topple over the edge.

He was dazed. In agony. For seconds he wasn't sure he could move at all. Henrik rushed down after him. Ryker wanted to shout out to tell him to go slow, to be careful, but he couldn't even find the strength to do that.

He regained some of his focus, some of his strength, when a plume of snow cascaded over the edge above Henrik and a barking dog came into view. The next moment another flurry, before the second dog sprang into view too. Its barks soon turned to a whimper when it reached the edge and its legs flailed as it tried desperately not to topple over.

Ryker willed it to safety. As much as he didn't want those beasts clamping their jaws around him, they weren't the enemy.

The dog managed to stay on top. Just about. A moment later

and the first of the men's heads bobbed into view. He called out to his friends.

Henrik landed on the ridge next to Ryker with a thud. Ryker had barely noticed him make his descent.

'You okay?' he said, pulling on Ryker's arm as if to encourage him up.

Ryker tried to lift his torso. It was agony, but he did it. He moved to his knees, then put his weight onto his feet. His brain was swimming.

'Follow me,' Henrik said. And he was off again.

Ryker glanced up once more. Two of the men were there now. The dogs weren't barking but were breathing heavily, their long, pink tongues dangling. No one looked like they were about to follow down the cliff.

Which only meant one thing. They would try to track back and intercept on the road instead. Ryker and Henrik were far from in the clear.

Ryker got moving. The last part of the descent was far easier, far less severe. When they were down below the tops of the last of the trees that sprinkled the cliff face, Henrik let go and jumped the rest of the way. He landed out of sight below Ryker with a gentle thud.

'Hurry!' Henrik said from beneath him.

Ryker decided against such a move. His knees wouldn't thank him for it, and he'd already taken enough knocks today, not to mention the lifetime of knocks before that.

He finally jumped down when he was a couple of yards from the verge at the side of the road. Even that sent a nasty shock through his bones.

'I'm getting too old for this,' he said to Henrik when he'd righted himself.

Henrik looked like he didn't know what Ryker meant by that.

Ryker glanced back above. No sign of anyone, or anything, at the top now.

'We don't have long,' Ryker said.

They'd certainly never make it back to his car before they crossed paths with the others.

But what would they do when they saw Ryker and Henrik on the road? Mow them down? For whatever reason, Ryker didn't believe the men wanted Henrik dead, otherwise he already would have been. But what about him? Was he expendable? Was his best chance out of this now to stand his ground and fight them off? He certainly didn't want to beg or bargain for his survival.

'Let's go,' Ryker said, eventually finding the strength to move his increasingly heaving body into a jog.

Henrik moved alongside him, both of them at the side of the road where the pristine-looking tarmac gave way to a slushy, muddy verge before the rock face. The other side of the road was the drop to the water, nothing between the tarmac and blue stuff other than an ageing metal barrier, and a thin row of trees.

'Move to the other side,' Ryker said, glancing behind him to check the road was clear before darting across. He jumped the barrier, took a couple of slippery steps on the snowy ground around the trees to correct himself. Much slower to move here than on the cleared road, but at least they had some cover.

They continued to move as fast as they could – conditions permitting – with not a word spoken between them. They rounded a bend in the road – a bend in the natural layout of the land – and in the distance the cluster of buildings making up Blodstein's industrial waterfront came into view. Potential safety. Potential warmth. It looked so close, but they were at least two miles away still. Plus the town would be full of the townsfolk. Each one a potential enemy.

'Engine,' Ryker said.

Henrik had heard it too, judging by the look on his face, and the two of them stopped their running and crouched down and pulled up against the side of the verge to try and hide themselves from the road just above them.

It was definitely the chasing pack. Even without seeing, Ryker could tell by the low rumble that he'd heard a car or pickup, rather than a lorry or anything else, and they were travelling slowly. Far too slowly for anyone simply passing by. They were looking for the spot Ryker and Henrik had scaled.

The car moved past. The engine noise slowly faded. But it didn't disappear.

'They're going to find us,' Ryker said to Henrik, who looked more scared than ever. 'We can't outrun them. And if we stay here, they'll see us.'

So what exactly was the answer?

In unison, in equal desperation, both of them looked away from one another and to the grey, rippling water beneath. Far from the most inviting prospect, but was the water their only choice?

'There's a boat,' Henrik said, pointing just north of the spot they were hiding by. Sure enough, ten yards into the water, tethered to a small and decrepit wooden jetty at the water's edge, was an equally decrepit-looking rowing boat. Were there even oars on it?

Voices. The dogs barking once more. Out of sight, but close by.

Without saying a word, Henrik peeled away. Ryker hesitated, but only for a second. The boy was rash, no doubt about it, but so far his instincts hadn't been bad. And Ryker wasn't going to leave him now.

Henrik turned just as he reached the edge and dropped out of sight. One, two, three seconds.

Splash.

Ryker peered over the edge. Henrik was flailing.

'Shit.' Ryker jumped after him. Smacked into the ice-cold water. Tried his hardest to stay relaxed even as his heart thudded erratically and his brain fuzzed over.

He took a couple of steady breaths to gain focus. Henrik, on the other hand, was panicking.

'Breathe normally,' Ryker said, gently treading water. He reached out and pushed Henrik's backside up toward the water's surface. 'Just relax. Lie back. Look up to the sky. Breathe.'

Ryker's words were delivered calmly, soothing, as though a meditation. He'd seen first-hand the effects of jumping into icy water – how that initial moment of shock and panic, heart beating rapidly and chaotically, could prove fatal.

His calming worked. Henrik's frantic movements dulled. His breathing slowed.

Just in time because the voices were getting louder.

Ryker let go and Henrik returned upright, slowly bobbing up and down as they both treaded the water. With one arm, Ryker pulled Henrik close, pulled them both right up to the edge so they were as hidden from sight as they could be. Certainly out of view from the road. Not so out of sight if anyone was to walk right up to the water.

If they did that, Ryker had no clue what his next move would be. Drag them in with him?

'Shhh,' Ryker said to Henrik, holding a finger to his lips.

The water gently lapped against them, the ripples from their initial entry subsumed by the natural movement of the water. Ryker let his body slip down a little further so the top of the water was above his chin. He held Henrik's eye. Neither looked away.

Voices louder still. Dogs yapping and yelping. Ryker couldn't tell what the men were saying but the look on Henrik's face showed he could.

Agonising moments passed by. How long had they been in the water? Seconds? Minutes? It felt like an age. Ryker's body shuddered from the cold. Henrik's face was white. Both of them were in trouble if they didn't get out soon. Probably mere minutes before severe hypothermia became a realistic risk.

Then, unexpectedly, Henrik's face relaxed. He very nearly smiled, the edges of his mouth twitched upward, before his face neutralised and he simply nodded.

Moments later, the voices faded.

'They're gone,' Henrik said.

17

'I know a place,' Henrik said.

He and Ryker had already sat shivering in the boat, bobbing up and down on the water, for several minutes. Ryker had initially pulled the boat right up to the shore, but was now torn between their two stark choices; move across the water – to wherever – and risk being spotted if the men were still out there, or sit and wait for the men to disappear, but in the process risk the men simply walking right up to where Ryker and Henrik were hidden.

In both scenarios, perhaps the biggest problem was the cold.

'Where?' Ryker asked, willing for an answer that swayed him.

'In the town. By the water. An old factory building.'

'They'll be watching closely in the town.'

For all Ryker knew, Erling and his gang – Wold too? – would be moving door to door to find them. Was anywhere in Blodstein safe?

'Not this place,' Henrik said. 'This place is safe.'

Ryker's eyes narrowed as he looked over the youngster. He seemed confident enough about his suggestion, even if Ryker was left pondering. He also noted that Henrik's communication, his English, was far more accomplished now than before. Just growing confidence?

'A safe place,' Ryker said. 'Does that safe place include a safe person?'

Ryker wasn't sure he'd trust anyone in Blodstein.

'No,' Henrik said. 'It's empty.'

Good enough for Ryker. He picked up the single rotten oar from the deck of the leaky boat.

'Show me where.'

The journey on the water took over an hour. Both of them were suffering badly from the cold, but they had little choice but to carry on, snaking as close to the water's edge as they could to remain unseen from the roadside. They ditched the boat a couple of hundred yards out from the first of the town's industrial buildings, entering a forested area once more at a point where the road had already veered off inland and was out of sight.

'We could find somewhere in the woods,' Ryker suggested, still unsure about moving into the town.

Henrik, walking a half step in front, carried on looking ahead. 'No. This place is better.'

Ryker remained as alert as he could as they carried on through the trees, but the only signs of life he saw were the little critters living in the wilds. Soon though, the sounds from the small town drifted over. Vehicles, and the whir and hum of machinery from the businesses lining the water.

They pulled up against a chain-link fence, six feet high, the metal mesh almost entirely disguised by thick, bushy creepers.

'This is it?' Ryker asked, indicating beyond the fence to the unseen.

'Not this one. The next one.'

Ryker looked over Henrik's shoulder. The fence in that direction went right up to the water, which meant they'd have to get wet again if they wanted to move around that way. Ryker didn't.

'We need to go onto the road,' Henrik said, answering Ryker's next question. 'But it's not far.'

Ryker nodded.

He moved off first, trailing alongside the fence. In spots the creepers were less dense and he was able to get glimpses of the space beyond. A simple building. Corrugated steel warehouse, with a small brick office block attached. A few cars in the car park. No sign of any people, despite the sound of machinery and banging inside.

No particular threat, though Ryker would be as cautious as possible. If they saw anyone at all, they'd hide.

They reached the corner of the fence. A road swept off in front of them, with a large metal barrier at the end of the tarmac before the forest, as though without it the traffic would accidentally plunge into the trees. Ryker spotted several vehicles parked in view. Vans, cars. No people.

'It's the next building,' Henrik said. 'We should move quick.'

Before Ryker could say anything, Henrik bounded forward and hunkered down behind the rear end of the first vehicle – a blue van. Ryker followed. Then they hopped from one vehicle to the next until they were past the first premises. The next one had a similar chain fence, though the perimeter was noticeably bigger, with not one building beyond but several. A huge warehouse, two smaller ones. A glass-and-aluminium office block. Clear signs of life, too, with multiple cars in the car park, a forklift truck whirring around.

'You can't be serious?' Ryker said, looking at Henrik.

He seemed confused. 'What?' He followed Ryker's line of sight before returning with an amused look. 'No. Not there. There.'

He pointed. Ryker hadn't spotted it at first glance but now realised a narrow lane sat between the two plots of land, enclosed by the non-stop security fence that ran along the front of both of the larger adjacent premises. He saw no gate, whatever lay beyond was blocked off from the road, with just a narrow run of space heading into the distance, metal fence either side. Odd.

'It's still the same,' Henrik said.

Ryker wasn't sure what he meant by that, but Henrik peeled away from the car they were by and raced over to the fence. He reached forward and pushed and a section of the fence flapped up. He squeezed his slight body through the gap, straightened up the other side and looked to Ryker.

'Come on!'

Ryker repeated Henrik's move. Except the gap was far smaller for him and he had to squeeze his way through, the metal scraping the skin on his sides and back in the process. Much to Henrik's amusement once more.

They moved off at pace down the narrow lane. Ryker flicked his gaze left and right to spot anyone from the neighbouring buildings looking on. He saw no one, and they soon came out to a small clearing by the water's edge, where a simple wooden shack stood in the centre. A boathouse? Shed? Warehouse? Who knew, but it was old and not far from falling down, its shingle roof intact but sunken into the structure, suggesting the rafters had given way some time ago.

One thing was for sure: it was empty.

'Let's get inside,' Ryker said.

18

Ryker was pleasantly surprised at what he found inside the abandoned building. Henrik wasn't. He'd known exactly what to expect. The building, little more than an enlarged storage shed, though for who or what, it wasn't clear, had likely been out of official use for some time given its state. The variety of rubbish, discarded both inside and out, evidenced its recent unofficial use. Rubbish that, in the case of Ryker and Henrik, had proved extremely useful.

Their first task was to build a small fire. A little risky, given the potential for the smoke to alert anyone of their presence, but a necessary step to helping them warm their frozen bodies and stave off hypothermia, if it hadn't already taken hold.

Henrik didn't need any tutoring, either in how to build, or how to the light the fire from scratch. Were all kids in this remote area as adept at outdoor survival or was Henrik an outlier?

The next step was to strip out of their cold, sodden clothing. Luckily, they had no need to sit starkers. Ryker found an old and thick bright-yellow worker's coat – stained, smelly, and with a large gash down the side through which the inner padding was spilling loose. Probably the reason it had been discarded, but Henrik didn't seem to care too much: it was warm and dry and big enough to cover him nearly head to toe.

For himself, Ryker found several discarded dust sheets. Decorator's sheets, most likely, given the many hardened white paint stains on the fabric. The sheets were equally smelly as the coat, and horribly dusty, but amply large enough for Ryker to wind around him – like a toga in ancient Rome – to keep him warm as they sat by and fed the fire to heat them through and dry their clothes.

'You have a lot of scars,' Henrik said as they sat, looking to Ryker's arms, which other than his neck and face and hands was the only skin visible. Still, when they'd stripped out of their wet-through clothes, modesty hadn't been Ryker's number one thought and clearly Henrik had noticed the patchwork evidence of past injuries across Ryker's body.

'Yeah,' Ryker said.

'Who are you?'

'I told you. My name's James Ryker.'

'And you're English. But... *what* are you?'

This was a conversation Ryker really didn't want to get into now.

'Your job, I mean,' Henrik said, as if the clarification would help. 'Do you have a job?'

'Not anymore.'

'You were in the army?'

'What makes you say that?'

Henrik shrugged. 'You look... tough. Maybe a fighter, a boxer or–'

'No. I wasn't in the army. And I wasn't a boxer. But I have been involved in a lot of fighting. A lot of bad things.'

Henrik looked as though he had no idea what that meant. Ryker didn't really know either, but he wasn't about to open up to this kid about his troubled past. He hated opening up about it to himself even.

'I'm here to help,' Ryker said. 'Let's leave it there.'

'But why are you helping me?'

'Good question. You tell me?'

Henrik went silent now as he stared at the flames licking up from the small fire. With a crackle, a small, glowing splinter of wood jumped out and landed a couple of inches from his bare foot. He didn't flinch. The ember went from orange to black as it cooled.

'Henrik? Why did those men have you?'

He looked up and caught Ryker's eye. Ryker was sure he saw tears welling. 'I don't know.'

'Is that the truth?'

Henrik nodded.

'They never told you? Never asked you any questions?'

Henrik looked back to the fire without saying a word.

'What do you know about Russians?' Ryker asked.

'Russia?'

'No. Not the place. The people. Two Russians, here in Blodstein.'

Easy enough to call them Russians, even if Ryker wasn't sure that was their precise nationality or affiliation.

'I've no idea what you're talking about.'

'They didn't take you? Never came to that house?'

'Russians? I don't know what you mean?'

Ryker sighed. 'Why don't you tell me about yourself.'

Better to get him to relax, talk freely, before they approached the hard stuff.

'What do you want to know?'

'You grew up in Blodstein?'

'A little.'

'Well, you knew this place?'

Henrik nodded. 'I don't know where I was born. But I don't think it was here in Blodstein.'

'You were an orphan?'

'Not really. I had a mother, I lived with her, but she was... taken away. Or I was taken away.'

'How do you mean?'

'I was so little, I don't really remember. I only know what I was told. I was two when I came to live here.'

'With who?'

'Foster, is that the word?'

Ryker nodded.

'They were my foster parents. I stayed with them for eight, nine years. But then...'

He trailed off and pushed his head down toward his bent knees. Sadness. Raw.

'Then?'

'There was an accident. Their car slid off the road. Into the water. They drowned.'

The room fell silent, except for the crack and pop of the fire. Ryker didn't know what to say. He'd suffered losses too. His old mentor at the JIA, Mackie, and the one person he'd truly loved – Angela Grainger – were the two most painful. They'd both died because of him, directly or indirectly, as had so many others over the years. Which was one of the very reasons why he'd pushed Sam Moreno away, Simona in Prague too. He couldn't let it happen again.

He was terrible at talking about his past, about his feelings and how those dark events had shaped him, although he knew it did help.

So what was he supposed to do here with Henrik? Ask more questions? Keep silent? Change the subject?

'I should have been in the car that night,' Henrik said. 'But I... I'm not a good kid.' He glanced back up to Ryker now. A look on his face Ryker hadn't seen on him before. Shame. Disgust. 'I treated them so badly. They were supposed to take me out that night, but I caused so much trouble they went without me. The neighbour looked after me. I never saw them again.'

Silence once more. This time it went on longer.

'What happened to you after that?'

'That same neighbour, I stayed with her. She was... nice. But I was horrible to her too. I just wanted my mamma and pappa back.'

A tear escaped his eye now, though he wiped it away in a flash, hung his head, clearly embarrassed by the show of emotion. He had no need to be.

'What was her name?'

'The neighbour? Trine. Trine Hansen.'

'Does she still live here?'

'I don't know.'

'But you didn't think about us going to her?'

He seemed to think about the question, but then didn't give any answer.

'I didn't stay with her long,' he said. 'I was eleven when they found me a new family in Trondheim.'

'And then?'

'And then... and then nothing. I was with them until...'

'Until those men took you?'

'I don't even know how long ago. One month. Two?'

Ryker shook his head in disbelief. Were his new 'family' not looking for him? Or was it just that the search, for whatever reason, hadn't come this far north?

'I think... maybe because I ran away a lot. Maybe they don't even care I'm gone.'

'I can't believe that.'

A strange silence fell over them, with Henrik in quiet contemplation. About his life, most likely. His mistakes. About

the people he'd let down, those who'd let him down. None of
that meant he deserved what was happening to him now.

But what was happening?

'Do you know any of those men?' Ryker asked.

'Not before,' he said, shaking his head.

'I thought everyone here knew everyone else.'

'I never cared.'

'What about now? What do you know about them now?'

Henrik pursed his lips and shook his head. 'Hardly a thing.'

'They never asked you anything? Never told you anything?'

'No.'

'They hurt you?'

'No. They fed me. Let me watch TV. But they never let me
leave that house. I mean, I was never supposed to.'

He smiled a little, but it was short-lived.

'Yesterday, on the road, when–'

'When you nearly killed me?' Henrik prompted.

'That's not quite how I saw it, but–'

'I ran. From the house. I wanted to get to Trondheim.'

'Why Trondheim?'

'It's safe. Safer than here. Like you said–'

'Everyone knows everyone else here. I'm sorry I stopped
you.'

Henrik's body quivered. Just a reaction to the cold, or was it
something that had flashed in his mind?

'You said you knew this place?' Ryker said, looking around
the room.

That little smile, that little indicator of hope and a better life,
crept across Henrik's face again.

'I used to come here a lot. To get away from everyone else.
You know?'

'Kind of.'

'It might not seem much to you, but here... I could just be

me. Could be free of everything else. I never brought anyone else here before. In a way, I've always preferred being on my own.'

Ryker didn't say anything to that, though he'd certainly spent much of his life the same way. Out of necessity, as much as out of choice.

'I'm probably more like you than you realise,' Ryker said.

'I doubt that.'

'I never had a real family either.'

'I had a real family. They're dead.'

'I always felt alone too. It can make a person much stronger.'

'I'm not strong.'

'Henrik, I don't know a lot of children, teenagers, but I can't imagine there are many stronger than you.'

'And you?'

'You think I'm strong?'

'You look it.'

Ryker wouldn't delve into the difference between mental and physical strength.

'Let's just say, I have a habit of surviving,' Ryker said. 'I think you do too.'

That smile again. Henrik looked genuinely flattered, but Ryker had meant it.

'We need some food,' Ryker said. He leaned forward and tested his clothes, hanging above the fire from the snapped rafters. Warm, a little damp. Another half hour and they'd be fully dry. Was it worth waiting that long? 'We also need to decide what to do next.'

'Take me to Trondheim.'

'To your foster parents?'

A forceful shake of the head. 'No. Not to them.'

Interesting. 'To the police then?'

Henrik didn't answer.

'Is there someone there who can help you?' Ryker asked, sounding a little less patient.

Henrik hung his head again. 'I don't really know.'

'I don't know how we'd even get to Trondheim now,' Ryker said. 'I have a car, but it's by that house still.'

Several miles of trekking to get there. And would Erling and the others have found it already? What would they have done if so? Trashed it? Towed it away? Ordered someone to lay in wait? The journey to the car would be a risk in itself, never mind the question of what they would find when they got there.

'You could steal a car?' Henrik suggested.

Ryker was sure he could. Did he want to?

'I'm not sure that's fair on the owner,' Ryker said.

'Depends on the owner,' Henrik said with a sly grin.

'How about Trine Hansen?' Ryker asked.

Henrik's face soured. 'I don't want to see her.'

'I don't think that's what I suggested.'

Henrik said nothing but he looked angry now.

'Do you know Inspector Wold?' Ryker asked.

Henrik nodded.

'Is he involved? In kidnapping you? In keeping you at that house?'

'I... he was never at the house.'

'But yesterday, he took you away in his car. I could tell you were afraid of him then.'

Henrik shot a glare at Ryker. 'I'm not afraid.'

'Did he take you straight to them?'

Henrik paused but then nodded. 'Near to the town. He stopped the car. Handed me over. That was it.'

'You didn't know before that Wold was involved?'

'I don't know what he knows or how.'

But Wold certainly hadn't helped Henrik when he'd had the

chance. Somehow he'd already been well aware of what was happening.

Ryker wanted to ask about Pettersen. Would Henrik know her? Trust her? For some reason he held back, for once unsure of his own instincts. Plus, he'd already badgered the boy enough. The kid was tired, cold, hungry, had suffered weeks of captivity for reasons he claimed he didn't know. Interrogating him wouldn't help.

That was one reason why Ryker stopped asking questions.

The other, was because of the sound.

Judging by the look on Henrik's face, both of them had heard it.

'There's someone here,' Ryker said.

19

Isabell had left their bed at seven thirty. Berg would have stayed under the sheets longer, he was tired physically and mentally, but instead, he rushed to get dressed and downstairs before she left, determined to delve into her plans for the day. First, they shared an awkward and near silent breakfast. Not exactly worth making the effort of getting up for, but he was awaiting his moment.

'What are you doing today?' he asked as he poured himself another coffee.

· 'How do you mean?'

'Are you staying home?'

She looked fidgety. 'Most of the day, yes.'

'But you're going out this morning?'

The fact she was up and dressed already confirmed that.

'Just some errands to run. A couple of meetings.'

'I thought perhaps we could have lunch today?'

'Together?' she said, as though it was a preposterous suggestion.

'No, over a video call. Yes, of course together.'

He moved closer to her, put his hand on her waist.

'Sorry, darling,' she said. 'I would have, but... you never ask me anymore. I'd love to. Another day though?'

She smiled and reached forward and kissed him on the cheek. Then checked her watch.

'I've got to go.'

With that she did.

Berg moved through the house. Stood at the window in the lounge, sipping his coffee, until her car was off the drive and out of sight.

Then he called Nyland.

'Where are you?' Berg said without pleasantries when the call was finally answered.

'I was right outside. I'll follow her.'

Berg was, for once, impressed. And he certainly hadn't spotted Nyland at all when he'd looked out the window just now, or earlier.

'What more can you tell me about Tronstad?'

Berg moved away from the window and back through the house to the kitchen.

'Not much more yet. He's forty-one. Unmarried. He's renting a house on the water, a few miles north of the town. One of those big ones.'

Berg knew the type. Huge cabins that rich folk from the cities bought so they could 'get away' from the rat race – for a few weeks a year at least. Properties that were way out of reach of the regular townsfolk, had plots that included acres and acres of land, but were so cut off from life that Berg had no clue why anyone would want one. He could have afforded one if he wanted. He didn't.

So Tronstad was one of those types. Interesting.

'That doesn't explain why he and my wife were in that house in town yesterday,' Berg said as he stared out of the kitchen window to the garden beyond. In summer their sprawling outdoor space was beautifully manicured and full of vibrant colours. In midwinter it looked bleak and barren. Kind of how Berg felt right now.

'No,' Nyland said. 'It doesn't. I need to do some further work on that. He doesn't have an office, as far as I can see, so perhaps that's what he's using that place for. It is possible that... I mean, it's possible this is all normal. He's seeing her professionally.'

Yes, it was possible. But even that would be a problem, as far as Berg was concerned. What need did Isabell have of a lawyer? Especially when she hadn't mentioned a word of it to him. Whatever the answer, she was keeping the truth from him. He would find out why.

'Let me know where she goes. If she meets him again–'

'I'll be there. I'll get as much information for you as I can.'

'And the other things I asked for?'

For some reason Berg couldn't bring himself to say those things out loud over the phone, as though a small part of him worried that someone was eavesdropping on him, in the very manner that he was asking Nyland to eavesdrop on his wife and Tronstad.

'It'll take me a bit longer. I've reached out to–'

'You've done what! I didn't tell you to speak to anyone else about this!'

Silence.

'Nyland, you shit–'

'Mr Berg, you have to understand I can't do all that you've asked on my own. But these people... they're very discreet. I can assure you of that. That's what you're paying for.'

'Damn right it is. If any word of this gets out, I'll tear your balls off and feed them to you.'

Berg waited for a response to the threat. It took him a few seconds to realise the silence was because the call had already disconnected. Bad signal or had Nyland ended the call? Had he heard the threat even? The doubt only made Berg's temper rise all the more.

Somehow he resisted tossing the phone across the kitchen.

He finished his coffee, got himself ready, and left the house.

Berg's temper remained piqued, but under control, as he arrived at work. He managed to make it to the office without anyone accosting him. A bonus. He checked his diary. Only two meetings during the day, both in the afternoon, which would mean he'd finally get a chance to get his head down and get on top of the numbers for the upcoming audit.

Seriously surprising his expectations, he managed to make it past lunchtime without interruption, though by that point his brain was weary and his thoughts were increasingly turning from work to his private life. He'd heard nothing more from Nyland. Should he call him?

Then came the inevitable knock on the door. The even more inevitable face that peered through the glass was Marius's.

'Come in.' Berg beckoned.

Marius did so. He took a seat opposite Berg without being invited.

'Can I help you?' Berg said.

'You never did tell me what that was about yesterday,' Marius said. 'With those Russians.'

That was right. Berg hadn't. In fact, he'd done everything he could to avoid Marius for the rest of the day, and he'd thought Marius was out all day today with suppliers. Clearly not.

'How did your meetings go?' Berg asked.

'I'll get to that,' he said. Berg didn't like his tone. 'I'm starting to get the feeling that you don't trust me. That, or you want to keep things from me?'

'Things? What things?'

'I'm not an idiot,' Marius said.

Berg kind of thought he was, though he decided against saying it.

'I know about your history with them.'

Berg grit his teeth.

'You thought I didn't? Like I said, I'm not dumb.'

'You're talking as though there's some dark secret. Just because I don't tell you everything that happens in *my* business, doesn't mean there's something bad.'

Marius humphed. 'Yeah, except I don't trust those guys. And I don't trust you around them.'

'Are you serious?' Berg said, hackles raised. 'Don't you dare–'

'I know what happened last time.'

Berg grit his teeth rather than bite back. Twice now Marius had said that. Berg really wanted to find out more. To find out exactly what this arsehole knew. But doing so would only open up the fact that there really was something Berg was trying to hide.

Perhaps Marius was only fishing.

'I know to anyone on the outside looking in, everything looks above board here, but the way I see it, this place is as much theirs as it is yours,' Marius said.

'What on earth are you talking about?' Berg said. 'They don't own anything here.'

'Those two from yesterday? Maybe not. You might be in charge here, but I'm older than you, Sigurd. I worked here while you were still at school. I worked with your father.'

'I know you did. I took you on as a favour to him.'

'I worked with him, but I always knew he was dirty.'

Berg felt ready to explode but somehow held it in. He wasn't sure that was a good thing. What happened when he eventually erupted?

'He was dirty, his money was dirty,' Marius continued. 'The money used to start this business, money which still sits as a debt on our books, came from him.'

'You piece of shit,' Berg said, getting to his feet. 'My father's been dead–'

'For a long time.' Marius got up from his chair too, standing his ground. A challenge? 'Yeah. I know that. I was at his funeral. He's gone. But those debts still sit on our books, don't they? So who are we going to pay back? His ghost?'

'Get the fuck out of my office–'

'Don't worry. I'm going.' Marius moved for the door. 'I've still got a real job to do.'

'No you don't. You're fired.'

Marius turned and looked at Berg. A snide look. Berg wanted to wipe it off.

'I don't think so, *Boss*. See what happens if you try.'

With that Marius opened the door and stormed out.

Berg was left stunned. He didn't move for what felt like several minutes.

Had that conversation really just happened? Had he really been threatened by that... that... he couldn't even think of the word. But Marius was proving to be a far bigger problem than Berg had ever anticipated. What worried him the most was that Marius had a big mouth. Who else had he already talked to?

Berg's phone buzzed on the desk. He glanced to the screen. Hoped it was Nyland. No.

'What do you want?' he shouted when he answered.

'Sigurd, it's me.'

Berg sighed in frustration and clenched the phone a little more tightly in his hand. 'I know it's you. What do you want, you dumb ape?'

Silence. Had the phone disconnected again like earlier with Nyland? What was wrong with this thing? He checked the screen. No. Probably the big bastard was just unsure how to respond to the insult.

'We've got a problem,' Erling said.

This was all Berg needed. 'What problem?'

'The boy. He's gone.'

20

Konstantin finished the treacly coffee and left a few coins on the table. He got to his feet and made his way to the door. The young waitress caught his eye as he moved. He smiled at her. The return look she gave was as though she'd seen a ghoul. Then, finally, a smile broke through.

Forced? No, he didn't think so, just that confusion twisted in her mind. Her reaction was common. He didn't have a ghastly appearance, at least not with his clothes on. In the past some women had commented that he was handsome, like a rugged movie star, even if he saw his jaw as a little too square, and his nose a little too Roman. No, there was nothing peculiar about his face. So why the odd looks from strangers?

His eyes. Anyone who looked closely enough, into his eyes, shared the look the waitress had given.

The eyes. The window to the soul.

He gave a playful wave to her before opening the door and moving into the cold.

She was pretty. If he was interested in that sort of thing. He wasn't. Not today at least. Perhaps before he left this country he'd make a point of seeing her again. Is that what a normal man would do?

He pulled his phone from his pocket as he walked over to his car and sat down in the driver's seat. Jesper answered on the third ring. Quick. Had he been sitting waiting on his golden throne for an update?

'I've been following the woman,' Konstantin said. 'Like you asked.'

'And?'

And? And why the hell was he here, in this poxy country, following this poxy woman around all day? That wasn't his skill set. Jesper knew that. Was Jesper punishing him?

'And I don't know why.'

A guffaw from Jesper. Konstantin could imagine the mocking look on his face. His grip tightened on the phone.

'She's important to me,' Jesper said. 'Carry on with what you're doing until I tell you otherwise.'

'She's been in that house now for more than an hour.'

'With the man? Do you have a picture of him?'

'I already sent it to you. And the other man too.'

'The other man?'

'There's another man following her.'

Silence.

'I did say that in the message too.'

'What other man?'

So clearly Jesper didn't know already about the other man, and also hadn't read the message. So perhaps he hadn't been waiting on Konstantin after all. He briefly wondered what Jesper actually did all day. Did he have an army of Konstantins all around the world, keeping him abreast of their movements all day, every day?

Konstantin explained what he'd seen. He'd arrived outside

Berg's house at six am, when it was still dark outside. He'd parked his car and moved closer on foot, hiding in foliage until sunrise. A little after seven am the other car had arrived. The one with the man inside. The man who had since been on Mrs Berg's tail for hours, keeping a distance, never too close, but always there.

'Security, do you think?' Jesper asked.

'No. He's not close enough to her,' Konstantin said. 'She doesn't know he's there. He's definitely spying on her.'

'Spying on her, not him?'

'I already said, he was at her house this morning.'

A grumble in response. Had Konstantin spoken out of turn?

'Has he seen you at all?' Jesper asked.

'I don't think so.'

'That's not a very clear answer.'

'If he has, he hasn't shown it. And I've been careful. You know I always am.'

'I'll find out who the men are. Both of them. I'll let you know. Until then, stay with her.'

The call ended. Konstantin brought the phone down. His eyes rested not on the building where Mrs Berg was cooped with her friend, but on the car further down the road, parked at the edge of an alley, where the watcher was... what was he doing? It was too far for Konstantin to tell even though he could make out the man's form behind the glass.

Konstantin sighed and sat back in his seat. He counted the seconds, then the minutes as he awaited the return call from Jesper. He hoped the wait was worth it. It was about time this trip got more interesting.

A police car rumbled by. The male driver glanced over in Konstantin's direction. Konstantin stared. Not a challenge, more curiosity.

Soon the car was past him and heading on.

What an odd little town, full of odd little people.

He was still waiting for Jesper's call when the woman came out of the house. The man too. They stood outside the closed door, chatting. Then she moved up to him and they hugged. Quite a long, tight hug. Mr Berg wouldn't be impressed. Or perhaps he would.

Was that why the follower was there, because of the husband?

Moments later she was walking away, alone, back toward her parked car. Across the street, the watcher shuffled out of view behind his car window.

Amateur.

She moved out of sight. But the watcher remained. Only as he reversed out onto the street did Konstantin turn his engine on.

He followed the watcher, as he had earlier in the day. Every now and then he caught a glimpse of Mrs Berg's Tesla further ahead, but only fleetingly.

Finally the call came through.

'The man she's with is Stefan Tronstad,' Jesper said. 'He's a lawyer. When you get a chance, I want you to approach him. Find out why she's with him.'

'Any way I can?'

'Do what you need to do. But don't make too much of a mess. You might be in that town a few days yet.'

Konstantin grimaced at the thought. 'And the other?'

'Jonas Nyland. He's a private investigator.'

A private investigator? As he'd thought, most likely the husband had hired him.

'He's a loner. An added complication,' Jesper said. 'Make him go away.'

Another call abruptly ended. Jesper's words swam in Konstantin's mind. The slashes on his chest, the most recent two in particular, ached as he thought.

This was what he'd been waiting for, wasn't it?

Yet he felt no better for it at all.

21

The sounds that alerted Ryker came from two directions: a low-pitched mechanical rumbling from the water side, and a more gentle patter and rustle from the road side.

An ambush? Or pure coincidence?

'Get dressed,' Ryker said to Henrik.

Both scrambled to get their clothes on. Ryker moved over to the ramshackle wall at the back of the building and peered between a two-inch gap where the slats of the wall had slid apart – not exactly a clear view because of the overgrown grounds which framed the grey, murky water beyond like a bleak postcard.

'There's a boat,' Ryker said, not taking his eye from the craft which bobbed up and down, heading slowly from left to right, about a hundred yards out.

'Let me see,' Henrik said, coming up behind.

Ryker shifted out of the way and Henrik stood on tiptoes to peer through.

'It's a fishing boat,' he said.

Ryker had thought the same. Did that mean it was no threat? He really couldn't be sure.

'It's not coming this way,' Henrik added.

Ryker agreed with that too.

'What about out there?' Henrik said as he turned back to Ryker.

Were they both being overly paranoid? Was it paranoia or simply caution? This was an alien place for Ryker, a place where he was already doubtful he could trust anyone. Perhaps the best thing to do, after all, as Henrik had suggested, was to steal a car and get as far away as fast as they could.

'Wait by the fire,' Ryker said. 'Keep yourself warm.'

Henrik nodded. Ryker grabbed his coat. By far the thickest garment he had, it was still horribly damp compared to the rest of his things, but it would provide better protection from the cold than nothing at all. He slung it over his shoulders and crept to the door, at the ready, as though he expected someone to rush through at any moment.

No one did. Ryker pulled the door open and peered out. No one in sight, but the sounds from the nearby businesses amplified. Was that all they'd heard in the first place?

No. Ryker didn't think so. He moved outside, eyes darting. Nothing he could see from this point other than fences, trees, bushes, rubbish, and the roofs of the adjacent warehouses, rising tall. Certainly he saw no one up there.

Ryker moved forward, trekking back toward the road. He was several yards from the roadside fence when a car swept past in front. It caught him by surprise and he ducked to the side and hunched down.

The car was soon out of sight. No indication of anything untoward.

Ryker peeled away from his position, straightened up, looked ahead to the side fence opposite and stopped dead, staring into the eyes of a man. Face heavily weathered, he stood the other side of the fence, next to a pile of discarded pallets.

Blue coveralls. A cigarette dangled between his lips. He nodded to Ryker as if in greeting. Ryker nodded back. Then the frail-looking guy picked up two pallets, effortlessly swung them up over his head, turned and sauntered off.

Ryker moved back to the shed and pushed the door open.

'What?' Henrik said.

'It's nothing,' Ryker said. 'Just a guy from the factory.'

'He saw you?'

'He saw me, but–'

'Then we need to go!'

'No,' Ryker said, though he wasn't sure why he was so hesitant.

'What if he tells someone?'

'Why would he do that?'

'We need a car,' Henrik said. 'We need to leave here.'

'I already said–'

'You don't have to steal one.'

Ryker paused, waiting for Henrik to explain. Hoping he had a good plan about to come to the fore.

'You don't have to steal one,' Henrik repeated. 'But I could.'

Said with pure confidence. Interesting.

'Same difference,' Ryker said.

'You said you didn't want to steal because it's not fair on the owner. But what if the owner is a motherfucker?'

Ryker cringed at the boy's bad language. He wasn't sure why. Except it just didn't seem necessary. He thought about pulling him up on it, but he wasn't his parent, nor was he exactly a role model for the younger generation.

'What are you thinking?' Ryker asked, more curious now.

'I know where one of them lives,' Henrik said. 'It's not far from here. Half a mile maybe.'

'One of them?'

'One of the men you fought at the house. One of the men who's been keeping me there.'

'I thought you said you didn't know them.'

'I didn't know them before. I looked in one of their wallets one time.'

Ryker thought. Did he believe him? 'No,' he said, even though the prospect of a little comeuppance for the kidnappers was genuinely promising. 'Not yet at least.'

Henrik shot Ryker a withering look.

'We're not ready,' Ryker said. 'It's too soon. First, we'll head into the town. We need supplies. Food. You need a coat. We'll come back here. Stay a little longer to recuperate. Then when we're ready we can get a car and get out of here.'

'Why not just get a car now? We can get everything else after.'

Ryker had to admit he flitted between his own suggestion and Henrik's, but he had more than one reason why he didn't want to run out of town right away.

'No,' Ryker said. 'Just trust me.'

'Then I'll stay here,' Henrik said. 'You're a stranger, but if anyone saw me and you together...'

Ryker paused. He sensed Henrik's fear, and the boy was right: the two of them together would draw a lot more attention.

'I won't be long,' Ryker said. 'Stay by the fire, stay warm. If anyone comes this way–'

'What? Fight them? Run? Swim?'

Henrik smiled, though he was far from amused by those prospects, Ryker knew.

'You'll be fine here,' Ryker said, hoping his words would reassure. 'But if you get spooked, run into one of the factories. You want to be around lots of people. Run there. Cause havoc. I'll be back soon enough.'

Ryker turned and left without waiting for another response.

22

Ryker continued to question his decision to leave Henrik as he pulled back the fence and clambered out onto the pavement. Yes, hiding in plain sight had worked for him in the past. The instincts of Erling and the others, having lost Ryker and Henrik on the road south of here, would surely be that the two of them had fled Blodstein for good. They would hardly expect to see the two of them casually walking the town's streets, would they?

Even if one of the bad guys spotted Ryker, what would they do in daylight, with other people around? Attack him? Shoot him? Stab him? Kidnap him? All possibilities, but all felt unlikely and would only draw unwanted attention to the gang.

He didn't want to be in this town any longer than necessary, but he also knew he'd find answers here.

Ryker would remain vigilant, particularly with the prospect that the gang had the police on their side.

He passed by few pedestrians on his walk. Where he could he crossed the street to avoid direct contact, and with his head down, no one seemed to pay him any particular attention.

He checked his phone along the way. It had stopped

working after their water adventure. Although he'd tried his best to dry it out, along with his clothes, the device still wouldn't boot up. It was only a cheap burner. The only stored number was Heidi's – the woman from the ferry. He could remember her number anyway, even if he wasn't sure he'd ever call her. He tossed the phone into a bin. Even if it came back to life, even if it fell into the wrong hands, discarding it would cause him no problems.

Along with the phone, the only other possessions he'd had on him when he'd left his car in the woods was a pocketful of cash, and the car key (also potentially now water-damaged). Inside the car was more cash, a few clothes, a few other provisions, one British passport in the name of Carl Logan. Nothing that couldn't be replaced, though he did want to at least try to recover what he could. Everything else he'd come to the country with remained in the safe deposit box in the bank in Trondheim where he'd first headed before leaving on his trip north. There his possessions would stay until he became desperate, or until he moved on. Not yet.

Cash would be the first thing he needed more of. The notes in his pocket wouldn't last long, but he could get more from his various deposit accounts through a money transfer shop, which he knew Trondheim had more than one of.

Not Blodstein though.

The town was quiet. The selection of shops poor. The convenience store, a few buildings down from the corner café, wasn't large but somehow contained all of the basic provisions Ryker needed; drinks, food, a penknife, an outdoor coat for Henrik (in the smallest adult size available), a cheap prepaid phone, and a basic backpack to carry it all in.

Ryker paid for it all with the crumpled, nearly dry cash, using up more than half of what he had. He received an odd look from the teller. To be expected really. Would the guy make a call to Erling or Wold as soon as Ryker stepped out? Ryker really didn't know anymore in this strange town.

As he moved outside, Ryker looked up the street, to the police station further along. No sign of any marked cars there.

Darkness was on the way, Ryker knew. He wanted to be back by Henrik's side before then. But he also wanted to make one more stop first.

He crossed over the road. Glanced back across to the café as he passed it by. Glanced along the long road heading south as he moved over the main crossroads. Kept his head low, his pace a little quicker as he walked on by the police station, the words 'hiding in plain sight' rattling through his mind as though the mantra would help him.

He carried on until he reached the library. He looked up at the building. A handsome structure, a touch of the classical with two grand columns at the entrance. Ryker moved up the steps. Pushed open the bare-wood door. The smell of oldness filled his nose. One step inside and he felt he'd been transported back in time several decades.

In his troubled childhood years, Ryker had been far from a bookworm, but a lingering memory in his mind was the smell of the old local library near to the council estate where he spent his early teens. Housed in what had previously been a bank, with high ceilings and ornate internal fixtures, the otherwise downtrodden building had a distinct smell of oldness, both from the fabric of the structure, but also the thousands of books. This library smelled, and felt, exactly the same.

Was it the very essence of a library to smell like that, or did more modern libraries feel... well... more modern?

He moved toward the counter, behind which a single worker – a grey-haired woman – sat, slowly typing at a worn-out-looking computer. She glanced up and gave Ryker a slightly suspicious smile. He smiled back. He'd seen her before, when he'd stopped here briefly the day he arrived in Blodstein. He noticed a look of recognition in her eyes, though she said nothing.

Ryker moved through and into the records room: a dark, wood-panelled space with no natural air or light. Ryker got what he needed from the filing cabinets and sat himself down at the sole terminal. A little red light, on a CCTV camera up in the corner, blinked away as Ryker worked, but he was otherwise undisturbed. It took him more than half an hour with the microfiche, then a further half hour at one of the aged computer screens, searching the free but painfully slow internet, to find what he was looking for. But at least he found it.

He made a mental note then headed for the exit.

Dusk. The street outside was gloomier than ever. Ryker looked left and right as he walked down the steps to the pavement. A figure to his right peeled away from behind a wall.

Ryker paused in his stride, but only for a moment.

'Pettersen,' he said.

She was in uniform. On foot. No sign of any colleagues or any car.

'What is it I should call you again?' she said as Ryker walked off down the street, retracing his steps. Pettersen followed alongside. 'James? Carl?'

'Call me whatever you like.'

'I thought you'd left here?'

'You thought you'd run me out, you mean?'

'I wish you hadn't come back.'

He looked at her and winked when she caught his eye. 'Liar,' he said.

She smiled. Sort of.

He thought about asking how she knew he was back. Had she simply spotted him walking around, or had someone tipped her off? The fact there was no Wold, no cavalry to take Ryker down, or at least into cuffs – for what, though? – was a good sign.

A sign he could trust her? He still wasn't sure about that.

'You've been out in the rain,' she said, looking straight ahead now.

He didn't respond.

'Your coat,' she added after a few silent steps. 'It's really wet. I can tell. Although, I don't remember it raining today. Strange.'

Ryker still said nothing.

'Where are you going to, anyway?' she asked. 'The hotel is the other way.'

'I'm not staying there anymore. Remember?'

'So where are you staying?'

'Is that an invitation?'

He caught her eye again.

'No,' she said, blank face.

They reached the main crossroads and came to a stop. The silence dragged out. Clearly something bugged her.

'What do you want from me?' Ryker asked.

The lights turned green and they moved across to the other side.

'I've been hearing some things,' she said. 'Not nice things.'

'Such as?'

'Such as an outsider causing problems here. Trespassing. Attacking some of the locals.'

'Didn't we already clear this up?'

'I'm talking about today, not last night at the bar. I've also heard some nasty rumours. Of a boy. Kidnapped. Being held against his will.'

Ryker looked down at her again. She remained staring straight ahead.

'That sounds like something the police really should investigate,' Ryker said.

'I said the same thing to my boss.'

'Wold? And what did he say?'

'That he was concerned by the rumours. That he was looking into it. That any information I had, needed to go straight to him.'

Ryker said nothing as his brain rumbled.

'Do you know anything about this?' Pettersen asked. 'I've heard the boy's name is Henrik. The same as the boy you were asking me about.'

Ryker stopped walking. She did too. They faced each other. A pickup truck trudged along the road behind Pettersen. Ryker eyed the driver as it passed by. No one he recognised.

'So?' Pettersen asked.

She was either someone who could genuinely help, or simply a good actor. Part of Wold's dirty little gang, sent to play games with Ryker to help find the boy. Ryker had to find a way to figure out which option was true. An ally could prove crucial.

'What's in the bag,' she said, indicating to his shoulder. 'Looks new. Very full too.'

'Food,' Ryker said. 'Haven't eaten all day.'

'Must be enough for two in there.'

'You mean you want some?'

'No,' she said, her voice more stern. 'That's not what I meant at all.'

An awkward silence built up. With darkness looming, Ryker wanted nothing more than to get moving and back to Henrik, but how was he supposed to get away from Pettersen now? Or should he take her with him?

'Where are you going to?' she asked.

Ryker's lack of answer only added to the look of suspicion on her face.

'If you need help–'

'I'm staying at the hotel by the water,' he said. 'A step up from Blodstein Gjestehus.'

'I don't believe you,' she said.

Ryker shrugged. Pettersen opened her mouth to say something else. Then her radio crackled to life. Pettersen lifted the device from the strap on her chest and rattled off a response. The conversation carried on for a few seconds before she pulled the radio away from her mouth.

'That was Wold,' she said. 'I didn't say anything to him about seeing you.'

'Why would you?'

'Because earlier he asked me to.'

'Why would he ask that?'

'Good question. Anyway, I have to go. I'm needed.'

With that she turned and broke into a jog as she headed back toward the station.

Ryker watched her for a few seconds before he got on his way too.

At that moment, he knew for sure he wasn't staying in Blodstein another night. One way or another, he and Henrik were leaving.

23

Street lights flickered on as Ryker walked along. Darkness fell quickly. By the time he approached the factories, no daylight remained, making every step that little bit more tense. At least the hour was still early, and the factories and warehouses still busy. Rather than threat, Ryker felt a certain comfort in the knowledge that so many people remained around him, going about their 'normal' days.

He soon made it back to the gap in the fence. He looked up and down the street, was about to pull back the metal slats when a van approached somewhere behind him, lights blaring.

Too late now, with Ryker there, hunched down, fence in hand. As the headlight beams swept over him, Ryker pulled himself through the gap. He spun on his heel to watch the van idle past. Too dark to make out anyone up front, or to spot whether they were looking at him.

Regardless, Ryker moved more quickly down the lane. The lane that was now black – the trees and overgrowth around him enough to drown out any illumination from the street and the buildings around. As Ryker's eyes adjusted to the renewed darkness, he caught sight of the form of the shed in the thin light from the cloud-shrouded moon. No sign of any glow of fire through the gaps in the walls of the structure.

Ryker slowed. Steps more cautious than before. He listened. Looked. Too dark to really see anything.

'Henrik?' Ryker called, his voice low.

He reached the shed. Pushed open the door. The fire in the centre of the space was all but out, just a few glowing embers remained, smoke twisting up into the air. Plenty of warmth still, but the fire was dying. And he saw no sign of Henrik.

'You took a long time.'

Henrik. Ryker spun around. Could barely see him in the dark outside. Had heard nothing of him.

The boy moved forward, his movement giving away his position, though he remained cloaked in darkness and Ryker's wariness peaked. Something about his voice.

'I got what we needed,' Ryker said, slipping the bag from his shoulders. He unzipped the main compartment to take out the coat.

'What we needed?' Henrik said. 'We needed some books from the library?'

Ryker paused. Henrik laughed. A short, sharp laugh.

'Why were you speaking to *her*?'

'You were watching me?' Ryker said, a little disturbed by the thought.

'Obviously.'

'You weren't following me though.'

Not directly, anyway. There'd been no one on his tail, street by street. Ryker would have known.

'I know this town better than you. It wasn't that hard to think where you were going. I got there before you. Waited. To see what you were doing.'

So he'd been hiding out somewhere by the shops? Ryker

wondered where exactly. The café? No, surely he wouldn't have made himself that vulnerable.

Either way, the kid was sneaky. Clever, though a little snide of him to do that.

'Why?' Ryker asked.

'You were talking to that policewoman.'

'Yes.'

'About me?'

'No.'

'I don't believe you.'

'Do you see her here now? Or any of her colleagues?'

Silence from Henrik. Silence, except for the sound of him shivering.

Why had he put himself through that?

Ryker pulled the coat out of the bag and outstretched his hand. Henrik didn't take it.

'You don't trust me?' Ryker asked.

No response still. Though after a few moments Henrik yanked the coat from Ryker's grasp.

'The fire's nearly out,' Ryker said. 'We could make another–'

'I'm not staying here.'

'Probably a good choice. So... what now?'

Even though he could see little of Henrik's face, he could sense a stark change in the boy's mood and demeanour. Was this where they parted ways? Though if Henrik didn't trust Ryker, and wanted to go it alone from here, then why had he come back to this place at all? He'd had the chance to run. He hadn't taken it.

Ryker knew why. This boy had more to him than Ryker had realised, but Henrik was also lost. In life. Fourteen years old. No real family, no one in this place who he truly believed he could trust to help him. Ryker was the closest person to breaking that, but they'd known each other for only a few hours. Of course

Henrik was hesitant and wary. But the fact he was standing in front of Ryker now proved a dead giveaway that he *wanted* help, and that he saw Ryker as his best bet for getting that.

'You said you knew where we could get a car?' Ryker said.

A short pause, before, 'Yeah. Follow me.'

Stealing a car wasn't as easy as shown in movies, Ryker knew. Gone were the days when a wire hook down the window, into the door, could be used to pop a door lock. Gone were the days when a plastic panel could be ripped out from under the steering column and two wires criss-crossed to hot-wire and get the engine rocking. Unless they could find a much older car, modern computer electronics, and security, meant they needed a key – or at least a key clone. Ryker knew how to clone key fobs, but he didn't have any of the equipment to do so. So getting hold of an actual key was the only way. And the only way of getting a key was to steal one directly off a person, or to break into a house, an office, and steal one.

Henrik seemed to know all this without explanation from Ryker, which only made Ryker all the more curious of the boy's life and experiences. Fourteen years old? Ryker certainly hadn't been an angel at that age, or at any age really. Had he stolen cars at fourteen? The answer wasn't the point. His was hardly a model path to take through life, and certainly not a path he'd wish for any other child.

The house they arrived at was a small, detached, wood-clad affair on a short street of similar-sized though not identical properties. In the dark Ryder struggled to tell exactly what state they were in, but the street seemed nice enough, and the houses' modest sizes suggested the occupants were working class. An assumption further cemented by the cars on the drives, and the few on the road, with a mixture of makes, ranging in age from brand new to ten years old, though none were high-end.

A single car – a nearly new VW Golf – lay parked on the driveway outside the house Ryker and Henrik spied on, Ryker hadn't seen the car before on his adventures around the town. Given who Henrik said lived here, Ryker had half-expected to see one of the more ubiquitous pickup trucks.

'How do you know this is the place?' Ryker asked.

'I just do,' Henrik said, without looking.

'Which one is he?' Ryker asked.

Henrik did now glance at him. 'He was at the house earlier. The smaller one. His name's Martin.'

'Martin what?'

'Martin Lindstrom.'

'And you know where he lives?'

'I told you. I sneaked a look at his wallet one day. When he was snoring on the sofa after too much beer. I found his driving licence.'

'Your one guard was drunk and asleep? Why didn't you make a run for it?'

'I tried. More than once. But not that day.'

Without further explanation, Henrik moved away from the car they were hunched by, into the road. Ryker followed. Lights were on somewhere in the house in front of them, the glow visible through the glazed window of the front door. Given the relatively early hour, whoever was home was likely still up.

'Do you have a plan?' Henrik asked as he looked around him. Somewhat nervously, Ryker felt.

'Back door. Smash and grab. It's the quickest and easiest way.'

'I could go to the front. Ring the bell. Add confusion.'

Ryker hesitated. Not least because he was unsure of putting Henrik directly in harm's way.

But before he could say anything, Henrik raced forward, up to the front door, and pressed on the bell then knocked. Ryker darted past him, around the car and toward the back, just as the front door opened and he heard an inquisitive female voice.

No time to waste. Ryker jogged toward the garage, where a wall and a gate blocked him from the garden and the back of the house. He jumped up, grasped the top of the wall and swung himself up and over.

A dark garden. Small. Lights all around him from the nearby properties to the side and rear of this one. All was quiet though. He moved quickly across the paving slabs to a back door – the top half was glazed with several small, square panes. Lights on beyond. A kitchen and dining room. No one in sight, though the stove was lit. A pan steamed away on top of it.

Ryker tried the door. Locked. But he could see, through the glass panes, the key in the lock.

He half turned, pulled back his elbow and smashed it into the pane closest to the handle. The single-glazed glass caved at the first try. Ryker reached in, turned the lock and pushed open the door.

He stepped in. A man's voice. Not Henrik. Questioning. A woman too. More panicked now. Henrik was also talking. Quickly. Trying to calm the woman?

Ryker looked around. Spotted the bowl on the side table. He moved over, grabbed for the VW-emblazoned key fob.

A figure appeared in the doorway. A man. A man Ryker didn't recognise. Short. Slight. Fifties, Ryker guessed. His shirt was dishevelled, like he'd had a rough day. He held a phone in his hand. He said something to Ryker. It sounded like a command – get out, or something similar – though his voice quavered. He was petrified.

Ryker rushed forward, the man caught in two minds. Attack or defend. He chose the latter and backtracked into the hall, nearly tripping over his own feet as Ryker closed in. But Ryker had no intention of attacking him. At least not if he didn't have to.

He didn't have to.

Ryker turned raced for the back door. He jumped up over the wall. His ankle twisted as he fell and he grimaced in pain. Not enough to stop him. He rushed for the car. Unlocked it. Jumped it. Engine on. Reverse. Henrik appeared in the mirror. He dove into the passenger seat. Neither said a word. Ryker hit the accelerator and the car jerked back. Ryker twisted the wheel and the tyres screeched as the Golf swung around in the road. First gear, Ryker floored it. He checked the mirrors as he sped away.

The man came out onto his front step, phone to his ear. No sign of the woman.

Ryker, teeth gritted in anger, retuned his gaze to the road.

Silence in the cabin. After a while, and a few more turns as they approached the edge of the town, Henrik finally spoke.

'What?' he asked, himself sounding aggrieved.

'You know what,' Ryker said.

'Do I?'

'He wasn't one of them.'

No response from Henrik now. Ryker wouldn't even look at him, he was too pissed off.

'So who was he?' Ryker asked.

A short pause. 'You really want to know?'

'That's why I asked.'

'He's a teacher. At the school. He's a real bastard. Believe me.'

Believe him? Ryker didn't know what to believe anymore.

'Don't ever lie to me again,' he said.

Henrik gave no response to that.

24

Berg stared around the living room. The sheet that passed as a curtain hung sloppily over the only window. It was dark out now, but with the single overhead bulb glowing a dull orange, Berg imagined the room was as gloomy and depressing as this even on a sunny summer's day. The brown carpet had stains all over, patches of fabric mottled and stuck together from spillages of who knew what. The mucky brown velvet sofa was threadbare and sunken. The cheap coffee table was littered with dirty plates, used cups and glasses and empty beer bottles. The room looked like it belonged to a bunch of teenage, drug-abusing dropouts.

Berg turned to Erling whose large frame took up virtually the entire doorway. He was in a sulk. Apparently even behemoths like him could have pathetic whiney tantrums when they didn't get what they wanted, or when things didn't go their way.

'What?' Erling said, a challenge in his tone.

'How can you stand this place?' Berg asked.

Erling shrugged. 'It's not that bad. It needs cleaning but so what? It's not supposed to be five star. Do you know how boring it is sitting here for hours on end watching that little idiot?'

'Sounds really challenging. Is that why you let a fourteen-year-old escape? From three grown men? Because you were all too bored to stop him?'

Erling glowered and cracked his knuckles. 'I told you already. He had help.'

'Yes. The mystery man. Who managed to evade you, your useless friends, and a pack of dogs, on foot, through snow and ice.'

Erling said nothing now.

'Talk me through it again,' Berg said, moving toward Erling. The big man stood out of the way and Berg walked into the corridor, glancing in and out of the pokey rooms as he headed on. Each space was equally gloomy, messy and stuffy as the living room.

Erling gave his recollection. The mystery man turning up, unannounced. The same one Erling had encountered at the logging site the previous day, asking questions about Lindstrom's Nissan. He explained, once again, how the man had felled Erling, Lindstrom and Jan, another useless lump. The boy had bitten Erling. So, too, had the mystery man – Carl Logan? A boot to Erling's head had opened a gash that needed stitches. He'd already shown Berg all of the scratches and cuts as if they were explanation enough for what had happened. Erling concluded the retelling with the failed chase through the forest which culminated in the unlikely escape. More like a disappearance, as if man and boy had vanished in a puff of smoke.

'Is there any part of this story that doesn't make you sound like a clueless moron?' Berg asked, turning to face Erling as they stepped out onto the deck.

Erling glowered – one thing he remained very good at – but said nothing.

'What do you know about this man?' Berg asked.

'I already told you his name, and what he looked like.'

'That's it?'

'No. We also found his car. Over in the woods, that way.' Erling indicated with his chewed-up hand. 'Rented. From a shop in Trondheim.'

'He hasn't been back for it?'

'Not much point. We burned it out.'

'You did what! Why–'

'We searched it first,' Erling said, enough to bring Berg's rising temperature down a notch.

'And?'

Erling dug in his coat pocket and handed a little dark blue booklet over. Berg knew even before he looked that it was a passport.

British.

'So that confirms his name at least. But who the hell is Carl Logan?'

Erling shrugged. Berg pocketed the passport.

'I need that boy,' Berg said. 'You'll get nothing from me otherwise.'

'I've had nothing from you so far anyway.'

Berg raised an eyebrow. Was Erling seriously questioning his integrity?

'You'll get what you're owed when you've done what was asked.'

Erling mumbled under his breath.

'Is anyone watching the car? In case our mystery man goes back there.'

'They were. But what's the point of having someone there, in the cold, day and night?'

'What's the point? What's the point! Are you fucking serious?

In case he goes back there looking for his fucking car, you stupid, ham-fisted imbecile!'

Erling bared his teeth like a dog. For a fleeting second Berg became seriously worried his impromptu outburst had sent Erling over the edge. The big man was an underling, he knew his place, but everyone could be pushed too far, and as dumb as he was, Erling could crush Berg into the ground if he wanted to.

The next second the scramble and rustle of tyres on the dirt track floated over. A new arrival.

'Put someone out in the forest day and night,' Berg said, reverting to authority – exactly what Erling needed. 'And call me if you see or hear anything of the boy or his new companion.'

Erling didn't respond. Berg walked off, around the side of the house, to the front where the police car pulled up. Wold, on his own. He got out of the car.

'Quite a day, from what I hear,' he said in his naturally condescending tone. Or was it natural? Perhaps he practised it at home every night, in front of the mirror, because he had nothing better to do and no woman to screw.

'We'll find him,' Berg said. 'Both of them.'

'That's twice the kid has gotten away from you now.'

Was Wold questioning Berg's aptitude?

'From me?'

'You know what I mean.'

Berg said nothing.

'Lucky last time I was around to help,' Wold added.

'Yes, thank you, Inspector. Your impeccable duty hasn't gone unnoticed.'

Wold's eyes narrowed. 'Careful, Sigurd. You might run these guys like your own little kingdom, but you don't tell me what to do. You don't own me.'

Berg ignored that. 'We have this.' Berg moved over to the

policeman and drew the passport from his pocket. He handed it over.

Wold took one look. 'I could have guessed.'

'You know him?'

'I ran into him the other day. More than once. The last time Henrik tried to get away.'

Berg already knew all about that and wasn't interested in hearing Wold's take.

'Find out everything you can about him,' he said. 'Actually, no, just find him. Bring him here.'

Wold glared, it was clear the inspector didn't like to be told what to do. Especially not by Berg. But he'd got himself into this mess. He might have been on the outside, looking in, but he was still part of it.

'I want this over with. As soon as possible,' Wold said. 'The longer this goes on, the more damage it does.'

'Damage? To you?'

Wold held Berg's eye.

'You want this over?' Berg said. 'Find Henrik. And find Carl Logan.'

Berg brushed past him and headed for his car.

25

The Bergs lived in about the nicest house Konstantin had seen in this crappy little town. A two-storey whitewashed mansion – at least it was a mansion compared to most other homes in the area – that sat on a plot of a couple of acres, on a short, leafy road with only five other houses. Each of the houses were big, and looking at their styles, they'd obviously been built at the same time, by the same developer, though the Bergs' was the biggest.

Not that Konstantin cared in the slightest about any of that, but the basic layout of the land, the road, the distance between the houses, was of interest because it decided his options of how and where to spy. The wide plots, the abundance of plant life, was also a key reason why it was at all possible for Mrs Berg to have two different people watching her, without her knowing.

When they'd arrived, Nyland parked his car behind a bush on a verge across the street from the house. Konstantin drove on past. He turned his car around further down the street then moved back toward the Bergs' home, pulling up on the road right outside, just the low hedge at the edge of the property blocking his otherwise unobstructed view of the building beyond.

Intentionally indiscreet.

Then he waited.

Waited.

Mostly not watching the house, but the glimpse he could see of Nyland's car.

Finally, there he was.

Out of the car. Not happy. He glanced to the house then, hunched over, scuttled across the street to Konstantin, right up to the driver's side window.

Konstantin did nothing. Just remained in his seat, looking out the windscreen.

A knock on the glass.

Konstantin turned, pushed the button to open the window.

'Hi,' he said.

'What kind of amateur are you?' Nyland spat, in his native Norwegian. Konstantin could speak the language just fine. How would he ever move around the world like he did if he didn't blend?

'Excuse me?'

'You. You've been following me around all day. Following her. You're ruining my work. You want us both found out?'

An interesting take on the subject. Though Konstantin was a little surprised – impressed? – at the suggestion that Nyland had long ago spotted him. Perhaps he was better at this game than Konstantin originally gave him credit for.

Not that it mattered much, in the end.

'Perhaps I'm a policeman,' Konstantin said. 'Ever think about that?'

A forced laugh from Nyland. 'I know every policeman around here. And I can tell from your accent you're not local.'

Konstantin shrugged.

'Who's paying you? Sigurd? That slimy arsehole.'

'You should calm down,' Konstantin said. 'She'll see you–'

'See *me*? It's you who parked right outside the front of the house! You who was right there outside the café earlier!'

'It's you who is in the street outside her home, shouting. Get in the car, I'll explain everything.'

Nyland seemed to think about the proposition for a few seconds. Then without a word, he quickly moved around the car and sank down into the passenger seat.

Silence in the cabin.

'So?'

Konstantin's scars ached once more. Did he have a choice here? Had Jesper given him a choice?

Make him go away.

To an everyday person such words could mean all manner of things. Jesper's instruction however was very clear.

Why else would Konstantin be here at all?

Konstantin reached inside his jacket and whipped out the knife. He twisted his wrist and slammed the blade into Nyland's throat. A spatter of blood hit the windscreen. Then a pulse of blood squirted out onto Konstantin's face. He flinched, but only because he hadn't expected it. Nyland gargled and choked. His body shuddered. His wide, petrified eyes bore down on Konstantin.

Not sure what else to say or do, Konstantin simply shrugged. Seconds later Nyland's head slumped and his body went limp.

Konstantin pulled the knife out and a fresh wave of blood oozed and pulsed from the gaping wound. The car's interior was ruined. He wiped the blade clean on Nyland's jacket, then put the knife back in his pocket. He reached into Nyland's coat and took his car keys.

Two choices. Dump his own car and drive around in a dead

man's car, or dump Nyland's car and clean the blood out of this one.

Konstantin sighed. Both choices presented inconveniences.

First things first, he had to get rid of the corpse.

He looked over to the Bergs' house. No sign of anything exciting in there. He'd catch up with Mrs Berg soon enough.

What was Jesper's endgame in that regard? Mrs Berg was an okay-enough-looking woman to spy on, but if he had to choose, Konstantin would much rather have that waitress.

He turned the engine on and caught sight of his blood-spattered face in the mirror. That same ache across his chest once more. More than an ache now. A stabbing pain. He squeezed his eyes shut for a few seconds as the pain grew and grew, and spread further and further through his body.

Tensing every muscle and sinew as tightly as he could, groaning with effort, the debilitating feeling eventually dulled back to a manageable ache. He was still staring at his own reflection in the mirror, his cheeks red now, his forehead bristled with beads of sweat.

'Later,' he said to himself, slightly out of breath. 'I'll do it later. I won't forget.'

Then he pulled out and headed down the road.

26

Two choices rumbled in Ryker's mind: Head straight for Trondheim, or take the short detour into the forest to find his rented car.

Curiosity won out over caution. He made the turn. Headed along the track, moving slowly, headlights off so he could watch the forest around him for any signs of light or life. With only dull moonlight coming from above, Ryker felt Henrik's increased tension as they moved through the darkness.

Ryker pulled off the road. Stopped the car ten yards from his rental. Even in the night, it wasn't hard to realise he was looking at a burned out shell. Not good. It wasn't that the possessions in that car were irreplaceable, but the fact that those possessions were now in the hands of his enemies.

'We should go,' Henrik said, fear in his voice.

Ryker thought about getting out and taking a closer look... No. What would be the point? He flicked his gaze from the car to the trees behind it. Had he seen movement there? A flash of light? Phone screen perhaps?

Nothing there now.

He could go and check...

Once again the answer was no. Keeping Henrik safe, and getting them both away from there, remained the first priority. His eyes never leaving that spot in the woods, Ryker put the car into reverse and backed out to the road.

———

The journey to Trondheim was long but hassle-free. Unexpectedly so. Ryker had been well prepared for a chase. A police car, or Erling and his gang, on his tail, chasing him and Henrik down. Or a roadblock even. After all, Ryker and Henrik had broken into a house, stolen a car. Both the wrong side and the right side of the law were looking for them now.

Somehow none of that happened. It was gone eight pm when they passed by a road sign marking the edge of the city. Residential streets came soon after.

'I could take you to the police here,' Ryker said.

'No.'

They'd chatted little on the journey, but they'd had this conversation already. Henrik didn't want the police involved. He only wanted to be taken to people he knew. Not his foster parents, but friends. People he trusted who would keep him safe. He'd explained little of what he meant by that, though Ryker understood his point, particularly given his own doubts about Wold and Pettersen in Blodstein. The Trondheim police were a different outfit altogether, but did that really mean Ryker could trust them more than people that Henrik knew?

'Which way?' Ryker asked as they approached a T-junction and a red light.

'Left. We're almost there now.'

Henrik seemed a little perkier because of it. Ryker made the turn. They left behind the rows of neat little timber houses with pointed eaves – the same traditional style that lined the pretty and historic waterfront in the city – and moved onto a street that was far more... basic. Low-level, flat-roofed terraces. A run of shops and takeaways. A small retail park. Beyond it a cluster of four high-rises. Not modern, glass-rich apartments favoured by young professionals in many cities all over the world, but bland-looking, hastily erected concrete blocks used to house those on or below the poverty line. Ryker hadn't seen this side to Trondheim before, though it didn't surprise him that it existed, even in a city as quaint as this one.

'This is it?' Ryker said, as he pulled off the main road and onto a twisting track that headed toward the blocks. Alongside the road, sitting lower than their bigger cousins, were a series of four-storey-tall brick blocks.

'Yeah,' Henrik said. 'This is it.'

He sounded more downbeat now. Ryker looked over. He was unhappy about something.

'What?' Ryker asked.

'You were expecting something nicer?' Henrik asked. 'A mansion with a swimming pool and somewhere to land my helicopter?'

'Not at all,' Ryker said. 'You said you were fostered. That you were bounced around. It's an unfortunate truth that kids like that, like me too, don't–'

'You're nothing like me.'

Ryker didn't bother to argue.

'Pull up here,' Henrik said, looking to the left.

Ryker did so.

'Are you sure you wouldn't be better off with your foster parents?' Ryker asked.

He knew exactly where they lived. Less than two miles away.

He'd found their address through his research in the library – a cross-reference of various open-access databases.

'I want to be here.'

'You're only fourteen years old.'

'It's my choice.'

Ryker wasn't sure it technically was.

'So who does live here?' he asked.

'None of your business.'

'I'm asking all the same.'

Henrik sighed. 'Friends.' He reached for the door handle.

'I'll help you inside.' Ryker moved for his handle too. He sensed Henrik's protest coming. Still, Ryker got out of the car.

'I don't want you to,' Henrik said, looking over the top of the car to Ryker.

'I don't really care.' Ryker shut his door. 'I've done all this to help you, Henrik. I'm not about to let you walk off into the unknown now.'

'Unknown? This place isn't unknown to me.'

'But it is to me.'

And Ryker wouldn't be swayed. He moved around the car to Henrik's side. So what if the boy was angry with him? He was young, rebellious, had a mind of his own, but he was still a kid.

They walked side by side along the verge and up the path toward some steps which led to the top level of flats. Ryker guessed each block consisted of two duplexes stacked atop one another. Various noises drifted over from the tightly-packed dwellings around them; talking, shouting, music, dogs barking, TVs. A door opened off to Ryker's right and a man stepped out. Tracksuit. Cap covering his face. He glanced up but then put his head down and sauntered toward the road.

'You really should go,' Henrik said. He moved a little quicker to step ahead of Ryker.

Ryker took no notice of the instruction. They made it to the top of the stairs. Henrik moved to the door. Ryker followed a couple of steps behind, hands in pockets.

Henrik reached the door and stopped. He turned back to Ryker, part anger, part apprehension etched on his features. Then he knocked. Ryker stayed back. The music beyond stopped. Ryker could make out voices. How many people were in there? The door opened. Two bright eyes were caught in the light seeping out from inside. A man. Tall. Slender. Young – early twenties – but he had a shaved head that shone with reflected light. His face was screwed up when he answered the door but as soon as he laid eyes on Henrik he beamed.

'Henrik!'

He reached out and ruffled the boy's hair then pulled him in for a manly slap on the back. He turned and called inside. Ryker didn't catch any of the Norwegian, but soon two others were by the skinhead's side. Similar age – early twenties, or perhaps late teens. Dark clothing. A few tattoos. Beer cans in hand.

The tall skinhead looked over to Ryker. Suspicion now on his face. He said something, but Ryker only caught a few of the words. It wasn't friendly. Henrik responded. *Engelsk* was in there. English. So too *hjelpe*. Help.

The skinhead tutted. 'You can go now,' he said to Ryker.

Ryker stepped forward, peering into the interior beyond. Various odours caught in his nose. Tobacco. Cannabis. Beer. Sweat. His gaze rested back on Skinhead. Ryker knew these types. Far from the worst guys around, but he would bet his life's worth they were little more than bums. Bums who partied and drank too much and smoked too much. Jobs? Unlikely, other than a bit of cash-in-hand work here and there. Petty crime? Far more likely. Perhaps some unfair assumptions in there, but regardless, Ryker knew this was no place for a fourteen-year-old.

'Henrik,' Ryker said, holding his hand out to him. He smiled

ROB SINCLAIR

to Ryker, then pushed past his chums into the house. 'Thanks for everything,' he called out before disappearing inside.

One of the other men followed him, leaving Skinhead and one companion in the doorway, both glaring at Ryker.

'You know he was kidnapped?' Ryker said.

The two guys didn't flinch.

'Kid. Napped.'

Nothing.

'He's been missing for weeks,' Ryker said. 'Did you even know? Care?'

'He's safe with us,' Skinhead said. 'Now fuck off.'

With that the two moved back and the door slammed shut. The men retreated out of sight behind the frosted glass. Seconds later the blaring music returned.

Ryker remained standing on the spot, brain whirring.

Disconsolately, he hung his head, and turned to go back to his car.

Once inside, he remained in the driver's seat with the engine off. Honestly, he was a little dumbfounded. Over the course of the day he'd risked his life to save Henrik. Had fought off those men at the house, had led the boy through the forest, through the water. Had kept Henrik safe while they recuperated. Helped him to steal a car to get him out of Blodstein. Had driven him all this way. Ryker had done all of that almost without question. A natural instinct of wanting to help a vulnerable person in distress, someone who was otherwise unable to help themselves.

Sitting in the car, he felt like a chump. He still had no explanation for why those men in Blodstein had kidnapped Henrik in the first place, or what they wanted with him, but he also now realised he knew so little about Henrik himself. Ryker had only seen a young victim of a horrible crime. Henrik was

176

still a young victim, but Ryker had no doubt the gloss had been taken off these last few hours.

Who was Henrik, really?

Regardless, Ryker knew one thing: he wasn't happy leaving Henrik in that house.

He stepped back out into the night. Strode over to the building. Up the steps, to the front door. He rapped the wood with his knuckle. The music stopped once more. Footsteps. The door opened. Skinhead. Face screwed in anger, he opened his mouth. Ryker reached out, grabbed him by the neck, lifted him off his feet and tossed him to the ground.

He strode forward. Through the grimy corridor. The stench of cannabis grew, almost overpowering, sending Ryker's head into a spin. He stormed into the back room. Four, five, six people. Three men. Two women. Plus Henrik. Sunken in a sofa, wedged between a man and woman. Well, they were barely adults, but they were older than Henrik. Henrik, who had a spliff in his hand.

There'd been smiles on the faces at first, but when they spotted Ryker looming, the happy looks disappeared in a flash, replaced by shock and anger.

'What the hell?' Henrik said, bouncing up to his feet.

'You're not staying here,' Ryker said.

'Where's–'

'Motherfucker!'

Ryker turned to see Skinhead lurching for him. Ryker shimmied. Skinhead stumbled past. Ryker slapped him across the back to aid his forward momentum and he plummeted to the floor.

Ryker heard murmurs and gasps of shock. The gaggle looked on at him as though he was some out-of-control beast.

He needed to rein it in. But he also needed Henrik.

'Come on, Henrik. You don't belong here. We'll find somewhere else.'

'Who do you think you are?' Henrik sneered.

'I'm not leaving you here.'

Henrik shook his head in disgust. 'You don't get it, do you?'

'Those men from Blodstein could turn up. What then?'

Skinhead rose to his feet. He rubbed at his neck. Then at his head.

'I'm safe here,' Henrik said. 'I'm staying.'

'Safe?'

Ryker glanced to Skinhead and the others. Did Henrik really believe his own words?

Movement behind Ryker. He half-turned. Spotted the glint of metal. A knife. He spun, reached out and grabbed the wrist. Balled his fist and threw it forward.

Crack.

Solid connection into the chest. The figure plummeted, gasping for breath.

The figure. A scrawny young woman.

'Shit,' Ryker said.

But she did have a knife in her hand.

The woman, girl, whatever she was, squirmed on the ground, moaning, hand clutched to her chest as she tried to breathe.

Ryker turned back to the group. They all looked shocked, abhorred. Like Ryker had just committed the most horrendous crime known to man. He wanted to argue against that. She'd been about to stab him. Hadn't she?

Ryker was well used to dealing with people trying to hurt him. Act quickly, forcefully. Subtlety wasn't exactly his thing, but then it was hardly normal for a teenage girl to attack him.

'Get out,' Henrik said. Angered, but the words were measured. Then... 'GET OUT!'

The power and forcefulness and emotion in the screech caused Ryker to step back.

He held Henrik's eye for a moment.

'Get out. I don't ever want to see you again.'

Other than grabbing the boy and hauling him out of there, what choice did Ryker have?

Feeling about as useless as he could ever remember, he turned for the door.

27

How the hell was Ryker supposed to know about handling kids? Teenagers? Yes, he'd been one himself many years ago, but he'd been an even bigger shit than Henrik. He had zero adult experience of being around children, up until today when he'd rescued Henrik. To say he felt out of his depth made him feel ridiculous, but what was he to do?

Walk away. That's what he should do. He knew it. Henrik knew it. Pettersen and Wold knew it. Erling and the other meatheads knew it. Ryker had done his bit. Walk away.

So why couldn't he?

The engine was on, but Ryker still hadn't moved. He stared up at the door to the apartment. As though Henrik would have a change of heart any second.

After ten minutes there'd been no sign of anyone coming or going.

Ryker knew exactly what he should do next. He should go find a hotel. Sleep. Get up in the morning and head to the bank to collect his things. Then head on his way.

Yet he knew he wouldn't do that. Whatever Henrik had said, however strongly he felt that this was over, it wasn't for Ryker.

Those men in Blodstein had kidnapped Henrik. Held him against his will. His captors had chased Ryker down. Sent dogs. They'd burned out his car. Ryker wasn't finished with them, and he was sure the men weren't finished either.

Ryker wouldn't leave until he'd figured out exactly what was going on.

It was getting late, but he'd travelled all this way. He had one more stop to make in this city tonight.

Pushing reluctance to the side, he released the parking brake and pulled the car into the road.

With the help of the stolen car's satnav, it didn't take Ryker long to find the address he'd earlier memorised. The house was a step up from the estate where Ryker had left Henrik, similar in size and appearance to the one in Blodstein where he and Henrik had stolen the car. Ryker clenched the steering wheel a little tighter as he thought about those moments. Henrik had lied to him. Had he enjoyed that? Getting what he saw as revenge on a teacher he didn't like? Manipulating Ryker in the process?

Ryker let go of the wheel, shut off the engine and stepped out. He could see no lights on in the house, no car on the drive. The lights from the properties to the left and right suggested the neighbours were home. Ryker moved up to the door and rang the bell. No answer. Not a good start. He stepped back and looked over the house. He moved to the front window and peered in. A lounge. Furniture all in place, but definitely no signs of life from within.

What was he supposed to do now?

He turned and was halfway down the drive toward his car when a figure appeared to his right. A man. Jogging. He pulled to a stop at the edge of the drive next door and leaned over, holding his knees, breathing heavily. Ryker paused and watched him. When the man straightened up and caught sight of Ryker he jumped back.

'Sorry,' Ryker said. 'I didn't mean to frighten you.'

The man took a moment to compose himself. His breathing slowed a little.

'You're English,' he said.

Ryker nodded. 'Do you know the people who live here?'

'I know them, yes.'

'They're not home?' Ryker asked.

The man shook his head. 'Haven't seen them for a few days.'

'They had a boy, Henrik?'

The man paused now. His heavy breaths stopped for a few seconds, before he let out a long exhale. The warm, moist breath billowed upward into the cold night.

'They did,' he said. 'Who are you?'

'My name's James Ryker. Henrik disappeared, didn't he?'

No answer now.

'I'm helping the family.'

The man looked dubious. 'Yes. Henrik disappeared. A few weeks ago. The police were here. They talked to me. My wife. We couldn't help them.'

'Do you know what happened?'

'Nobody does. Everyone was concerned at the start, no one knew what had happened, but...'

'But what?'

'I don't think it was anything bad. I'm just the neighbour, but from what people say, I think Henrik just had enough. He ran away. Not the first time.'

'Not the first time?'

'Do you know Henrik?'

'A little.'

'Then you know what I mean. He's trouble. I hate to say this, but perhaps it's for the best that he's gone.'

The calmness in the man's delivery astounded Ryker. The suggestion that it was best that a fourteen-year-old boy had disappeared, regardless of why, or what had happened to him? Ryker couldn't comprehend that, even after the run-in he'd already had with Henrik.

'And the Johansens?' Ryker asked.

'I think they were relieved really.'

Ryker clenched his fist at that response. 'No. I meant, where are they?'

'Oh. Sorry. I haven't seen them for a few days.'

'They're on holiday?'

'I don't know. The last I saw them... three, four days ago. There were people here. Some men from up north.'

'Up north?'

'I recognised the accents.'

'What can you tell me about them?'

'The men? They were... I don't know really. What do you want me to say? There were two of them. They drove a Range Rover. Nice car. Expensive. You don't see many around here.'

The man stopped. Ryker held his tongue, waiting to see if the guy would add anything else. He didn't.

'That was the last you saw of the Johansens?'

'That's what I said.' His tone more than a little snarky now.

Ryker decided to quit.

'Okay, thank you.'

The man, looking a little perturbed about something, stood his ground as Ryker moved for his car.

He jumped in. Pulled off down the street.

Okay, so Henrik was a troubled kid. That much was clear. Ryker had been too. That didn't mean that Henrik deserved to be kidnapped. And the Johansens were missing? Two men from up north? Ryker didn't like that one bit.

Earlier, on leaving Henrik in that house, Ryker had been torn as to whether he should be involved here at all.

Now he was absolutely crystal clear.

He wasn't going anywhere. Whether Henrik liked it or not, this remained his fight after all.

28

All in all it had been one hell of a shitty day. The run-in with Marius – what was Berg going to do with him anyway? Nyland and his lacklustre investigation. Henrik running away with Carl Logan, whoever the hell he was. And looming over all of that? The constant threat of the Russians.

The Russians, who'd been unusually quiet today, Berg pondered as he shut down the engine and stepped out onto his drive. He looked to the darkened street beyond. No sign of Nyland there now. Not unusual. Berg hadn't spotted him there that morning either. Though he was becoming increasingly agitated that the PI wasn't now returning his calls or messages. The last he'd heard from Nyland was that Isabell had once again met with the lawyer, Tronstad, in that house in Blodstein. Berg had been well minded to jump into the car at that point and head to the house to confront that bastard. He hadn't. Next time...

But more to the point, why the fuck was Nyland now on radio silence, particularly given the extra money Berg had transferred to him?

He turned for the front door. He never made it. His phone

vibrated. Unknown number. On this day, of all days, Berg decided it was probably a good idea to take it.

'It's me,' the accented voice said. 'Valeri Sychev.'

'It's late,' Berg said. 'Come and see me tomorrow.'

'No.'

This time the voice echoed. Berg turned to where the sound had come from and Sychev appeared at the bottom of the driveway.

Berg's heart thudded a little harder in his chest.

'Was it really necessary to call me then?' Berg said, not impressed by the little trick.

'This way,' Sychev said. 'We're going for a little ride.'

Berg's insides curdled. What could go wrong?

Andrey, the Bulldog, drove. Sychev and Berg sat in the back seats of the Audi, Sychev on the driver's side. The streets were dark and quiet on the outskirts of the town so late at night. The town centre likely would be too. They never made it there. Bulldog pulled into a narrow lane and stopped the car.

'A busy day,' Sychev said.

Berg had watched him closely the whole way. His hands – empty – had remained on his lap, but was the Russian armed? A knife or gun in his jacket, or stashed somewhere down the side of his seat?

'A challenging day for sure,' Berg said.

Sychev sighed. 'Tell me about it.'

Silence. Was it a serious command?

'Please,' Sychev said. 'Tell me about this boy. The one causing you problems.'

How the hell–

'What boy?' Berg said. The response sounded lame even to his own ears.

The smug look on Sychev's face broadened a little.

'I have to admit, you surprised me, Sigurd. When I came here, I'd heard a little of your father's reputation. But you? I knew nothing about you. Not really.'

Berg said nothing to that, though the mention of his father angered him. He hated his father, even if he wouldn't have been where he was in life without him.

'I suppose I had certain ideas about who you were,' Sychev continued. 'Businessman. A rich man. Rich enough, anyway, because there are so many levels to wealth. But you're not a man who made himself rich. You used your family's money. I'm not saying that's bad, but even before I met you I imagined someone spoiled, arrogant, confident, entitled. Someone who has to always get his own way. A big baby really.'

Bulldog laughed. Berg caught the hardman's stare in the rear-view mirror for a moment.

'I have to say,' Sychev added, 'a lot of my ideas were right, but you still surprised me. There's more to you than I thought.'

Berg still said nothing, even if he felt as bruised as he did angry, as he did apprehensive by where the conversation was headed.

'Tell me about the boy,' Sychev said. 'Who is he? What does he mean to you?'

'No,' Berg said.

Sychev raised an eyebrow.

'No,' Berg said again. 'It's nothing to do with you.'

'It isn't?'

'You came here, to *my* corner of the world, for business. To deal. You want to deal? Fine, let's talk about it. Anything else in my life? Nothing to do with you.'

'That's not your choice to make.'

'Then you'll never get anything from me.'

Sychev shook his head and let out a long sigh. A sigh so long Berg was surprised the guy's face didn't turn bright purple.

'You're not as powerful in this town as you think you are,' Sychev said.

Silence again from Berg. Did he think himself powerful here? Well, of course he did. Look at the rest of the people around him. He was superior on almost every level.

'I can say the same to you,' Berg said. 'This is *my* town.'

Sychev's face remained neutral now. For some reason it riled Berg all the more. 'You're probably wondering how we know about the boy,' he said.

'If I knew which boy you keep on referring to, then–'

'Please, Sigurd. Please, stop. The boy you kidnapped. Henrik is his name, I think. The boy you had some men watching over in that house in the forest. The boy who today managed to escape from that house and has now run away from you.'

Berg grit his teeth.

'You want to know how I know all this?' Sychev said.

Berg didn't answer.

'Because I asked. I asked all sorts of people all sorts of questions about you. It didn't take long to get some interesting answers. The very men who were looking after him told me. You think these men are loyal to you, that they would never turn on you. But, unfortunately, that's not true. Perhaps the biggest problem is, you believe you're better than them. I think they see that too. They see your arrogance. The way you look down on them, mistreat them. So it was easy for me. All I had to do was ask about you, offer a little in return, and here we are.'

Sychev shrugged, extreme nonchalance.

'Except you're sitting here, with me now,' Berg said, 'asking questions about who the boy is, why he was there. So yeah, perhaps one or two of my guys mentioned something to you, but you're not as clever as you think you are either. Because you know virtually nothing.'

'I know your men would betray you. They were going to hand the boy to me. Money. That was all it took. We met them in a bar last night. Did you know that?'

Berg ground his teeth harder. So hard his jaw ached.

'You didn't know?'

'And how is it that he's now missing,' Berg said. 'Was that down to you too?'

'I'm afraid not,' Sychev said, shaking his head. 'It seems we're not the only ones in this town capable of making trouble for you.'

Sychev looked at his watch and sighed.

'Get out,' he said.

'Excuse me?'

'You heard. Get out. It's late, and I'm tired.'

'Then take me home,' Berg said, his temperature rising.

Before Sychev said another word Bulldog shot into action. He heaved open his door, stomped out. Yanked Berg's door open. Reached in and grabbed Berg by the scruff of his neck.

'Okay, okay!' Berg shouted. Bulldog dragged Berg out and only removed his hands from Berg's coat when they were both standing out in the cold.

'We'll come to your office in the morning,' Sychev called from the warm interior. 'Then you can tell me everything. I want to know exactly what you're planning with this boy. And I want you to have your final offer ready for me. Or we'll be done playing nicely with you.'

Bulldog kicked the passenger door shut. He glared at Berg in a momentary stand-off before getting back into the driver's seat. With spinning tyres the Audi shot off down the road. Berg held an arm up to his face to stop the grit getting into his eyes.

Was this how Nyland had felt the other day when Berg had left him stranded?

Berg pushed that thought away. When the red tail lights faded into the distance, he finally let out a sigh of relief.

He shivered in the cold. His home was a good thirty-minute walk away, along dark, unlit tracks. Not a pleasant walk by any means.

At least it would give him plenty of time to think.

He set off, brain moving at warp speed.

Today had been one hell of a shitty day. Even worse now than when he'd earlier arrived home. At least the Russians had finally put all their cards on the table.

It would need some thought, but one way or another Berg would come out of this on top. Whatever it took, he'd win.

He always did.

29

Isabell appeared much more circumspect – at least compared to recent days – when Berg found her in the kitchen the next morning. Or was the apparent change just because of how Berg felt himself?

She was sitting on a stool at the worktop counter, two hands wrapped around a steaming coffee mug. It was gone eight am but she still wore her dressing gown, her head huddled down into the thick pink ruffles of the neck and hood.

'Morning,' Berg said as he moved over to make a coffee for himself. Unlike her, he was already showered and dressed. He'd be out of the door within ten minutes. Another busy day ahead, another day of fighting off the circling vultures that closed in day by day.

The story of his life.

But vultures were nothing except scavengers, feeding off scraps. Berg was a lion.

'You look tired,' Isabell said. Had she even looked at him?

'Yeah,' Berg replied.

'You were late again last night.'

It hadn't been that late. She'd been in bed when he'd eventually made it into the house after first being accosted by the Russians on his driveway, then left in the middle of nowhere by them. She'd been in bed, but awake.

Had she seen Sychev outside?

He'd suspected last night that perhaps she'd heard him when he'd initially arrived home, and had been at the window, looking down while he was in discussion with Sychev. That thought grew now. How would he explain it?

'I'll try to be earlier tonight,' he said.

She murmured – consent? approval? – then finished her coffee and got up from the stool.

No make-up. Her hair was mussy. Had something happened with Tronstad – a lover's tiff – the previous day? Did Berg want that to be the case? No doubt he found some satisfaction in the thought that her own scheming and cheating had caused her misery.

'What are your plans today?' Berg asked. He took a sip from his coffee. Too hot. Damn it. He'd wanted to drink it quickly and go. Now he risked getting stuck, trying to make small talk for several minutes while he struggled to finish it off – the last thing he needed.

'Not much. I'll probably be here all day.'

She gave a meek smile. Then left the room.

Berg sighed. Something about the conversation... was that a knot in his stomach?

He swallowed another large mouthful of overly hot coffee. That'd take the feeling in his stomach away. It did. Kind of. Because, instead, his insides burned from the liquid. He grimaced. He heard her soft footsteps, padding up the stairs.

That knot again. Guilt? Remorse? Regret?

Sod this. He put his coffee down on the side, moved out into the hall, slipped on his shoes. He grabbed his car keys and his coat and headed for the door.

No Russians. No Marius. A good start to his working day.

No Nyland. A bad start. Where the hell was he? Perhaps he'd taken the opportunity to spend some time digging into Tronstad, rather than tailing Isabell, who'd given a clear indication that she was staying at home all day. But that still didn't explain why the idiot wasn't answering his phone, or responding to messages.

Berg grumbled and slapped his phone down onto the desk.

He checked his watch. Ten am already. He had to expect that Sychev would be here at some point. He'd said as much last night. Today was the day. Do or die. Well, perhaps not die, but–

A knock on his office door. As he looked up, Berg expected to see Marius's smug face there, or – even worse – Sychev's. No, just one of the lackeys.

Berg beckoned him in.

'The police are here to see you. Inspector Pettersen.'

This was all he needed.

'Of course,' Berg said with a broad smile, as though it was the most normal thing for the police to turn up at his place of work. 'Send her in.'

The lackey turned, and the next moment Pettersen walked in, her prompt appearance suggesting she hadn't been ready to take no for an answer.

'Shut the door, please,' Berg said.

The underling did so. Pettersen was alone, it seemed. Was that a positive sign? She remained standing, coat still on, as she looked around the office with an air of disdain. What was that about?

'What can I do for you, Inspector?' Berg asked.

He was aware of Pettersen. Wold had talked about her, and he'd seen her around the town, but this was the first time they'd ever been face to face.

'You're Sigurd Berg?' she said.

He frowned. 'I am.'

'My father knew your father.'

Berg's eyes narrowed as his brain rumbled. 'Is that right?'

'Inspector Lode,' Pettersen said.

Berg took a couple of moments as his memories fired. 'Ah, yes, I remember him. He was...' Berg really didn't know what to say. 'How is he?'

'He's dead,' Pettersen said. 'Has been for a long time. Just like yours.'

Berg clenched his teeth. Something about the tone of her voice that he didn't like.

'I remember your father though,' Pettersen said. 'I was young, but people talked about him. He was the rich businessman every kid in school wanted to be. Big house, BMW, fancy clothes.'

Berg sniffed and nodded. 'It wasn't–'

'You look just like him.'

It was true. He did. Berg hated that. Every time he looked in the mirror was a reminder.

She looked around the room again, turning this way and that.

'It's nice that you get to carry on his business. His legacy.'

He really didn't like her tone. 'Same for you, really. An inspector, just like him.'

'Oh, no, Mr Berg, I'm nothing like my father. For one, he was corrupt.' She let that hang. Berg said nothing. 'I know that now. Small town like this, it doesn't take much. Everyone knows each other, people are so ready to do each other favours, even if it means breaking rules, the law. I imagine that was even worse in those years. What about you?'

'What about me?'

'You and your father? Are you the same as he was?'

Berg paused before he answered that. The open insinuation, particularly given the mention of her father's corruption, was that she was also accusing Berg, and his father, of the same.

'I'm sure you're not really here to talk about our fathers, good or bad.'

She shrugged.

'Do you want to sit?' Berg said, pointing to the seat right by her.

'I'm fine,' she said. 'We found a body this morning.'

Berg's stomach tightened. His immediate thought was about the barrels in the sea. Surely neither of those had come ashore. That was impossible, wasn't it?

If not those, then... Henrik? His saviour, Carl Logan?

'Mr Berg?'

Berg shook his head to focus. 'A body?'

'Just north of the town, in a patch of woodland by the water. There was a car there too. The person who called it in thought it was a crash at first, but... it doesn't seem that's right.'

'That's awful,' Berg said. 'But... why are you here?'

And he really was confused, and worried, by that.

'The car had Trondheim plates,' she said. 'And the body, a man's, was...'

She sucked in a lungful of air, as if a coping mechanism for whatever nastiness she'd seen that morning.

'The body was very badly mutilated,' she continued. 'The face was unrecognisable.'

'Perhaps an animal?' Berg said, though immediately he felt

foolish for doing so. Better to keep his mouth shut until he knew where this was going.

'Not an animal,' Pettersen said. 'Not many animals use big rocks to smash skulls in.'

Berg quivered at the images forming in his mind.

'The really strange thing, though, is that I don't think it was the rock that killed him. Maybe the damage to the face was supposed to disguise it, but I think he was stabbed. In the neck. A post-mortem may help to clear things up.'

'This is horrible,' Berg said, and he really did mean that. 'This doesn't happen in our town.'

Pettersen pursed her lips and shook her head. 'Unfortunately it happens everywhere, one way or another.'

Berg said nothing to that, though his brain continued to rumble with thoughts as to what was to come next from her, as to where the conversation would go, who the dead man was. There weren't many options, he knew, and none of them were going to be good for him.

'It's really strange,' Pettersen said. 'Because the water was right there. Anyone wanting to hide their tracks, hide what they'd done, could have easily pushed the body and the car into the water. I think we'd have still found out, but maybe not so quickly.'

'Perhaps,' Berg said.

'A very amateurish move.'

'Amateurish?' Berg said. 'You say it like you'd expect a killer in our town to be more accomplished.'

'You haven't asked me who he is yet?'

'I thought you didn't know.'

She frowned. 'I never said that.'

'No, but you said about... his face.'

'Of course we know who he is,' she said. 'That's why I'm here.'

Silence. She was testing him. But honestly, what was he supposed to say?

'So, do you want to know?' she asked.

'I'm not sure I do really,' he said with a slightly nervous laugh.

She looked like she didn't know how to take that. 'His name is Jonas Nyland.'

What the hell?

'Do you know him?' she asked.

Of course she already knew that he did, which was why she was there.

'The thing is, Mr Berg, we found no wallet on him. No ID. No phone either. But his fingerprints confirmed his identity. He's on the system because he used to be a policeman, a few years ago in Trondheim.'

Berg kept his mouth shut.

'Strange that he was up here, so far from home, and not to have those things on him. Almost as if the killer, who butchered the poor man's face, who left the body and car hidden, but very poorly hidden, took those belongings from him to try to stall any investigation.'

'Or maybe this man... Nyland, just didn't carry a wallet, or phone with him.'

Pettersen shrugged. 'I can't say that's not possible. Anyway, we found where he was staying. A rented house. I've already been there this morning. A busy morning. I need a break.'

She laughed. Berg didn't.

'Perhaps I'll take a quick break after this.'

Berg still said nothing. He was too busy thinking. Thinking of what the hell had happened to Nyland, and exactly how much trouble he was in because of it. Was someone setting him up, or were the police just heading down the wrong path?

Or was this because of Wold? Wold was trying to hurt him.

'Mr Berg, we found Nyland's things. We found his phone. We found notes of his work. We found several mentions of the work he was doing for you. On his phone we can see all of the calls and the messages from you.'

Berg shook his head in disbelief.

'Mr Berg, did you have anything to do with Jonas Nyland's death?'

'What!' Berg said, genuinely bemused by the question. Then a little more forcibly, 'Why the fuck would I kill Jonas Nyland! He was working for me. I was paying him to spy on my wife!'

Pettersen didn't blink an eye at his little outburst. She remained stony-faced. A cool character, that was for sure.

A knock on the door. Berg's heart dropped. The same lackey at the window, but undoubtedly more bad news.

'Inspector Wold,' the lackey said, before the senior policeman barged his way in. He took one look at Pettersen, then at Berg, then shook his head.

'Karina, a word please,' Wold said.

She looked less than impressed. Berg felt emboldened all of a sudden as Pettersen skulked off out of the office with her boss. Berg got to his feet, took a couple of steps toward the door, as if doing so would help him eavesdrop on the conversation now taking place outside.

No use. Wold appeared in the doorway once more. He strode inside, alone, and shut the door behind him. Like his colleague had, he remained standing, glaring over at Berg.

'She's quite a piece of work,' Berg said.

'She's a brilliant inspector,' Wold responded, almost affection in his voice. 'But sometimes these youngsters need to learn their place before they get bitten.'

Berg relaxed a little more at that statement.

'But just because I sent her away this time, doesn't mean you're off the hook.'

'Off the hook for what?'

'Nyland. He was working for you.'

Wold said this as though it was his outstanding detective skills which had led to the discovery of that fact.

'I already told Pettersen that he was,' Berg said, indicating to the door and the now departed policewoman.

Wold stared. 'See, in a way it's a shame I have someone on my team so keen. Anyone else and they'd have been a step or two behind. But her? She works fast. Gives me less chance to make things work. For me. If you know what I mean.'

Berg did. Wold didn't like Pettersen because she was good at her job and honest about it. That said so much more about him than it did about her.

'But then,' Wold said, his face screwing up as if he was deep in thought, 'I'm not so sure this is so simple. Perhaps Nyland wasn't working *for* you, but against you.'

'What? That's–'

'Your wife, or perhaps someone else entirely, hired Nyland, an out-of-town investigator, to come and look into you. It's not as though you're without problems, without enemies now, is it, Sigurd?'

Berg decided to keep his mouth shut, whether or not Wold knew he was talking nothing but falsehoods.

'Perhaps Nyland even spoke to you. Laid out his cards. That explains the phone calls between the two of you. Perhaps he even got funny ideas. About not just investigating you, but blackmailing you.'

Wold nodded, clearly pleased with himself.

'I know you, Sigurd. I know you're not the type of man who'd sit and take a threat like that. So the two of you met up. Unfortunately for Nyland, he really doesn't know you at all. He doesn't know what you're prepared to do, to keep ahead.'

No. Nyland hadn't known. Did Wold?

'You know that's completely untrue, don't you?' Berg said, trying to sound as commanding, and as calm and confident as he could.

'Do I?'

Berg ground his teeth. Wold thought he could play games. But Pettersen... she was involved in this murder case too. She wouldn't fall for Wold's nonsense if he was seriously going to try to frame Berg. Perhaps her keenness really was Wold's biggest pitfall.

'Don't you see what's going on here?' Berg said.

Wold pursed his lips and turned out his hands.

'Someone is trying to cause problems for me,' Berg said. 'This has to be connected.'

Wold's eyes pinched as he glared, but he still said nothing.

'The boy. That Carl Logan. Nyland getting murdered. This is all connected.'

He conveniently left out mention of the Russians in that hypothesis. But actually, was them being the culprits the most simple explanation? The Russians were heaping more pressure on him.

'What else have you found out about Carl Logan?' Berg said, looking for any diversion he could find.

'No one's seen or heard from him. He's not in town. If he was, I'd know about it.'

Wold spoke with supreme confidence, as if he really believed his own words. What a joke he was.

'But do you know anything more about who he is? Why the hell he's in our town in the first place?'

'No,' Wold said.

Berg wasn't sure he believed him. For one, it was unlike Wold to be so blunt in his answers.

Wold checked his watch. 'Funny old world, isn't it?' he said.

'I bet a few days ago you thought you were untouchable around here. How quickly a man's position, his outlook, can change.'

Wold turned and grabbed the door handle.

'See you soon, Sigurd.'

He walked out, leaving Berg shaking with anger, mixed in almost equal measure with worry.

30

Ryker decided he'd had enough travelling for one day. As tempted as he was to ride back to Blodstein, by the time he got there he wouldn't be able to do anything useful, except for slinking through the night-time streets – for what? Instead, he decided to rest up, and would look at his options with a fresh mind in the morning. In theory. Except he chose against going to a hotel in Trondheim – for one, he had virtually no cash left, until he could get to his reserves. He'd sleep in the stolen car. Not exactly luxury comfort, but he'd certainly seen far worse.

Before he got ready for some shut-eye, he did have one more stop to make. He found a used car garage, whose outdoor forecourt was bathed in darkness, and which had a large and even darker yard at its rear. A couple of security cameras here and there, but Ryker scaled the metal security fence with ease and sneaked to the back, to the far corner of the yard, where the least attractive of the available cars were left to rust. He unscrewed the licence plates, jumped back over the wall, and swapped out the plates on the stolen car. Not a perfect ruse, but hopefully it would at least allow him to move more freely in the stolen car for a little longer.

With the new licence plates secured, he drove back across the city and to the estate where he'd earlier left Henrik. He turned off the main road and onto the twisting street, eventually pulling to the side of the road a couple of buildings before he reached the one Henrik and his chums were smoking and drinking in. Lights were still on, though Ryker guessed it wasn't really that late.

Why was he there? Simple. Where else?

He shut the engine off, pulled the hood of his coat up over his head, pulled the zip as high as it would go, then pushed back into the seat and headrest and closed his eyes.

The knock on the window brought Ryker out of his half-sleep. Not a horrendous night, all in all, but he'd never fully settled, had always been just on the verge of deep sleep, his eyes naturally flitting open every now and then – subconsciously – to check everything was okay.

Except he hadn't spotted this person approaching his car, so perhaps he hadn't been as alert as he'd thought.

It was light outside. Eight thirty. Later than he'd normally sleep. He shuffled up in the seat, blinked a couple of times to get his focus before he set eyes on the young woman at the window. He recognised her. The same woman who'd tried to stab him the night before. Who he'd smashed in the chest with his fist.

He pulled the window down.

'Good morning,' he said.

'Why are you here?'

He looked beyond her where two friends – both female, both teenagers by the look of it – were standing a little further along the street, glaring back at Ryker. Neither of those two had been in the house last night, Ryker noted.

'You know why,' he said.

'He doesn't want you here. None of us do.'

'I'm helping him.'

'He doesn't need your help.'

'Is he inside still?'

She pulled back a little, looked to her friends. As if debating whether she would answer. Or whether she'd give a truthful answer, perhaps.

'Yes, he's in there,' she said. 'I told you, we'll keep him safe.'

'Do you even have any idea what's happening to him?'

She scoffed. 'Do you?'

Ryker didn't answer. Perhaps he shouldn't underestimate this bunch. Well, not their intentions, at least. It certainly appeared as though they had Henrik's interests in mind, but physically, were they really up to it if Erling and the others descended here en masse?

'I'm going for a walk,' she said. 'You won't be here when I get back.'

She let the command hang. Ryker held her eye but still said nothing.

'If you are, I'll call the police.' She unzipped her coat a little, pulled down the neck of her jumper to reveal the patch of swollen, purple flesh that sank further below the fabric. 'I'll tell them you attacked me. Tried to rape me. My friends stopped you. I've got plenty of witnesses.'

She looked over to the glarers, then back to Ryker. The expression on her face could only be described as wicked.

Then she walked away.

Ryker shook his head. For more than two decades he'd travelled all over the world, had become embroiled in some of the most horrendous and violent plots, coups, terrorism, had been tortured, had come across the most cruel and vicious people imaginable. He'd survived all that, had come out on top, over and over.

For some reason he felt as out of his depth dealing with these youngsters as he could recall at any of those points in the past. With the conniving on display, and the delicacy needed by him, this was an unfamiliar and very different challenge for sure.

He glanced back to the house, then started the engine and pulled away.

The sky was blue, the sun was out and provided plenty of warmth inside the car as Ryker drove north, though the temperature outside was a frigid minus four. Thick snow remained on the peaks, with a patchwork of white within the piney forests around him. A beautiful sight, even if the roads had iced over in the night, and were treacherous as a result. The danger of the drive only added to the knot of apprehension in his stomach as he travelled back to Blodstein. He was riding into town in a stolen car. Riding back into a town where the previous day he'd had a run-in with a gang of men, from whom he'd reclaimed a kidnapped boy. A boy who was now languishing in a squalid apartment with people who were strangers to Ryker.

Today he needed sense. He needed to come away from Blodstein with real answers and a real plan of how to get to the end of this mess.

His starting point was Trine Hansen. The kindly neighbour who, according to Henrik, had taken him in when his foster parents of several years had died in a car accident.

She lived on a street of nondescript houses, more or less carbon copies of the home where Ryker had stolen the car the previous evening. In the middle of the working day, he wasn't sure if he'd find Trine home or not. If not, he was quite tempted to take a look around inside anyway. He wasn't going to get through this unless he stepped up his actions a notch or two.

He parked on the road outside. No cars on the small drive. No pedestrians or other vehicles moving up or down the street.

Ryker got out and moved toward the house. He headed to the front door and rang the bell. No answer. Was that what he'd wanted? He pushed his face closer to the small frosted panes of the front door. With poor natural light, he found it difficult to make out what lay beyond, but he certainly saw and heard no signs of anyone coming to the door. He knocked for good measure. Nothing.

'Kan jeg hjelpe deg?' came the voice from behind.

He turned to see the woman, shopping bags in hand, at the edge of the driveway. Her words rattled in his head. He assumed, 'Can I help you.' Whatever it was, the question wasn't delivered in a particularly friendly manner.

'I'm looking for Trine Hansen.'

The flicker in her eyes suggested he'd found her. 'Who are you?'

'My name's James Ryker. I wanted to talk to you about Henrik.'

A twitch on her face. She glanced along the street and then back to Ryker.

'Let's go inside. It's freezing and my arms will fall off.'

He assumed she meant because of the shopping, rather than the cold, though perhaps her lack of English vocabulary made her meaning ambiguous.

'After you,' Ryker said, trying an easy-going smile. She looked at him like he was an idiot. Well, he'd tried at least.

Trine Hansen's home was as modest on the inside as on the outside. Three small rooms downstairs, and Ryker presumed three small bedrooms upstairs. Trine was mid-thirties. No indication in the few photos about the kitchen, where she led him, that she had a partner or children.

'You're not at work?' Ryker said, as she unpacked one of the bags of shopping into the fridge-freezer.

'Not today.'

'What do you do?'

She straightened up and turned around and glared at him. The kettle clicked as it finished boiling.

'Coffee?' she asked.

'Black. Please.'

She grabbed a fresh milk and moved over to the kettle.

'When did you last see Henrik?' Ryker asked.

She didn't answer for a couple of seconds, busying herself with the mugs and a jar of instant coffee. Convenient delay?

'Not for a while. He moved to Trondheim when he left me.'

'Why did he leave?'

She turned around again, a more exasperated look now.

'You have met Henrik, haven't you?'

Ryker nodded.

'If you really know him, you'll know how difficult he is. I liked him, I felt for him when the Rosteds died. It was awful. He was so young, and had already had so much trouble.'

'Trouble?'

'Different families. I don't even know what happened to his real mother and father. But the Rosteds treated him like their son. I'm sure he would have stayed with them until he was a man if they hadn't died.'

'They sound like good people.'

'Better than almost everyone I've met. I don't know how they did it. Henrik was hard work for them–'

'In what way?'

She paused and stared at Ryker as though he should know the answer.

'You were a boy once, I'm sure you can imagine. Perhaps you were like that too. Fighting. Smoking. Staying out. Not going to school. Breaking things. Stealing–'

It all sounded very familiar to Ryker, though he didn't appreciate the knowing look Trine gave him as she reeled off the misdemeanours.

'–but, despite it all, and even though they, of course, did punish him in their own way, they were always so happy and relaxed. I think he needed that.'

'And you took him in–'

'I had to. He was lost without them. I did it for them as much as for Henrik.'

'It didn't last long though?'

She tutted. 'I get the feeling you're asking me questions you already know the answers to?'

'Just making sure I understand.'

'Understand what?'

She finished making the coffees and handed a steaming mug to Ryker.

'Do you know the Johansens?' Ryker asked.

'In Trondheim? I know that's the name of the family Henrik went to. I never met them.'

Was that odd?

'You never visited him either?' Ryker asked.

A flicker in her eyes again. Remorse?

'I wanted to. I think... time just slipped by.'

Ryker wasn't so sure about that. He got the feeling Trine had been relieved to see the back of Henrik. That she'd not looked back since. But was there something else?

'He was kidnapped,' Ryker said.

She paused, the coffee mug a couple of inches from her mouth.

'The Johansens are now missing too.'

She shook her head. 'I don't know what you're saying. Why are you telling me?'

'Some men took Henrik, a fourteen-year-old boy. Men from this town took him. One of them's called Erling. Big guy, big beard. You know him?'

A flicker once more. Her eyes were not good at concealment.

'No,' she said.

'Another is Martin Lindstrom.'

She didn't say anything, but the look on her face...

Ryker shook his head to show his disapproval of her deceit. 'Those men were holding Henrik at a house outside the town. In the forest, near a logging site. You probably know where I mean.'

She shook her head and pushed her mug down on the worktop.

'Please, this is too much. I need a moment.'

She went to stride past but Ryker held his arm out to stop her. She looked up at him, fear in her eyes now.

'I'm not the bad guy.'

His words hung in the air. Her face didn't change. She was scared. Of him? That wasn't his intention.

'I found Henrik at that house,' Ryker said. 'I took him away from there, and back to his friends in Trondheim. He's safe. But those men are still out there. I want to know why they took him. Erling's just a doer. I want to know who made this happen.'

'Please? I just want to go to the toilet.'

What was he going to do? Grab her and refuse?

He moved aside. She walked off. Padded up the stairs. A bang as a door closed. He looked around as he waited. Her phone had been on the counter before. Gone now.

Ryker sighed. Though he was intrigued as to who would turn up. A friend? Erling and his crew? The police?

Progress, at least, he guessed.

A toilet flushed upstairs, then the door opened and Trine padded down the stairs, more slowly than when she'd gone up. Without catching Ryker's eye she moved back into the kitchen and picked up her drink.

'Nice coffee,' Ryker said, taking a sip from his mug.

She looked at him meekly. 'Thanks.'

'Tell me what you know about Erling,' Ryker said.

She opened her mouth, then closed it, then shook her head. 'I don't know him at all.'

'You know of him?'

She looked confused by the question.

Ryker sighed. For whatever reason, it was clear she was holding back on him. The question was why, and how was he going to get her to change her mind?

'Who around here drives a Range Rover?' he asked.

'Excuse me?' More confusion. Genuine?

'A Range Rover. It's a big, expensive car. Who around here could afford that?'

She frowned. 'Not many people. There'd be...'

She paused. Not to think, but because she'd heard the sound too. The engine noise.

He glared at her. She looked petrified all of a sudden. The coffee mug shook in her hands.

Ryker placed his cup down and strode out of the kitchen, into the front room. He peered out of the window. Just one car. That was good. But it was a police car. Not so good.

Wold? Pettersen? He couldn't yet see, though it was interesting that the car had come down the road steadily, no lights or siren.

Ryker turned and moved back into the corridor. He stopped

when he spotted Trine in the kitchen doorway. No mug in her hand now, but a seven-inch kitchen knife, pulled up to her chest.

'Please,' she said, the single word catching in her throat. Did she really think he was going to attack her?

He ignored her and turned for the door. He moved out into the cold as Pettersen stepped from her car. No sign of any backup.

'Back so soon?' she said.

Ryker remained standing a couple of yards from the front door, looking up and down the street. No one else around.

'Back?' Ryker asked.

How did she even know he'd left?

She looked to the car parked on the street.

'There was a car theft last night in Blodstein,' she said. 'A couple of streets from here. A car just like that one. Except that one has a Trondheim registration.'

'Obviously not the same car then.'

'Obviously not the right plates, as those tell me that car is fifteen years old. I could run them to check which car they actually belong to.'

Well, Ryker had done the best he could, under the circumstances, picking a crappy car he hoped no one would notice was missing its plates. Clearly the plan had pitfalls if anyone looked closely enough.

'Interesting too,' Pettersen said, 'that the description they gave me of the thief matches you.'

'What? Big? Handsome? Accent like James Bond?'

A slight smile from Pettersen. 'They also said there was a boy. A teenager. So, perhaps it wasn't you after all. I don't see a teenage boy with you now.'

Ryker moved a couple of steps toward her. She backtracked closer to her car, to the boot. He knew she had a shotgun in there. Perhaps she should have pulled it out already. She'd never do so now before he tackled her if that was her intention.

'Trine didn't call 1-1-2,' Ryker said, referring to the emergency number for the police. 'Did she?'

Pettersen shuffled a little closer to the boot.

'There'd be more of you here. But why did she call *you*? Your personal number, I'm presuming. How would she even know your number?'

'Because I expected you might show up here.'

Ryker moved another two steps forward.

'Where's Henrik?' Pettersen asked.

'I'll take you to him if you want.'

Her eyes pinched.

'He's safe,' Ryker said. 'For now. But there are people after him. After me too.'

'Or maybe it's just you. Maybe it's all you. You're the bad guy.'

'I think you know that makes no sense.'

'Doesn't it? Everything was fine until you arrived.'

'If you believe that then you're an idiot.'

Ryker went to step forward again. She popped the boot open.

'Another step and I get the shotgun.'

'And what? You'll fill me with lead out here on the street?'

'If I have to.'

'Have you ever even fired it before?'

Her lack of answer meant no.

Ryker looked along the street. Thirty yards up a man headed their way with a dog. Except he spotted the police car and froze, staring, as though wondering whether he should get any closer or not. Out of the corner of Ryker's eye, he realised that Pettersen had followed his line of sight.

He took the opportunity. He burst forward. A shriek of panic from behind him – Trine, on her front step? Ryker ignored her.

Pettersen tried to move, tried to defend, but Ryker was too close. He grabbed her wrist, spun her around by her shoulder, twisted her arm behind her back and pushed her up against the metalwork of her car.

'Don't fight,' Ryker said. 'I don't want to hurt you.'

'You... already are,' she said, squirming.

'I'll let you go, but listen.'

She breathed through gritted teeth, seething. She said nothing.

'You don't have many options,' he said. 'You were going to take me to the police station? Put me in a cell? Worst thing you could do. Henrik is safe, for now, but those men will find him. And I think you know Wold is involved somehow. Is he a bad cop? I don't know. But I don't trust him, and I'm not sure you do either. That's why I always see you alone, right?'

She squirmed a little more forcibly but still didn't say a word.

'I'm going to make this better,' Ryker said. 'I'll find everyone involved. They'll all answer for what they've done. Wold included.'

'What? You're going to go around killing them all?' Pettersen said, her clenched teeth making her words rasp.

'No,' Ryker said. 'Not unless I have to.'

'You're crazy.'

'Maybe. But your only sensible option is to listen to me. Work with me.'

She laughed. 'See? You're fucking crazy.'

Ryker let go of her and pushed off, taking a step back. She spun around.

'We'll take your car,' Ryker said. 'To Trondheim. I'll take you to Henrik. You'll see he's fine. He'll tell you what happened. Then we'll come back here and we'll finish this.'

She shook her head, her face was red, her features screwed in anger.

Ryker looked up the street again. The man was still there. Trine remained on her doorstep.

'If it makes you feel better, for the benefit of these lot, you can cuff me. Perhaps it will help you explain all this to your bosses later on. But we're going in your car, together, and we're going to Trondheim. Got it?'

She didn't answer, but Ryker turned around and placed his hands behind his back. After a few tense seconds he heard Pettersen move up to him. She hadn't gone for the shotgun. A good start at least.

Click. Click.

'Get in the car,' she said.

Ryker smiled. Then did as she'd instructed.

31

'I 've heard a lot about you,' the man sitting next to him in the back of the car said.

Interesting. Because Konstantin could say the same thing back to this man – Valeri Sychev. Though the same wasn't true of the man in the front, in the driver's seat. Andrey. Konstantin had never met him before, had never seen the ugly face, though one look into his hard eyes had told Konstantin exactly what kind of man he was. Hard. But simple.

Boring, really.

'Don't you want to know what I heard?' Sychev asked.

'No.'

Sychev laughed – entirely forced. 'Hey, Andrey, you two would be good friends. You're both men of very few words.'

Andrey didn't say anything in response to that – very apt.

'I don't think we're anything alike, really,' Konstantin said.

Sychev shrugged. 'And I know we haven't met in person before, but you do know *who* I am, don't you?'

Konstantin nodded.

'Good. Then you'll understand what I'm about to say. You'll

take orders from me, from now until we're done here. That is what Jesper has asked for.'

Konstantin said nothing, but he didn't like the idea at all. Jesper, and only Jesper was his paymaster. But what could he do?

'I understand you had a problem last night?' Sychev said.

'No. There was no problem.'

Disposing of Jonas Nyland's body had been simple enough really. On the clarification of Jesper, he'd decided against making the body disappear. It wouldn't have been hard, out in such a remote area. Water, woodland, burning, burying, a combination of those, the choices were many. The ultimate choice was far less work, which in a way Konstantin was pleased with. He'd dumped the body by the water, but not before smashing the face in. He'd later dumped Nyland's car there too, before spending a couple of hours cleaning the blood from his own car to make it usable again. Taking Nyland's personal possessions from his corpse, together with the pummelled face, would mean the police would have to work that little bit harder to figure things out, but if they were at all competent, it wouldn't be long before questions were directed toward Sigurd Berg. Which was exactly what Jesper had wanted. Last night, at least. Now, with the appearance of these two, Konstantin wasn't so sure.

'No problem?' Sychev said. 'You stabbed the man to death, destroyed his face with a rock and dumped his body by the road.'

'It's what Jesper wanted.'

'It was?'

A silent stand-off ensued, both men holding the other's eye.

'My mother was Ukrainian,' Konstantin said. Sychev raised an eyebrow. 'She was from the east and spoke Trasianka. I spoke it at home as a boy but when I left for Moscow I soon turned to our real mother tongue. Your Balachka sounds very similar to me. I always hated the way you people speak. Like you couldn't make up your mind who you wanted to be so you had to pretend to be two different people. One foot in each place.'

A scratching noise up front. Andrey's hands twisting around the steering wheel. As though he was wringing Konstantin's neck, angered by what he saw as a slight on his heritage.

'I like people who know who they are,' Konstantin said. 'Who talk simply. Act simply. You know what I mean?'

'Putting aside any insult, yes, I think I do,' Sychev said. 'I'll talk plainly to you. I tell you to do something, you do that thing. Not anything else. If you do that, we'll all get along just fine.'

Konstantin wasn't so sure, which was why he didn't say anything.

'I want you to find out what they know about the boy. That's all.'

'You say that's all, but–'

'We're not here to play games. Find out what they know, anyway you can. But if you make a mess, it's yours to deal with. And next time, deal with it properly, or this will be the first and the last time we work together. Do you understand?'

'Very clearly.'

With that, Konstantin opened the car door. He stretched as he got out. The car remained by his side and Konstantin stayed where he was for a few moments, looking across the street. His chest ached, though the pain there lessened with each day that passed. The most acute pain now was across his right shoulder. Where he'd delivered yesterday's atonement, yesterday's punishment. He'd dug deep with the knife, into the nerves and muscles that lay below the surface. Nyland was a nothing, his death had been quick and near painless for him – certainly by

Konstantin's norm – but for some reason his own punishment had been all the more severe.

Why was that? The only answer he could grasp was the pure frustration of this place. He already hated it, though he couldn't fully explain why. It wasn't the cold, he was well used to that, it wasn't even the people... or perhaps it was, especially now that Sychev and his little dog were here.

Yet Sychev's direct order should have taken his frustration away. Wasn't that what Konstantin wanted? To have his shackles removed?

The two sides of the coin didn't reconcile at all. On the one hand, Konstantin's life of violence had left the countless scars on his body. Every line, every lump of raised flesh represented a life gone, a life taken, pain and suffering – both his and theirs. He'd never accept that what he did was 'good' – that was why he had those marks. Yet without killing... what else did he have? Did his life have any other meaning at all?

He checked the road, then moved across the street. He knocked on the door and waited. He heard footsteps the other side. Hard shoes on a wooden floor. Locks released. The door opened.

The man was smartly dressed. Shiny black shoes. Neatly pressed navy trousers. Light blue shirt, tucked in, the top button undone, but the collar tidy. His hair was neatly coiffed, his face was strong – nice proportions to the jaw, nose, and overhanging brows gave an altogether manly appearance.

'Can I help you?' he asked in his native Norwegian, his smile relaxed and pleasant.

'That choice is yours,' Konstantin said, before thrusting his arm forward. Electricity fizzled and crackled as he pushed the taser into Tronstad's gut. His eyes bulged in shock as he reeled backward... then he collapsed to the floor.

Konstantin looked over his shoulder. No one in sight, except for the car across the road. Andrey glared at him, but then the engine started up, the car pulled away and moved out of sight.

Konstantin stepped inside and shut the door behind him.

32

Konstantin sat back in the chair and watched Stefan Tronstad, naked body swinging back and forth in front of him. One end of the rope was tied around his ankles, which were clasped together, tightly bound. The other end of the rope hung from the ceiling fan above. An old style, almost ornate ceiling fan – the type used decades before air-conditioning became the norm. The fixture seemed an oddity here, in this northerly part of the world. Did it really ever see use? He couldn't imagine the summers were so warm as to require it.

He smiled to himself as a thought hit him. Childish, really, but it amused him. He imagined turning the fan on, watching the rotors build up speed, poor Stefan spinning around and around, faster and faster, his body lifting through the centrifugal force until he was nothing but a blur. Like a cartoon caper.

No. Konstantin wouldn't try that.

Tronstad groaned, though his eyes remained closed. A drop of blood pooled on his brow and dropped from his skin and to the floor a couple of feet below, joining the ever-growing small puddle there. Not much blood really, not yet. Tronstad had only been given a gentle introduction so far.

Unfortunately, the guy didn't seem to have much stomach for ill treatment. A couple of simple body blows, and a couple of slaps around the face, which had caused his nose and lip to bleed, and he'd passed out. From sheer fear, Konstantin could only presume.

With the captive out of it, Konstantin had taken the opportunity to look around the place. Just a small place, it hadn't taken long. This room, the kitchen, the toilet. An office, given the functional fittings, and about as basic as they came, and sparsely furnished like it wasn't yet in full use. He saw plenty of paperwork, mostly boxed up. Plus a computer, which Konstantin would look through if he got bored. For now he sat quietly, waiting.

The guy was definitely stirring. Perhaps he was even already awake, and only pretending to be unconscious, as though doing so would help him now.

Konstantin got up and moved forward. He grabbed the water glass from the desk and crouched low in front of his prisoner. He tipped the glass up against Tronstad's swollen lips.

'Drink,' he said, even though he knew it was impossible to properly drink in the poor guy's position.

Tronstad did a lousy job of lapping at the cool liquid, but at least it was clear now that he definitely was awake. Konstantin put the glass down and pulled the knife from the sheath attached to his side. Tronstad stared at Konstantin's chest – at the scars? – but then his eyes rested on the blade. He whimpered.

'You're wondering about my body?' Konstantin said, twisting the knife in his hands. 'That's my story. But, how about this? You tell me yours, I'll tell you mine?'

Nothing from Tronstad except for some simple begging.

'Do you know what it's like to skin a person?' Konstantin asked. 'Dead or alive?'

'N-no. P-please.' Was that no, he didn't know, or no, don't skin me?

'I think a lot of people imagine it's very difficult. We're human. We think we're superior to other beasts. We think our bodies are temples, that we're strong and capable and durable. But you know what? Have you ever bought a whole, raw chicken?'

No answer now. Just an incoherent mumble.

'You get a chicken from your shop, it still has skin on it. It's not hard to remove, is it? It peels right off. It's the same for almost any animal. Rabbit, chicken, dog, pig. The skin is an organ, it's strong, it stays together, but that doesn't make it harder to take off, it makes it easier. You can pull it right off like a sheet. All you need is...'

He wafted the blade past Tronstad's face, pushed the tip onto his skin and drew it as lightly as he could up his torso, over his waist, along his thigh to just above his knee.

'All you need is a little cut to start...'

He quickly drew the knife across the surface, skin deep, three inches across. A tiny incision really, probably not as much pain as banging his leg on a table. Except Tronstad screamed and bucked like his limb was severed.

'Please, come on. That's nothing. But you see, just a little cut is needed. Then you take the edges...'

Konstantin applied pressure to the skin.

'And you *yank* down.'

He drew his hand down at speed...

For effect. He hadn't taken hold of the sides. But it took Tronstad a couple of seconds of writhing and screaming to realise that.

Konstantin laughed. 'So easy. You'd be amazed how few cuts are needed to entirely peel a person's skin. Sometimes I try to do it with the least I can, just for the challenge.'

Konstantin's manner turned deadly serious.

'It's easy, but I'm very sorry to say for you, that it isn't painless. No, really, it's probably the worst pain you could imagine.'

Tronstad's phone, on the floor by Konstantin's feet, vibrated with an incoming call. Konstantin didn't show his frustration at the interruption, but moved over to look at the screen. He laughed. Tronstad's eyes flickered.

'It's her,' Konstantin said.

'Isabell,' Tronstad mumbled, as though in plea. To her, or to Konstantin?

The call ended.

'I'm glad she called,' Konstantin said. 'We have a lot to talk about, you and me. And a lot of it is to do with her.'

Tronstad shook his head. 'Why?' he said, panting, as though he'd already suffered. He really hadn't.

'My friend, that's exactly why I'm here. To find out.'

'He sent you.'

'He?'

'Sigurd.'

Konstantin smiled. This man was a lawyer apparently. He was supposed to be clever. He didn't seem it to Konstantin.

'No. Mr Berg didn't send me here. But I am interested to know why you and his wife are so friendly with each other.'

The phone vibrated again. Another glance to the screen. Her again.

'She's c-coming here,' Tronstad said. 'We have a m-meeting. If I don't answer she'll know there's a p-problem. She'll call the police.'

Konstantin turned and moved back over and crouched down in front of Tronstad. He lifted the bound man's head a little so they were eye to eye.

'Seems unlikely to me. Woman has meeting with lawyer.

Woman calls lawyer twice. He doesn't answer, so she calls the police? Please try harder.'

'P-please.'

A loud knock on the front door echoed. Tronstad squeezed his eyes shut.

'That's her, isn't it?' Konstantin said.

No answer. Konstantin's brain whirred.

Another knock. Louder this time. The phone vibrated once more.

'She's very keen.'

Then.

'Isabell!' Tronstad shouted out, at the top of his voice. He sucked in a deep lungful of air. Opened his mouth, ready to bellow again...

Konstantin's fist to the belly put paid to that idea. Another fist to the face. Konstantin's knuckles crunched onto the bridge of Tronstad's nose and his head flopped. A fresh wave of blood trickled down his forehead. Konstantin sighed.

The phone stopped vibrating. Then immediately restarted with yet another call. Had she heard the call for help?

Only one way to find out.

'Let's go and welcome our new arrival,' Konstantin said, straightening up. 'We wouldn't want her to miss out on all the fun.'

He pulled the taser from his coat pocket, and moved for the front door.

33

Silence, and an acute sense of apprehension, filled the inside of the car as they drove out of Blodstein. Even Ryker was a little surprised Pettersen had agreed to his suggestion of going with him to Trondheim.

He remained in the back seat of the car, his cuffed hands behind his back.

'So you're really not taking me to the police station,' Ryker said, turning to look out of the back window where Blodstein faded into the distance.

He faced front again and squirmed, trying to get his hands into a better position.

'Do you want the key?' Pettersen asked, catching his eye in the rear-view mirror.

He said nothing, strained a bit more.

Click.

He pulled his hands to the front. One wrist free, from the other the cuffs dangled.

'Go on then,' he said.

She shook her head and pulled the key out and handed it back to him. 'Nice trick.'

'I've had a lot of practice.'

She didn't say anything to that.

'Pull over, I'll come up front.'

She did so, and they were soon on their way again.

In front of them the twisting road was clear of traffic. The sun, low in the sky to the west, created long shadows that reached out from the trees separating them from the water. Like giant tentacles, uncoiled and waiting, ready to worm around them, hold them back. Crush them.

Ryker shook the thought away.

'You trusted me,' Ryker said, staring ahead. They passed by the turning for the logging site.

'I'm not sure I do, really. But I want to find out what's really happening. Find Henrik, who took him and why.'

Ryker nodded. A few moments later they passed the turning for the house where he'd found Henrik.

'Do you know who owns the house up there?' Ryker asked. He was tempted to tell her to go there now. See who was home. Spend some time asking them questions. His way.

'I didn't even know there was a house there.'

Her face remained passive, though Ryker wasn't sure he believed her. But then, why would she lie about it?

'Tell me what you know,' Pettersen asked.

Ryker thought for a moment. Best to just start from the top. 'The day I arrived, I nearly knocked a kid off his moped, on this road, but quite a few miles south of here.'

'That kid was Henrik?'

'Yeah. Turns out he was trying to escape, back to Trondheim, but I didn't know that then. But I knew I didn't like the situation. Your boss, Wold, turned up, then a Nissan pickup truck. Wold took Henrik, claimed he was taking him home. The pickup wasn't there randomly either. The guys in there knew what was happening. They took the moped.'

Ryker paused for a few beats as he thought back, hoping doing so would trigger something useful he'd not considered before. He expected a follow-up question from Pettersen but nothing came.

'I arrived in Blodstein. And I have to say, I felt something was up from the start.'

She glared at him now, as though offended. 'What do you mean?'

'The attitude of your boss, for a start. When you saw me in the café?'

Still a little offended. 'Wold thinks he's more powerful than he really is,' Pettersen said. 'Big cop in a small town. But I really think he means to do good. He tries to protect Blodstein.'

Maybe she was right about that, but it didn't make Ryker trust him any more, and he still thought that Pettersen didn't fully trust him either.

'I asked Wold about Henrik in the café,' Ryker said. 'You saw the reaction yourself. You even made the point of asking me about Henrik outside, when Wold had gone.'

Pettersen sighed.

'Why did you?'

'I'd heard rumours.'

'What rumours?'

She didn't say anything right away. 'You were giving me your side of the story.'

He thought about pushing her. Not yet. 'I decided to start asking questions, to try and find the guys who took the moped. First, at the logging site. Next, I came across that house. Then in the evening I went to the bar where a group of locals were drinking. Erling is one of them. A woman named Sonja too. You know her?'

She sighed. 'I know all of them, one way or another.'

'Two Russians turned up. Or, kind of Russian.'

He glanced at her. She looked confused.

'Their language, their accents, tells me they come from an area of Russia near the Black Sea, near to Ukraine, where the Cossack people originally came from. Nowadays it's part of Russia, but it's not always a happy relationship. Some of the areas are more or less self-governed and they speak regional dialects, generally concoctions of Ukrainian and standard Russian. Anyway, the point of where they come from may or may not be relevant. Regardless, I was set on by Erling and his crew, but I think it was at the say-so of those Russians. I'd already asked too many questions. You saw what happened there at the bar. You stopped it getting out of hand.'

Silence from her now.

'I'd asked too many questions. But the reaction I got told me they'd been the right questions. So the next day–'

'Why didn't you just leave then? When you had a chance.'

'You don't know me very well, otherwise you wouldn't ask that. I went back to that house. Henrik was there, along with Erling and two others. I fought with them. Henrik ran off. I chased him. Found him. We were hunted through the forest, men and dogs after us. Somehow we escaped and ended back up in Blodstein.'

'When I saw you?'

'Getting supplies, and also information to help me help Henrik.'

'Including where Trine Hansen lived?'

Ryker nodded. 'I took Henrik back to some friends in Trondheim. He insisted. Though I'm worried I made a mistake.'

'A mistake?'

Ryker decided not to delve into that. 'Next, I went to find his foster parents. The Johansens. Except they're missing.'

The worried look on Pettersen's face suggested she hadn't known that.

'So next I went back to Blodstein. To Trine Hansen's home.'

'Where I found you. You really came all the way back from Trondheim, where you left Henrik, just to speak to her?'

'Not exactly. Before the Johansens went missing, men were seen visiting them. Men from up north, I was told. Driving a Range Rover. I don't believe that's coincidence. Whoever that car belongs to, it might be the person who's behind everything.'

Ryker stared over at Pettersen, trying to gauge a reaction on her face.

'I think I know who you're talking about,' she said.

'Who?'

'His name's Sigurd Berg. He's a local businessman. About the wealthiest man in our town, but that might not be much to anyone else. Have you met him?'

'Not yet. What would he want with Henrik?'

'That's what we need to find out, isn't it?'

Ryker smiled and chuckled. Pettersen's face screwed with offence.

'What?'

'Just the way you said *we*. The dynamic duo.'

She rolled her eyes and looked back to the road.

'Who are the Russians?' Ryker asked, taking on a more serious tone once more.

'I honestly don't know. But I do know they don't belong in Blodstein.'

'Just like me.'

'No.' She caught his eye. 'Not like you.'

'They seemed pretty cosy with Erling and his gang.'

'I can't figure out why,' Pettersen said. 'Those other people all work for Berg, one way or another. He owns one of the factories by the water. They make turbines. But Berg also owns the logging company, plus a lot of land and property here too. And I know he hates the Russians.'

'You know that?'

She rolled her eyes. He wasn't sure why. 'Rumours,' she said.

'You hear a lot of rumours.'

'I talk to a lot of people. A lot of what I hear is nonsense, but not everything. For example, I know the Russians have a history in Blodstein. Ever since Berg's father set up his business here, there's been talk of Russian involvement. Talk of their money running our town for years. Not just our town, in fact, but many along the coast.'

She sighed. It was a strangely solemn gesture.

'Do you know the history of our area. Of our country?'

'I know Blodstein literally means blood stone. Or blood rock. That the town was named hundreds of years ago when there was a metal mine here, one of the biggest in Scandinavia, the ore from it used by the Vikings to make axes and swords that they took on their bloody conquests around the world.'

She gave him a strange look.

'I meant more recent history, but I'm impressed you knew that.'

Ryker smiled but said nothing.

'Most of what I know comes from my own family,' she said. 'From my father and grandfather, though it was my grandfather who actually lived it. It started when the Germans took control of Norway during World War II, in 1940. They stormed our cities, flooded into our seaports. It wasn't even much of a fight. Don't ask me why – negligence, arrogance, corruption? – but we weren't prepared. In only a few days the Nazis controlled our whole coastline and were marching into Oslo almost without challenge. The story goes that at the front of the invading force in Oslo was nothing more than a brass band, cheerfully playing their propaganda music.'

She shook her head, as though ashamed about an event that she'd had no control over.

'Our coast has always been a huge part of our lives, even back then when the Vikings sailed off to everywhere. When the Germans took over, it was like our heritage, our everything, was taken away. They controlled our waters to help their military, they wanted to dominate the North Sea and the North Atlantic beyond, but they cared little for us. People had no jobs, no food, they were starving and penniless.'

Ryker sighed as the words sloshed in his mind. Of course, no country in Europe had survived untouched by the savagery of World War II, but he was less than familiar with the particular story of this country.

'That was 1940. We were still occupied as the war came to a finish. The Soviet army first advanced into Finnmark, in our far north, in 1944, but the Germans, even knowing they were defeated, were cruel to us. They burned everything. Homes, factories, forests. There was nothing left but scorched earth and ruined lives. Our country became one of the biggest battlegrounds in the last days of the war, but also a place where the Nazis retreated to. Before Hitler killed himself there was even talk of moving the Third Reich headquarters to Norway because they'd built such a large force here to repel the Russians. At the end of the war we had nearly half a million Nazi soldiers in our country.'

Ryker hadn't known that, but could understand now where the story was going.

'When the war finally ended, when all those foreign soldiers were finally expelled, and our own people returned to the ruins, they had nothing. They needed help to rebuild.'

'That help came from the Russians.'

'Not just the Russians, but yes. A lot of money did come from there, and a lot of it was, I'm sure, with the best of intentions. But not all of it.'

'No, not all of it.'

'Rich men like to get richer, after all.'

'They certainly do. And not all rich men like to play by the rules.'

'Ever since then there's been talk of which businesses, which families in our town, are controlled in the dark by the Russians. And by dirty money.'

'Sigurd Berg is one of them?' Ryker asked.

'Actually, I was referring to his father. He died many years ago, but it seems perhaps that Sigurd isn't too different.'

'That explains why the Russians are here. Perhaps why Erling and those others were with the Russians in the bar even. But it still doesn't explain why Berg would kidnap a fourteen-year-old boy.'

Pettersen sighed. 'No. It doesn't.'

The car went strangely quiet once more. Ryker was deep in thought. He assumed Pettersen was too. Were Henrik and the Russians simply two separate issues, both related to Berg in one way or another, or was everything connected?

Ryker glanced over to Pettersen a couple of times as they carried on their way. Even after the retelling of her country's and her family's dark times, she certainly appeared far more relaxed now than when they'd first set off, with her shoulders down, her chin up. His eyes rested on her hands on the steering wheel.

'What?' she asked.

She took her hand from the wheel. The one with the ring on it. She caught his eye. Looked a little angry.

'Go on then,' she said.

'Go on what?'

'Ask.'

Ryker raised an eyebrow.

'You were looking at the ring.'

'Was I?'

'Yes, I'm married. Does that matter to you?'

'Why would it? I just–'

'What?'

'It doesn't matter.'

He looked out of his window.

'Yes, it does matter,' she said, antsy, though he didn't know why. 'What were you going to say?'

He caught her eye again. Definitely pissed off. 'What does he do?'

'Whatever he damn well pleases.' A sarcastic-sounding laugh accompanied her response.

Clearly her marriage was a sore subject. Ryker said nothing more about it.

'What about you?' Pettersen asked.

'No, I'm not married,' Ryker said.

'Well, that's obvious.'

'Is it?'

'Have you ever been?'

'No.'

'Have you ever loved someone?'

'That's pretty deep.'

'Not really. It's a simple question. A yes or no answer.'

'Yes,' he said.

'You're still with her. Him?'

'Her. And no.'

'It's not easy, is it?'

'Definitely not.'

'You still love her?'

He paused before answering. Felt bad for doing so. It had been years since he'd been with Angela. Years since she'd been killed because of him. Her body buried in the red dirt next to the home they thought was a hideaway from their former lives. He still thought of her, though tried his best not to. A horrible thing to do to her really, but the pain of losing her remained so raw, even after everything else he'd been through since. No one would ever fill that gap in his life. Sam Moreno had come close, even if their relationship had remained platonic. Simona in Prague? Too late now.

'You still love her?' Pettersen asked again.

'Yes,' he said.

'But you're not together.'

'She's dead.'

Pettersen looked away quickly, as though ashamed or embarrassed by the answer.

'I'm sorry,' she said.

'Not as sorry as I am.'

'I did have a point,' she said, then laughed. A nervous laugh. Ryker found himself smiling in return. 'I definitely did. But I'm not sure what it was now.'

'Love conquers all?' Ryker suggested.

'No. Not that. In fact, perhaps for me, love alone wasn't enough.'

Ryker closed his eyes and tried to push the memories, and the emotions those memories dredged up, back to the darkest corner of his mind.

'The stupidest thing is,' Pettersen continued, 'I knew how hard being in the police was. I saw my parents struggle with it, right up until my father died. Even after everything they went through, all that he put her through, I still wanted to be just like him. And now, I really am. In more ways than I like to think.'

'Then he must have been a good policeman.'

She squirmed a little at that comment. His words had been intended as a light-hearted compliment, but clearly not taken as one. Obviously there more to the story of father and daughter.

'And you?' she asked.

'My father?'

'No. Your job. What is your job exactly?'

Ryker thought about the question. 'I help people.'

She laughed. 'You sound really lame sometimes. Ooh, me big man. Me help people, really good. Rah. Show me the baddies.'

Ryker tried not to laugh but he couldn't help it. When he caught her gaze he noticed a sparkle that hadn't been there before. She whipped her eyes back to the road.

'So let me guess,' she said. 'You weren't in the police. You're too... messy.'

'My clothes?'

'Your head. I don't think army either.'

'Because soldiers don't get messed in the head?'

'Interesting that you didn't question me saying you're messed in the head.'

Ryker raised an eyebrow as he stared at her. She glanced back and smiled. 'Okay. So not police, not army, but probably something similar. Government work. Am I right?'

'You're not far off. But that's in the past. Now I really am on my own.'

He went quiet, deep in thought. But only for a moment. He could see out of the corner of his eye that she kept looking over at him. He turned and saw the smirk on her face.

'What?' he said.

'Rah.' She lifted her arm and kissed her bicep. 'Big man help little lady. Perhaps she kiss me one day.'

'You're an idiot,' he said, once again unable to hold a straight face.

34

The inevitable. Berg was in the car park, heading toward his car, when he spotted them, on the other side of the security fence, Andrey sitting on the bonnet of their rented car, arms folded. Sychev was by the back passenger door, facing away, phone up to his ear.

Berg had intended to go to his car, to head into town. He wanted to find Erling and find out what the hell they were doing to locate and retrieve Henrik. But with the Russians right there, he couldn't do that now. Perhaps he should turn around and rush back inside before they spotted him.

Too late. Andrey nudged Sychev in the side and the taller man pulled the phone away and turned and waved with a stupid smirk on his stupid face.

Berg looked around him. A couple of guys were in the yard, one on a forklift, another checking a clipboard as he stood by one of the boats. Neither paid Berg any attention.

He sucked up some courage and moved forward quickly, up to the security fence.

'Why are you here?' Berg said to Sychev.

Sychev frowned. 'I told you we'd be back today.'

'But why are standing out here, like this?'

Sychev looked down to his feet, bemused. 'Standing like what?'

'You know what I mean.'

'Would you like us to go inside with you instead?'

No. He didn't want them anywhere near his factory.

Sychev shrugged. 'No? Then get in the car. We can talk in there.'

'Your car? What, so you can dump me miles from anywhere again?'

Andrey snorted in amusement.

'No, so we can take you into town. Away from all your colleagues here who are surely beginning to wonder now what is happening with you, and us. That's what you're worried about, isn't it?'

Berg grit his teeth. Sychev's proposition wasn't the worst. Plus Marius would be back soon too. Out of all of the men in the factory, Berg was most worried about Marius, following their last run-in. He got the distinct feeling that the guy was planning something.

'If you're that concerned about our intentions, you can follow us in your own car,' Sychev suggested.

That option certainly appealed more.

'Okay,' Berg said. 'Where to?'

'Are you hungry?'

'Not really.'

'Do you want us to buy you lunch?'

'Not really.'

Sychev smiled. 'We'll meet you at the café.'

'That's hardly inconspicuous.'

Sychev shrugged. 'No, but it is close to what we need to show you.'

He and Andrey turned and got back into their car. Berg

waited for only a second before he retreated to do the same.

———

Five other people were eating. Whatever time of day, the place was never empty, but it was also never full. Five people, at least, wasn't as bad as it could be for Berg. He recognised all but one of the faces, though no one paid him much attention.

Marie took their order, engaging in minimal chit-chat. Unusual for her. Normally it was a trick to get her to go away. For Berg at least. He'd known Marie since before she could walk, had known her father for more than twenty years, and had employed him for a lot of that time until he'd divorced Marie's mother and moved out of the area with his younger wife.

Perhaps not a bad move really.

Marie brought over the food. Berg didn't really want to eat, but Sychev had insisted they all order, and was also paying, so what would have been the point of Berg declining and then sitting there empty-handed, watching the other two stuff their nasty faces?

Still, he didn't like the situation at all. The air of deceit remained high, the tension rising further with every beat of his heart.

'Fish,' Sychev said.

'Excuse me?' Berg responded, looking up from his food.

'You people eat a lot of fish.'

'*You people?*'

Berg didn't like the way the guy had said that.

'Yeah. *You people*. People like you. Around here. This town.'

'We're by the sea. The sea has fish in it.'

Sychev slapped his fork onto his plate, his face showing his irritation. 'No shit,' he said. 'I meant no disrespect.'

Berg nodded to Sychev's food. Both he and Andrey had burger and fries.

'You didn't want to try the local cuisine?'

'Tried it,' Sychev said. 'Not for me.'

'You prefer American.'

'More than Norwegian, yes. I like American food, but I hate the people. Here, it's the opposite.'

Berg had never been to America, but he liked to imagine the big cities – New York, Chicago. What kind of man could he have made himself out there, with so much opportunity in front of him?

'That's what I don't understand about men like you,' Sychev said.

Berg's face screwed. 'So now it's *men* like me?'

'You're very sensitive today,' Sychev said, glancing around the café, looking smug, as though content at riling Berg, and hoping other people were taking notice. They weren't.

'What do you expect?' Berg said.

Sychev shook his head. 'My point was, men like you. Intelligent. Hard-working. Materialistic.'

Berg bit his tongue. What was Sychev playing at?

'You're telling me you're not those things?' Sychev asked.

'Materialistic?'

'Look at you. Nice car, clothes, house. Pretty wife. You like expensive things. But you stayed here, in Blodstein.'

'You want to know why I stay here?'

'I do.'

'Because it's my home. My family's home. Has been for generations. This is where I belong.'

'No, not that,' Sychev said as he wiped a blob of ketchup from his chin. 'You stay here because you feel like a king here. And if you went somewhere else you wouldn't be. You would be a little man in a big place. You're scared.'

Berg chewed through a mouthful of fish to stop himself from biting back.

Sychev shrugged. 'I'm only saying, it's a shame. Almost a waste. But you can still become bigger. You know that, don't you? You know that's why we're here?'

'Yeah, that's right. You're here only for my benefit. The charity of Jesper the Great.'

Sychev laughed. 'No need to be like that. Of course it's not all about you. We all get richer our way. What's wrong with that?'

'What's wrong is that the more you get your claws into my business—'

'The more money we all make together? You only don't like the idea because you're too proud. Who cares who controls what. By the time you retire, all you'll need is money, not control.'

'And when we die, all we need is a wooden box and a big hole to put it in. We all end up the same, in the end.'

Sychev nodded as though he saw the statement as deeply profound.

'All the more reason to *go with the flow* as they say.'

Berg sniffed, trying to quell his agitation.

'You know you're not the only businessman in this country we deal with.'

'Then why not just take your offers somewhere else.'

'Because we haven't got what we came for yet. And Jesper always gets what he wants.'

Berg said nothing.

'Tell me about the boy,' Sychev said.

'No,' Berg responded.

'You seem to be under a mistaken impression that you have a choice here.'

With that Andrey suddenly reached over. He grabbed Berg's wrist, pulled it under the table and twisted it around. His grip strength, his arm strength, was something else. Berg couldn't fight back at all. Andrey pushed Berg's wrist to bursting point and he grimaced, his whole body tensed, trying to stop his bones from snapping while showing no reaction so as to not draw attention from the other people around him.

'Tell me about the boy,' Sychev said.

'He's nothing,' Berg said, through gritted teeth. 'Just a stupid plot.'

'What plot?'

Sychev nodded to Andrey who released Berg's arm. Berg nursed his throbbing wrist and tried to regain his composure as he looked around the café.

'The kid is Rosen's son,' he said, quietly.

Silence for a couple of seconds.

'Erik Rosen?' Sychev said.

Berg nodded.

'Illegitimate son,' Berg said. 'Rosen had an affair, years ago. Henrik is his, but Rosen doesn't even know it.'

'So why did you kidnap him?'

'Why do you think?'

Sychev crossed his knife and fork over his plate, even though he'd barely half-finished his food. He sat back in his chair and wiped his mouth with his napkin.

'You're a sly dog, aren't you?' he said, smirking. 'You're going to blackmail Rosen? How? Threaten to kill the boy?'

Berg said nothing now.

'How much?'

'I hadn't got that far. We've had... complications. I think you know about that.'

Sychev laughed now. 'Sigurd, Sigurd, why didn't you tell us this before?'

Berg said nothing once more.

'If I'd known about this before we negotiated with Rosen, we could have helped each other even more.'

A lie. There'd been no 'negotiation' with Rosen. The way Berg understood it, the Russians had wrenched most of the business out from under him. Dirty money, dressed up as a big investment. Yes, Rosen Tech as an enterprise – despite the recent 'issue' at the factory – was now well set up for the future, bigger than ever, but Rosen's own share of the business was tiny. The exact same ploy Sychev had attempted to push onto Berg.

'You know, if you're telling me the truth–'

'Of course I'm telling you the truth!' Berg interrupted.

Sychev paused a moment. '*If* you're telling me the truth, I have to say I may have made a big mistake. And I can only apologise for that.'

'What mistake?' Berg said, a strange feeling brewing inside his gut.

'If you'd told me sooner...'

Sychev looked to Andrey and the two of them had a quick exchange in their native tongue. Berg's nerves continued to grow.

'The problem is, Sigurd, that these issues arise when people aren't honest with each other. Unfortunately you weren't honest with me. At least not soon enough.'

'What have you done? Nyland? Is that it? You killed Nyland because of this? You're trying to frame me?'

Sychev looked around the room then leaned in, across the table. 'You might want to keep your voice down, talking like that.'

He had a point. But Berg's head was in bits.

'But no. I'm not talking about Nyland. Come on, we've something to show you.'

Sychev pulled some notes from his pocket and placed them neatly on the table. The three of them headed out. Berg kept his eyes to the floor, he didn't want to know whether or not Marie or the other customers looked his way.

Outside, he took a couple of steps toward the car, but then noticed Sychev and Andrey pulling away.

'Not the car,' Sychev said, before turning and looking across the street.

That building. Berg had been keenly aware of the building the whole time they'd sat inside. The same building Nyland had seen his wife go into before, with that Stefan Tronstad.

The horrible feeling in his gut ratcheted.

'Come on,' Sychev said.

The three of them crossed the road. Sychev pulled ahead and knocked on the door of the building. He turned back to Berg, an apologetic look on his face. Genuine? Berg didn't know, nor was he sure it even mattered.

'There's no one here,' Berg said after a long and silent wait.

'There is,' Sychev said, tapping into his phone. 'Just be patient.'

Nothing more was said. One, two, three minutes passed. Berg looked around him as they waited. What was he hoping for? An intervention? Wold or Pettersen or someone else to come to his rescue?

The door opened. Berg turned to see... a man. A normal-looking man. Normal dress. Although he looked like he'd just come out of the shower with wet hair and flushed cheeks. He pulled back from the door. Sychev moved in first. Berg followed, Andrey behind.

The door closed, Berg went to spin around but Andrey grabbed him. Vice-like grip. Andrey pushed Berg's right hand up in between his shoulder blades.

'Don't do anything stupid,' Andrey said, his voice a callous whisper in Berg's ear.

The other man scuttled in front. 'Through here,' he said.

Sychev turned and smiled at Berg, then moved forward. Andrey applied more pressure and Berg shuffled along.

He couldn't be sure what hit him first. The sounds, or the smell. The smell... wet, metallic. The sounds... nothing more than murmurs. Groans even. Not quite human. Almost mechanical in nature, but... not.

As grim thoughts rattled in his mind, it was the sight that caused his legs to give way.

Andrey pulled him upright. Berg didn't know where to look.

Two bodies. Both bound. One – a man – hung upside down. The other – a woman – was slumped in a chair. The man... gaping flesh on his thighs oozed dark blood which drenched his torso. His torso, which had slashes and gashes all over. His head glistened with blood which pooled beneath him. Surely he wasn't alive?

The woman...

'Isabell,' Berg said, the name trembling in his mouth.

Her head remained bowed. She didn't move. But she did try to speak. 'Si-Sig... Ssss...'

'What have you done?' Berg said to Sychev.

The Russian turned to him, a look of stern concentration.

'No, Sigurd, not me. This was because of *you*.'

Thud.

A blow to the back of his head. Fist? Bat? Berg had no idea. The next moment, he toppled face down onto the blood-soaked floor.

35

They'd driven in silence for some time. Ryker felt increasingly awkward, though he didn't know why. Perhaps because of the overarching sombre mood of them both. They'd smiled, they'd laughed a little earlier, but this mission – if it could be called that – was fraught and deadly and serious. Maybe Pettersen felt embarrassed by her earlier joviality.

He looked across at her. She must have sensed him doing so and glanced back, her stern look melting away. A surprise to him.

'Okay, here's one,' she said, before smiling. 'Two Swedish police officers are patrolling the Norwegian border. Have you heard this one?'

Embarrassed by her earlier joviality? Okay, perhaps not. A good thing, really.

'I don't think so,' Ryker said.

'It's Friday afternoon and they're in a good mood. They're talking about how much they look forward to going home to their wives for a nice meal and some fun in bed. But suddenly they see a man who has hanged himself from a tree.'

She paused, as if for dramatic effect. Or perhaps she now

doubted the choice of joke, given the subject. No, soon she was back on track.

'The first officer goes, *Damn it! Now we have to write a report and wait for the transport... we won't be home until late!*'

Ryker already found himself smiling – largely because of the effort she put into the officer's voice.

'The second one says, *I have an idea... The Norwegian border is right over there. If we hang him from a tree on the Norwegian side it will be their problem and we'll still be home on time.* So the two officers take down the hanged man from the tree, carry him across the border, and find a tree there to hang him from. They go home to their wives. After a while two Norwegian police officers walk by and notice the hanged man. One of them says to the other. *What the hell, he's back again!*'

She laughed. Ryker tried his best not to.

'Do you know any good ones?' she asked after a few moments.

'Not really.'

'Any bad ones?'

Ryker thought. 'Okay. A Norwegian goes to the psychiatrist. *What brings you in today?* the psychiatrist asks. The patient says, *I've just been so depressed. I wish I was never Björn.*'

Silence. Pettersen looked at Ryker as though he was an idiot. Then she burst out laughing.

'Your face,' she said. 'Not bad actually. But... it doesn't really work in Norwegian. Born is født. Björn, født. Not exactly the same.'

Her smile slowly dropped away and she sighed. Ryker felt he knew what she was doing. Trying to lighten the mood, with her continual reversion to joking, but he sensed that even for her the battle was becoming tougher.

'Someone was murdered,' she said, no hint of light-heartedness now. 'Last night, we think.'

Her eyes were dead ahead, focused only on the road. She sighed again.

'In Blodstein?' Ryker asked.

She nodded. 'The body was dumped just north of the town. In the trees by the side of the road.'

'Who was it?'

'A man named Jonas Nyland. Do you know him?'

'Never heard of him.'

She glanced over, as if to check his face for any hint of a lie.

'I shouldn't even be telling you this,' she said.

'Then why are you?'

A laugh, but a nervous one. 'It's a long journey,' she said.

'You think his murder is relevant?' Ryker asked.

She didn't answer.

'You must do, otherwise there wouldn't be any point in bringing it up.'

Yet another sigh. 'He was a private investigator. Used to be a policeman. In Trondheim. Sigurd Berg hired him.'

'So Berg's unlikely to be the murderer then,' Ryker said. 'Why murder your own PI?'

'I guess so.'

'What was Nyland investigating?'

'That's a good question. But even more important is why is he dead?'

Ryker said nothing. Pettersen, too, was quiet until, 'Did you do it?'

Ryker snorted and glared at her. 'Are you seriously asking me that?'

'I'm not judging. Perhaps he was a terrible man. Threatened you. It was self-defence. But it's not unreasonable for me to ask, given everything you're involved with here.'

'None of this mess is my making.'

'That didn't answer my question.'

'No. I didn't kill him. I've never heard of him, never met him.'

'But you have killed men before.'

Was that a question? Ryker didn't bother to answer. She didn't say anything more.

The now more tense silence stretched out until they were approaching Trondheim. Night-time was almost upon them, the dusk only adding to the downbeat mood somehow. By the time they made it to the outskirts of the city, the street lights were on, and headlight beams and tail lights jostled and rolled around them.

'Take the left turn here,' Ryker said.

Pettersen flicked her indicator on, but then pulled the car into the right-hand lane at the junction.

'We've somewhere else to go first,' she said.

'We do?'

'You'll see.'

They carried on into unfamiliar territory. At least for Ryker. Did Pettersen know this area? Wherever she was taking them, it wasn't to the Johansens either. A few minutes later they turned into a street of ramshackle, single-storey homes. All timber built, each one unique, but all of them small and looking in various states of disrepair. Some empty, even.

'What are we doing here?' Ryker asked.

'We're looking for twenty-eight.'

Ryker stared out of the window. The street lights lit up the road well enough, but their beams barely reached to the set-back houses making it near impossible in the dark to see the numbers.

Pettersen slowed right down.

'There,' she said, looking out her side.

She pulled over and shut down the engine.

'So go on then? Why are we here?' Ryker said.

'To speak to Henrik's mother. His real mother.'

Pettersen opened her door. Ryker followed her out.

'You know her?' Ryker asked, mixed thoughts rumbling in his head.

'No,' Pettersen said. 'I'm just a good investigator.'

She moved toward the narrow path that led to the house. A thin glow around the edges of one of the two front windows suggested the house was occupied, although the street around them was deathly quiet.

Ryker glanced over his shoulder a couple of times as they headed for the door, an eerie feeling creeping over him.

Pettersen reached the door. Stopped. She turned around.

'I'm still in my uniform,' she said to Ryker.

'Is that a problem?'

'I have no authority here. In fact, I'll be in a lot of trouble if the local police see me, or if my boss finds out.'

'If.'

She sighed.

'We've come a long way for you to suddenly change your mind,' Ryker added.

Was that it? Or was she just nervous?

Ryker went to brush past her, but Pettersen stood her ground to stop him. 'No,' she said, before breaking out into a smile. 'I mean... look at you. We're not trying to scare her.'

'Very funny.'

Pettersen turned and knocked on the door. Footsteps beyond. No locks released, but the wooden door was yanked from its closed position, the fixture catching on its frame and popping open with a snap.

A man held on to the door. He was tall, looked like a carbon copy of the guy Ryker had left Henrik with – the skinhead. Except this skinhead was twenty years older. He wore a hoodie and shorts. His face was mottled, the skin on his forehead heavily creased. He had deep-set eyes, his pupils the size of pennies – drugs, was Ryker's immediate thought, though the darkness didn't help the matter.

The man glanced from Pettersen to Ryker. Then Pettersen started the ball rolling and soon the two of them were in an unfriendly back and forth in Norwegian.

Eventually all eyes turned to Ryker. The man glared – practically a snarl. Pettersen looked at Ryker pleadingly.

'Have you got any money?' she asked.

'How much?'

'Two hundred?'

Ryker fished in his pocket. Handed the money to Pettersen who slapped it into the man's hand. He shouted back inside then moved out. He paused in front of Ryker. They were the same height, and the man leaned in, his eyes wide. High as a kite. But angry about it. A dangerous combination.

'Fucking English,' he said, before he turned and walked away, muttering under his breath.

'He's gone to get some more beer,' Pettersen said. 'We've got about ten minutes. If we're not gone, he's calling his friends.'

'Great. Beer. Friends. We're going to have a party.'

Pettersen shook her head, smiling. 'I'm not sure that's what he meant.'

'Shame. But I'd love to know how you persuaded him to leave.'

'I'm very good at it. If you're lucky, I might tell you.' She winked before she turned and walked into the house.

Ryker looked over his shoulder once more, then followed her in.

The inside of the house was as dilapidated as the outside. Messy too, with clothes and rubbish strewn. Even despite the unnecessary anger directed at him from the man, Ryker felt sorry for the occupants living like this, however much the situation was down to them.

They moved through to a back room. A lounge. A colourful game show of some sort played on a widescreen TV, on the floor in the corner. The TV – obviously new and not exactly cheap-looking – looked seriously out of place.

Upon the single sofa in the room lay a woman, stretched out, cigarette dangling from her hand, which hovered above an ashtray on the floor.

She looked up. Then jumped up. Then rattled off a worried response when she realised two strangers were staring at her. Pettersen talked calmly. Ryker recognised the word *politiet* – police – more than once.

The woman sat upright on the sofa, her face sullen, the now stubbed-out cigarette slowly smoking in the ashtray. Both Ryker and Pettersen remained standing. Largely because they had nowhere else to sit.

Ryker guessed the woman was late thirties, early forties, and although her features retained a natural youthfulness, she had a gaunt appearance. He could see Henrik in her. Their faces, their noses, had a similar shape, their eyes were near identical except hers were bloodshot.

'Can we speak in English?' Pettersen said to the woman. 'My friend is helping.'

It wasn't often Ryker was referred to as a friend. The woman glared at him.

'I can try,' the woman said.

Pettersen turned to Ryker. 'This is Ingrid.'

'I'm James,' he said to her.

Her face showed no reaction at all.

'How is he?' she asked Ryker.

'Henrik?'

'She says you met him.'

Ryker glanced to Pettersen. Had she explained about the kidnapping already? Ingrid certainly didn't seem too concerned.

'Henrik's not doing too well,' Ryker said. 'Some men are trying to hurt him.'

Still no reaction on Ingrid's face.

'They kidnapped him,' Ryker said. 'Do you know what that means?'

'But *she* says you got him back.'

'I did. But the men who did it are still out there. We want to find out who they are. Can you help us?'

She looked down and shook her head. 'I haven't seen Henrik since he was two. I think he wouldn't even know me.'

'I wouldn't be so sure,' Ryker said.

'What does it matter?'

'He's here, now,' Ryker said. 'In Trondheim. You could see him.'

'Why would I want to?' Then she laughed. More like a cackle. 'You think this is some sad story for me? A poor mother, her child taken from her. You're wrong. I wasn't always like this, but I never wanted *him*. I asked them to take him away. I wanted *my* life back.'

Some life, Ryker thought.

'Do you know why anyone would want to hurt Henrik?' Pettersen asked.

Ingrid turned her attention away from Ryker and the two women carried on a conversation in Norwegian at warp speed. Eventually Pettersen faced Ryker again. She looked worried.

'Some men came to see her,' Pettersen said. 'Two, or three months ago.'

'What can she tell us about them?'

'She's already told me what she can remember. One of them sounds a lot like Erling.'

'And Berg?'

'No, I don't think so.'

'Have you got a picture of either of them to show her?' Ryker asked. 'Or the Russians?'

Pettersen checked her watch. 'I could try and get something, for the locals perhaps, but we only have a few more minutes.'

'A few more minutes, if we really care what happens when her boyfriend gets back.'

'I do.'

Ryker sighed.

'What did the men want?' he asked Ingrid.

She looked a little angrier now. 'They were asking about Henrik. Where was he. Where was his father. Who was his father.'

'His father?' Ryker said. 'And who is his father?'

She rolled her eyes. 'Same as I told them. I don't know. And I don't care.'

Ryker and Pettersen exchanged a look.

'You're sure you don't know,' Ryker said.

'I. Don't. Know,' Ingrid said.

She held Ryker's eye. Until a thud came from the door and her gaze switched to a spot behind him. He turned. Skinhead was back. He wasn't alone. Three men in the hallway. A couple of bats. A knife. No beer.

'We didn't need any more beer,' Skinhead said with an evil grin, his strong accent making the words almost indecipherable. 'Time's up.'

Ryker stood his ground. Then moved up to him. Eyeball to eyeball. Neither man flinched. Ryker glanced to the other two.

'Come on,' he said, calmly to Pettersen.

She scuttled past him to the front door. Ryker thought about saying something else to the man inches from his face. He didn't. Instead, he turned and followed Pettersen out.

36

One of the reasons Konstantin excelled was because he carried out his 'work' without emotion. He felt no sorrow, anger, disgust, squeamishness, or even apprehensiveness in what he did to others. As long as he made sure to properly atone for his acts, he slept at night perfectly well. No visions, no horrors or gore. But that didn't mean he was a man without emotion. He was no psycho, his brain wired no differently to anyone else's. Some things gave him pleasure, some things didn't. Some things annoyed him, some things didn't.

Valeri Sychev annoyed him. Really annoyed him. The man had a smugness, a perceived superiority that made Konstantin's skin crawl. The same feeling he had inside him now, as he drove from Blodstein to Trondheim, was the very feeling that had set him on this path in life. The first person he'd ever killed, had been because he allowed his own anger, his hatred – his jealousy? – to take over.

After that day he swore, to himself, to Jesper, too, that he'd never do the same again. He'd never again kill with emotion. Nobody needed a man like that. He'd stuck with that promise for more than fifteen years. Each subsequent life he'd taken...

yes, it had taken a little bit of him with it, too, and every glance of his reflection in a mirror reminded him of all the bad things he'd done in his life.

But when it came to how to deal with a man like Sychev? Perhaps some rules were meant to be broken.

Konstantin pulled his hand from the steering wheel and dug his nails into the fresh wounds on his side. He grimaced and then shouted out in pain. He pushed deeper, trying to find the most agonising spot, but after a while the pain only faded. Disappointed, he sighed and sank down in his seat a little – defeated. He pulled his finger away and wiped the blood onto his trouser leg.

He didn't want to make this trip. Not at Sychev's behest. He'd wanted to stay in Blodstein, in that house, and finish what he'd started. That man, Stefan Tronstad, was dead. He'd told little. But only because he'd known little. The woman, Isabell... he'd only started to work on her. She would have talked too. She would have told her whole life story without once stopping for breath. Konstantin had already carried out all the hard work on the man, to ensure that was the case.

And Sychev had pulled him away from there.

Konstantin was outraged to have his work interrupted in that way. He already had the mark for her too. A mark for each of them, criss-crossed one over the other on his side. He had the mark but she was still alive. That wasn't how this was supposed to work.

He'd been robbed.

But there would be plenty more marks by the end of the day. Sychev's orders assured that outcome – his orders! That man, how dare he.

The lights of the city drew him in, making him realise he'd spent too long already in that poxy little town. As much as he felt aggrieved to have his work in Blodstein interrupted, he sorely missed real civilisation, with real, civilised people. It was only a shame he wouldn't get to stay here tonight. Before long, he'd be on the road again, back to that shithole of a place. For the last time, he was certain of that.

And at least on the return journey he'd have some company. Kind of, he thought with a wry smile.

He parked by the side of the road, the house off to his left. Although it was dark out, the hour was early, and Konstantin remained in the driver's seat as first a dog walker idled by, and then a group of four teenagers. One of them glanced at him through the windscreen but it was nothing more than a fleeting look, and the foursome carried on their way without any further interaction.

Konstantin sucked in a deep breath then stepped out into the cold. He looked around him. Not exactly deserted here, but quiet enough. He'd try to be quiet too. This wasn't a big, old, disused warehouse in the middle of nowhere, where screams and begging would go unheard except to his ears, and those of the tormented. Here he needed to act smartly, and quickly.

That was fine. No information needed here. Only the boy.

Konstantin moved toward the house. Up the stairs. To the front door. Sounds of a TV programme filtered from beyond. Or perhaps a games console. A light-hearted conversation too. Laughter.

He knocked on the door. The sounds continued, but moments later the door edged open.

A girl. Teenager, to be more precise. Eighteen, nineteen perhaps. Blonde hair, blue eyes. She was pretty. Probably got a lot of attention from the boys her age. Men too. Men were beasts. Her dress sense though... scruffy, unkempt. He had no idea what style the youngsters called that.

'Can I help you?' she asked, looking at him as though he was an idiot.

'I'm here for Henrik,' Konstantin responded.

Her face changed now. From confident and cocky, to worried. Which meant she knew who Henrik was.

Okay, so at least he knew he had the right place.

He whipped the knife from inside his jacket and thrust it up into her neck. The five-inch blade glided in with ease, up into her mouth and beyond. She gargled, her body quivered. He lifted her off her feet by the knife handle and pushed his way inside.

37

'What do you think?' Pettersen asked as they drove away from Ingrid's house.

'That I feel even more sorry for Henrik now than I did before.'

'I'm not sure you answered the question I asked.'

'No? Still, my point stands. When I was growing up, all I ever wanted was to know my real mother and father. I never did find them, but I always imagined they would be...'

He trailed off. He didn't know how to finish the thought. He'd never known his real parents, had bounced around from foster home to foster home, in some of them for mere weeks or months. Never settled, either physically or mentally, until he'd finally gone off on his own at sixteen – when he'd been taken under the wing of Mackie, who eventually turned him into the man he became for the JIA. But in those lost childhood years, he'd often thought about his real parents. Had imagined all sorts of things, ranging from them being the kindest, happiest people imaginable, to them being mega-rich, to them being nasty, vindictive down-and-outs. Whatever the truth, he'd never found it. But to find a woman like Ingrid, who'd seemingly happily abandoned her child and had never looked back since... it shook Ryker, and brought back a lot of angst that he thought he'd left behind as a boy.

'But Henrik did have a loving family,' Pettersen said. 'The Rosteds.'

'He did. And they died. Then he went to the Johansens. Perhaps they're dead now too. To say he's had it hard is an understatement. The kid is lost in life.'

Pettersen sighed. 'This isn't what I meant at all by my question.'

'No?'

'What I'm asking is why would Erling be questioning who Henrik's father is?'

'It's obvious, isn't it?' Ryker said. 'One way or another, all this is because of who Henrik is. Whose blood is running in his veins.'

'You think Berg's his father?'

Ryker thought about that for a moment. Possible, certainly, but why kidnap your own son?

'I don't think so,' Ryker said.

'Then who.'

Ryker didn't answer. They were already approaching their destination.

'It's right over there,' he said, pointing to the house along the street. 'But don't get too close.' He was still abundantly aware of the fact they were driving around in a police car. He didn't want Henrik, or any of his friends, spooked before he and Pettersen even got to the front door.

Pettersen said nothing but pulled the car over and shut the engine off.

'So now what?' she asked. 'We both go over there and drag him out?'

Ryker shrugged. 'We can ask him first.'

'Why do we even want him to come with us? Maybe he really is safest here.'

Ryker didn't respond to that. He got out of the car. Pettersen followed. He could tell in the way she moved, the way she flicked her gaze all over, that her nerves had ramped since they'd left Ingrid's house. He wasn't sure why. Both times she'd been heading into the unknown.

'This time I'll lead,' Ryker said as he moved off toward the house. Pettersen didn't say anything but he could hear her soft footsteps and her controlled breathing behind him. Ryker headed up the steps. A couple of yards from the front door he heard a noise from inside. Nowhere near as loud as the last time. Just a TV, he thought. But with a subdued silence over the top of it.

He paused at the door. Pettersen came up to his side.

'What?' she said.

Ryker lifted his hand to knock but his knuckles stopped a couple of inches from the wood.

'There,' he said, indicating the smudge on the door, just below the handle. Hard to see exactly at night, against the dark painted door, but definitely a smudge. Something wet.

Ryker uncurled his fist and reached out. He dragged the tip of his forefinger across the mark. Lifted the finger close to his face. The smell was enough.

He looked to Pettersen. He didn't even need to say what it was. The panicked look on her face told him that she knew too.

Ryker stepped back. Lifted up his knee, then hauled the heel of his shoe into the edge of the door.

'Ryker, no!' Pettersen said.

Ryker didn't listen. He did it again. On the third strike the lock and the door finally failed. The wood splintered, metal bounced and clanked to the floor as the door swung open. The noise of the TV grew louder. No other sounds accompanied it. But the smell... and the sight...

'No,' was all Pettersen could muster, a hand to her mouth in shock.

'Henrik!' Ryker shouted out. No response.

He stepped inside. Glanced at the young woman slumped in the hallway. Blood drenched the front of her clothes and the floor around her.

Ryker moved past her. Pettersen rushed up to the woman. To check for a pulse? No point. She was dead.

Another body lay in the doorway to the lounge. A young man. Not Skinhead. A black hole where he used to have an eye. Blood streaked out of the gap, his mouth wide open as if in a perpetual last scream of pain, or begging. His blood-covered shirt was punctured with several stab wounds too. Dead, no doubt.

'Henrik?' Ryker said again, but quieter this time.

By now Ryker's heart thudded in his chest like a bass drum. He couldn't yet see fully into the lounge. Was the attacker still in there? Hiding? Waiting?

Ryker crouched a little, a more defensive pose. Hands at the ready. He had no weapon. He'd have to make do.

'This only just happened,' Pettersen said behind him. 'She's still warm.'

Ryker pushed the grim thoughts away. Stepped into the room quickly, bouncing on his toes, left, right...

No attacker. Not now. Just two more bodies. One man, one woman. The woman, laid out on the sofa, had a deep slash in her throat, her panicked eyes reaching out toward where Ryker was standing. The man was slumped, on his knees. Not much blood on him, but his neck hung at a horrific angle. No way he was alive.

'Is that him?' Pettersen said, the emotion – horror – in her voice clear.

Ryker didn't think so. He cautiously moved over. Reached out for the man's head. He went to lift up the chin to see his face, but the movement somehow caused the body to lose its balance and it rolled over onto the floor, splayed out, the head lolling.

Pettersen moaned in shock.

'It's not him,' Ryker said, trying to hold back his own emotion as much as he could. The one trying to burst free, above revulsion, was rage.

'Then where is he?'

'They've got him,' Ryker said. 'We were too late.'

He turned and caught Pettersen's weary gaze.

He opened his mouth to say something to her. What? Offer comfort? Swear he'd punish whoever had done this?

He didn't say anything.

Above the grim silence, the sound of sirens drifted over.

38

Berg's head felt like a tonne weight. How long had he been here, suspended, swinging upside down? Thirty minutes? Two hours? More?

Isabell remained on the chair, next to him. The mutilated body of Stefan Tronstad was on the floor, barely a foot away, his bloodied face turned, his accusing death stare fixed on Berg.

'If only you'd been honest with me sooner,' Sychev said. Not for the first time. As though it was Berg's fault that Sychev's guy – that beast – had carved Tronstad up, and had surely been about to do the same to Isabell.

'You make a lot of mistakes for a man who thinks so much of himself,' Sychev added. 'Who thinks he's such a success.'

The Russian came into view now. He strolled from behind Berg and rested just in front of the doorway, arms hanging by his sides. Hands empty. Good. But what about Andrey? Berg knew he remained somewhere behind him, even if he was as silent as... as silent as Tronstad.

Andrey had a knife. Perhaps other tools too. Berg knew that because he'd already watched Andrey cut his wife. Slicing across her forearm like it was a piece of chicken. Not the worst injury, not compared to what Tronstad had suffered, but Berg knew they were both at the mercy of these two.

'You're animals,' Berg said, as a wave of nausea washed over him. His stomach heaved at the thoughts, the sight in front of him. He closed his mouth and somehow managed to keep the bile down. Or up?

Isabell drifted in and out of consciousness. Shock, Berg believed, more than anything. Or had they drugged her? He wasn't even sure if he'd been conscious the whole time he'd been strung up. Everything about the situation felt so disorientating and surreal.

Except he knew it was real.

'You think... you think this will get you what you want?' Berg said.

Sychev didn't answer. Instead, he walked back and forth in front of Berg. Or was Sychev standing still and the perceived movement was because of Berg swinging?

'What exactly did you think was happening between him and your wife?' Sychev said, and Berg was sure he said it smiling.

He moved closer. Crouched down. By Isabell.

'Isabell! Oh, Isabell!' he cooed, as if rousing a baby. He reached out and went to lift up her chin. Berg flinched when Isabell jerked and snarled and gnashed her teeth. Sychev jumped back, laughing.

'Wow, she is fierce,' Sychev said. 'In a good way. Tell him, Isabell. Tell him what you were doing with your dear friend here.'

Sychev kicked the corpse on the floor. Isabell said nothing now. Andrey appeared from behind Berg. He went right up to Isabell and threw a fist into her stomach. Then another to her jaw that elicited a horrible squelch. Berg flinched when specks of blood hit his arm.

'Don't touch her!' he somehow managed to shout.

Silence. Then, 'You're so loyal,' Sychev said. 'I'm a little surprised. You hired your man Nyland because you thought your wife was screwing someone else, didn't you?'

Berg didn't answer.

'I know you did. But she wasn't. She wasn't screwing Tronstad. She was screwing *you.*'

Sychev laughed, he was enjoying himself way too much.

'No,' Isabell said.

No what? Berg didn't know because she said nothing more.

'She *hates* you,' Sychev said. 'Tronstad and her were concocting ways to punish you. She knows about our money. She knows about everything. The boy even. I also heard how you were trying to screw *us.*'

No. That wasn't possible. How could Isabell and that lawyer have known all that? Sychev was wrong.

'She was trying to ruin you,' Sychev said. 'You should be pleased because we've found this out for you. I thought, a strong man like you, you'd want to finish her off yourself.' He paused. 'You can, if you want. I'll untie you right now. You kill her. We'll tidy up for you.'

Berg said nothing, but he couldn't deny that his brain whirred with the idea...

'We'll conclude our deal,' Sychev said. 'You get to live the rest of your life a free and rich man.'

'Free?' Berg said. 'I'll never be free.'

Sychev sighed. Then his phone rang. 'Wait for me,' he said, though Berg didn't know who the words were aimed at. Sychev moved out of the room.

Andrey stood guard by the door. No one said a word. A couple of minutes later Sychev walked back in with a broad smile on his face, though with Berg upside down it looked misshapen and ghoulish.

'We've got him,' Sychev said. 'Henrik. He's coming home.'

Berg closed his eyes, not sure what to feel about Sychev's statement. Good news? Well, it certainly could have been worse. The boy was alive. This could all still work out. Couldn't it?

A knock came from the front door at the other end of the building. A tense silence ensued. A knock echoed again a few moments later – harder, louder this time.

Andrey and Sychev said something to each other that Berg couldn't understand. But neither looked happy. Clearly they weren't expecting anyone.

Sychev disappeared off. Andrey moved quickly across the room, gathering... what? He ended up back in front of Berg, standing to the side of the doorway, a foot-long machete in his hand, raised up high. Berg winced just at the sight of the blade, the macabre thoughts in his mind all the worse because of the sight on the floor in front of him. He certainly didn't want to end up like Tronstad. He'd much rather take a single fatal blow.

No... he could get through this.

The front door opened. Voices. Several. Andrey rolled back and forth on the balls of his feet, his face strained, ready to strike anyone who came through the doorway that wasn't Sychev.

'Andrey!' came the panicked cry from out of sight, before a series of shouts and thuds... Then a shadow in the doorway...

'Watch out!' Berg screamed.

The figure burst into the room... Lindstrom. He didn't see it coming. Andrey swooshed the machete down. Berg winced as the blade dug several inches into Lindstrom's shoulder. He cried out in pain, hunched over. Andrey tried to pull the blade out but it was wedged deep in muscle and bone.

'Sigurd!'

Erling. He bulldozed into the room. Andrey yanked the machete free. Lindstrom collapsed to the floor screaming in agony. Erling swung the bat in his hands and it cracked into

Andrey's side. The machete went flying. The next moment... two other people appeared. Sonja... Sychev? Who else? It was difficult to tell, hanging the wrong way up, shouting, screaming, bodies scuttling back and forth.

'No!' someone shouted. Sonja? 'They're getting away!'

And just like that the room cleared. Except for Lindstrom, who clutched at his shoulder where his arm hung by a thread. He propped himself up against the wall, breathing heavily as he stared over at Berg.

'Thank you,' Berg said to him. Lindstrom didn't respond.

A few moments later Erling and Sonja came back into the room, both bloodied, both breathless. No sign of Sychev and Andrey. Berg only hoped they were dead.

Erling moved forward. 'Come on, we have to go.'

He reached forward, toward Berg's feet.

Snap.

Berg's body collapsed to the floor, though Erling's meaty arms helped to soften the fall.

Berg shuffled and righted himself, pushing his weight down as his head recovered and blood flowed down through his body.

'I'm sorry,' Erling said.

No clarification, but Berg felt he knew what the big man meant. Erling had his hand stretched out.

'We'll get you safe.'

Berg reached up and grasped his hand, and with Erling's help managed to get to his feet.

'And her?' Sonja asked.

Berg looked at his wife, tied to the chair, her head up. She looked petrified, even though she was in a room with her husband and his friends now, and not those mad butchers.

'Bring her with us,' Berg said, before turning for the door.

39

'Who called them?' Pettersen asked.

'It doesn't matter,' Ryker said. 'We need to go.'

He moved out the room, toward the front. Through the open door, he could already see flashes of blue, the sound of the sirens closing in.

Pettersen went to go past him. He grabbed her shoulder.

'We can't go out that way,' he said.

'It's the police. They're here to help.'

'The best thing we can do now, to help Henrik, is to get on the move. Find who took him and get him back.'

'And the police can't help with that?'

'They can. Will they do so in the next five minutes? Or will it be hours of questioning and them trying to figure out if we're the bad guys or not?'

'*Them*? I'm one of *them*.' She spoke defensively, as though Ryker had offended her.

'Except you're not one of them here, are you? And what about me?'

She paused for a moment, but then shrugged him off.

'I'm not going out there with you,' Ryker said.

She stopped and turned. 'We don't have time for this.'

Ryker at least agreed with that.

'You have your phone?' he said, pulling his cheap prepaid handset from his pocket. Time for a first use.

'Yeah.'

'Give me your number.'

She rattled it off. Ryker typed it in and hit call. Her phone buzzed. He ended the call just as screeching tyres echoed from the outside.

'I'm going out the back,' Ryker said. 'I'll move around. Do what you need to do, but you need to get back to your car. I'll wait for you. But not for long. If you're not done–'

'Just go,' she said.

Ryker didn't hesitate. He turned and raced into the small kitchen. Looked out of the window by the overflowing dining table. Dark garden below. The window was locked. He grabbed a knife from the side, stuck it into the gap between window and frame and jimmied the fixture open.

Voices outside now. Pettersen included. She talked calmly. Assuredly.

Ryker didn't look back. He slunk through the window, twisted around, grasped the edge with both hands as his body hung down, then he dropped. He landed in a prickly bush and rolled out onto frozen grass, grimacing in pain. Just a few scratches and scrapes. He pulled himself up. Looked around. Darted across to a fence. Clambered over. Another two fences as he headed along, in parallel to the homes. A few dogs barked, but nothing else to worry him. More fences, then eventually he emerged onto a side street.

A police car blasted past, its lights flashing but no siren. Ryker reeled back and watched as the vehicle rounded the corner in front and disappeared. He let out a sigh of relief, then, hood up, he carefully walked back toward the front of the houses.

He stopped twenty yards away from Pettersen's car. Four other police cars were there, too, right outside the bloodbath house. One ambulance. More would arrive soon enough. A few bystanders milled, gawking – always the same.

Where was Pettersen? A uniformed officer rushed about rolling out police tape to stop any of the bystanders getting too close. Two of the police cars were within the cordon, but Pettersen's was well outside of it. All she needed to do was find a way to leave.

Ryker hunched down by a hedge and watched as his brain fired with disparate thoughts. Most dominant were thoughts of what he'd do when he caught up with whoever had slaughtered those youngsters. Police and courts and lawyers and prisons were one thing... but Ryker didn't believe they fitted every situation. That kind of 'justice' wasn't what was required here. And he really didn't want to leave Henrik's fate in the hands of the police. He'd get to Henrik first. He knew he would. He'd solve this before the police even got a plan together.

Ryker spun on his heel when he heard movement behind him. A man approaching. Ten yards away. Hood up, head down, hands in pockets. Oblivious. Until he looked up. Now he saw the police. His face remained cloaked in darkness, but doubts burned in Ryker's mind. Was the man looking at the police or at *him*?

The guy stopped walking. Ryker's brain continued to rumble. He thought back over the murder scene. Four bodies. No Henrik. But no Skinhead either. Was that who Ryker was staring at? Would Skinhead think Ryker was the culprit?

The next moment, the man turned and walked off in the opposite direction. Ryker thought about following.

He didn't. Because Pettersen's voice drifted over. A little more wary than before, Ryker looked back to the action. Spotted her. Right by the edge of the police tape. Just her and a uniformed policeman who towered over her, his arms folded. His face stern as he looked down at her, though Pettersen appeared relaxed and chatty. Would she try to get away from there? Or was she relaying everything. About him. About Henrik.

He'd give her a couple of minutes. But nothing more. He willed her on.

'Don't let me down,' he whispered.

Pettersen talked away, pointed to the house, pointed to her car. Ryker shuffled back a little more, further out of view, until he could only just make her out.

After a few moments she reached out and the policeman shook her hand. The next second he was speaking into his radio as he turned back to the house. Pettersen looked around her, then ducked under the tape and marched toward her car. She didn't let up, didn't look back. She was a couple of yards from the car when Ryker burst out from his hiding spot and raced over, keeping low.

'Get in,' Pettersen whispered when she saw him.

Ryker flung himself into the passenger seat. Pettersen stepped in much more gracefully. She started the engine up, swung the car around, and they were on their way. Ryker righted himself in the seat. Put his seat belt on. He leaned over and looked out the back window. No one was watching. No one cared at all.

When he went to turn back around he stopped to look at Pettersen. A half smile crept up her face.

'You're so tense, James,' she said.

'What did you say to them?'

She shrugged.

'You really do have the power of persuasion, don't you?'

'We all have our strengths.'

Ryker sat back and sighed. He could tell by her tone that her intention was to try to lighten the mood. Just like she had done on the drive down from Blodstein. Ryker wasn't sure he wanted the mood lightened this time though. Not after what they'd just witnessed.

'It's a long ride ahead,' he said.

'Yeah,' Pettersen said with a sigh.

'But I'm glad you chose to come with me.'

She didn't say anything to that.

40

The inside of the house in the forest was dark and cold. Berg shivered as he moved into the poorly lit lounge, the only light coming from an overhead bulb and a flickering lamp in the corner. At least someone had cleaned the place up a little since he'd last been.

'We're going to find them,' Erling said, coming into the room behind Berg, his fists balled, his face creased with anger and streaked with blood – not his.

Before Berg could say anything a man's harrowing scream rang out from one of the other rooms. Erling and Berg glanced at one another. Sonja walked in, her face ashen.

'How is he?' Berg asked.

'Bad,' she said. 'He needs a doctor.'

'A doctor?' Berg scoffed. 'You think some antibiotics will solve this? His fucking arm is hanging off!'

'Then what?'

Berg didn't answer that.

'He's losing blood too fast,' Sonja said, focusing on Erling now, as though Berg was too irrational to be part of the adults' conversation.

'Give him as many painkillers as you can,' Erling said. 'Vodka too, whatever there is. Keep him calm. It's the best we can do for now.'

Sonja glared at him. But what did she expect him to say? The local doctor in Blodstein wouldn't be able to offer anything better for Lindstrom. The nearest hospital was more than an hour away, but it was hardly a huge place with endless resource and expertise and it was doubtful even they could help properly. Plus, someone would need to take Lindstrom there and they couldn't afford to be another man down now.

'We could at least take him into town,' Sonja said. 'Leave him somewhere safe and call an ambulance. Let them deal with it.'

'Nobody leaves this house,' Berg said. 'Everyone stays until I say so.'

Sonja fixed her dissatisfied gaze squarely back to him now.

'He could die here,' she said. 'He's bleeding to death, for trying to save *you*.'

Berg said nothing to that, but apparently she wasn't finished.

'Should we have just left you in there with those psychos instead?'

The question went unanswered, only adding to Sonja's frustration.

'He's got a wife and a kid. A girl, two years old.'

'Is that supposed to make me feel more sorry for him?'

'Doesn't it?'

Berg shook his head and turned away. He winced in pain as he moved over to the sofa. Erling stayed right by his side, and helped to ease him down like a nurse attending to a rickety old man in a retirement home.

'I'm fine,' Berg said, swatting him away, which only made his hastily dressed wounds ache and throb all the more.

'Yeah, *you're* fine,' Sonja said. 'But Lindstrom isn't.'

'You want to help him?' Berg responded, his tone harder, his voice raised. 'It's on you. *You* take him to town. You dump him there. But if anyone sees you, if you bring anyone back here–'

'Thank you.'

She didn't sound like she meant it. She spun and strode out.

'Is there something I don't know about?' Berg said, catching the big man's eye.

'Huh?'

'Her and Lindstrom?'

Erling shook his head. 'Don't think so.'

Berg rolled his eyes. Silence for a few moments. Erling hovered, like he wanted something.

'What happened?' he asked. 'Tell me everything.'

Everything? Berg wasn't so sure about that. So he gave Erling the basics. What the Russians had done to Tronstad, what they'd found out about Henrik. The fact that the Russians' friend – the one who'd butchered Tronstad – had called just before the cavalry arrived to say they now had Henrik in their hands.

'You think Carl Logan is with them?' Erling said.

'There's nothing to suggest that,' Berg said.

Which did beg the question, where was he? Had the Russians killed him, too, in retrieving the boy?

'Do they know who Henrik is?' Erling asked. He held Berg's eye now.

'I told them he's Rosen's son.'

No reaction on Erling's face. No follow-up question.

A shout from down the hall. Not Lindstrom screaming this time, but a woman. Not a shout of pain, but anger.

Isabell.

'She doesn't want to be here,' Erling said.

And Berg didn't really want her there either, but what choice did he have?

'Just find a way to keep her quiet, keep her in one place. Do what you have to do.'

There were bigger issues at play tonight than keeping his wife comforted.

Erling nodded and turned to head out. Berg reached out and grabbed his hefty hand. The mammoth turned around, looked down at Berg.

'I know what you did,' Berg said.

Erling whipped his hand away but didn't say anything.

'I know you met with Sychev and his little lapdog. In the bar.'

Erling's face remained passive, and despite his size and intimidating position, looking over Berg, something in the air confirmed exactly who was in charge – and the answer had nothing to do with bicep size.

'I didn't know it would end like this,' Erling said.

'You were trying to sell me out.'

Erling said nothing.

'What?' Berg said. 'I wasn't paying you enough? I haven't done enough for you and your family over the years?'

'I told them nothing.'

'Maybe. And maybe only because of Carl Logan showing up that night.'

Erling's head dropped. Ashamed? Was he scared too?

'But you saved me tonight,' Berg said. 'Perhaps I can look past the rest. If we get through this.'

Once more Erling gave no response.

'Believe me, though: if you ever go behind my back again... what you saw of Tronstad tonight will be just the start compared to what I do to you.'

Erling sucked in a lungful of air through his nose. His chest rose several inches as he did so. If he wanted, Berg knew the guy could squash him, pulverise him, mash him into the ground with his meaty fists.

Instead, the big man simply nodded, then headed out.

Berg woke up with a start. He was on the sofa still. Panting. His face dripped sweat, his body clammy, even if his skin prickled with cold. The last remnants of violence flickered in his mind as he pushed away the gory horrors of his sleep.

How the hell was he supposed to sleep properly again after what he'd seen?

Why the hell had he fallen asleep at all with everything that was happening?

He wasn't alone in the room. Erling, Sonja, two others, were sitting around the circular table in the corner, a couple of bottles of spirits and piles of coins and notes in the middle, cards in their hands.

Berg grumbled and shuffled up in the sofa.

'Is it really the time for gambling and drinking?' he said.

A few eyes looked his way but no one said anything.

Only as Berg achingly got to his feet did he properly register that Sonja was now back from her little outing.

'Any word on Lindstrom?' Berg asked.

Sonja glared at him. As if to say, 'do you really care?'

Berg did. In so far as it affected him.

'Nothing,' Sonja said. 'With any luck he'll be in good hands by now.'

Berg glanced at his watch. He'd been asleep for well over an hour.

'No sign of anyone else?' Berg asked, to no one in particular.

'No sign of the Russians,' Erling said.

What was Berg expecting? For them to simply drive up to try and finish the job of killing him? No, whatever they had planned next it wasn't that. He checked his phone. No calls from them either. They'd be in touch soon enough, one way or another.

Perhaps he and Erling and the rest should head out and try to find *them* first. This was Berg's town, not theirs.

Except he had no clue where they were. Perhaps they'd simply fled Blodstein and he'd never see them again. Was that a possibility? Particularly if they really did have Henrik, and especially if they knew who Henrik really was.

Did they?

Berg moved out of the room, along the corridor to the first bedroom. He paused at the closed door. Put his hand to the handle. Pushed the door open slowly, as though worried that whatever was inside might escape. Well...

He peered in. Darkness. Except for the light leaking into the room from the hallway.

'*Fitte,*' came the rasping insult.

Berg paused in the doorway as he looked down at his wife, sitting on the floor in the corner of the room, knees up to her chest. Her wrists were cuffed together, the cuffs laced around the thick pipes of the radiator.

'My love,' Berg said, wanting to sound genuine. In fact, he thought he did, but the look on her face... if looks could kill...

She spat toward him. He didn't react. The globule landed by his feet.

'This is for the best,' he said. 'I'm keeping you safe, here, until this is all over.'

'Get out. Just get out of my sight.'

She sank her head to her knees, covering her face. He thought about going up to her, putting his arms around her, comforting her. Did he love her still? Of course, though he knew they could never go back to what they'd once had. Not after what she'd planned with Tronstad. Whatever she felt right now, *she* was the one in the wrong. In time he'd make sure she realised that.

Berg stepped back and gently pulled the door closed.

He was about to head further along to the toilet when he paused. A crackle of static from the lounge. Then Erling's low-pitched voice echoed along, vibrating through Berg's body even though the big man talked quietly.

Berg followed the sound. Erling headed toward him as he reached the room.

'Wold's here,' Erling said with distaste, the radio held up to his chest in anticipation of relaying Berg's response.

'Is he alone?'

Erling nodded.

'Are you absolutely sure?'

Erling repeated the question into the radio then held the receiver toward Berg so they could both hear the response.

'He's in his patrol car. In uniform. But he's definitely alone,' came the crackly response.

'Send him through,' Berg said. 'On foot. Just one of you.'

Acknowledgment on the other end before Erling brought the radio down.

'You sure about this?' he said.

'Better to have Wold on the inside with us, than out there causing problems.'

Erling huffed but didn't say anything.

'Come on,' Berg said, heading for the front entrance.

He grabbed a thick coat from the rack by the door. Whose, he had no clue, but it was big and warm and dry and cleanish. Erling didn't bother with one. They stepped out into the cold. Not dark. The clearing around the house was bathed in bright white from the security lights – usually motion-triggered but tonight they were on permanently. Berg nodded to the single sentry on duty at the front. They had another at the rear. Two on the road, who'd intercepted Wold. Another four within the treeline around the house. Twelve people all included, fourteen including Berg and his wife. A mini army. All at Berg's beck and call. Well, mostly at Erling's really, as the guys – and Sonja – were largely loggers, who worked cash in hand for him, and were being paid cash in hand for tonight. But Berg called the shots to the big man.

As he stood waiting in the cold, a renewed shiver ran through Berg. Having the security lights wired on definitely helped in illuminating the area directly around the house, but it also meant that the area beyond appeared all the more dark and lifeless. Berg could see nothing out there, in any direction. He shivered again.

He heard them before he saw them. The soft shuffle of feet on frozen ground – the only sound he could make out above his and Erling's breathing and the otherwise eerie silence of the night-time forest, where, in midwinter, even the night creatures didn't care to venture.

Berg kept his eyes on the spot straight ahead of him where the sound came from. Finally they came into view. Wold, and one of Berg's guys, walking next to each other in silence. Wold had his hands by his sides. The sentry had a huge wrench dangling from his fist. Not the most sophisticated of weapons but better than nothing. Between them all they had two shotguns, but as far as firearms were concerned, that was it.

As they neared, their warm breaths billowing above them, Berg saw that Wold was not happy. He and Erling remained rooted. Wold's exasperation only seemed to grow as he closed in, perhaps for the very fact that Berg stood there waiting rather than closing the gap.

'Are you deliberately trying to annoy me?' Wold said when he finally came to a stop a few yards away.

'I'm being careful. After the night I've had–'

'Quite a night.'

What did he know about it?

'Two dead bodies,' Wold said. 'I'm presuming both because of you?'

Two? Berg didn't react.

'Lindstrom worked for you, didn't he?' Wold said, turning his attention to Erling.

So Lindstrom hadn't made it. Sonja wouldn't be happy.

'I found him slumped in the café car park in a pool of his own blood,' Wold said. 'His arm cleaved off. The ambulance arrived a few minutes after but there was nothing they could do.'

Berg grit his teeth.

'And right over the road from there...' Wold bowed slightly and shook his head as if in despair. Genuine? 'I've never seen anything like that.'

Berg still kept his mouth shut. He would until he understood Wold's intentions.

'Stefan Tronstad,' Wold said. 'He was found hacked to pieces in his new office. And when I say hacked, I mean his skin was peeled from his body. I've got a forensics team on the way to help figure it all out, but I'm pretty sure that happened to him while he was still alive.'

He said it as though he had experience of finding tortured bodies. Did he believe his own crap?

'The thing is, there's several sets of bloody footprints leading out of that house, and plenty of other evidence to suggest something big went down there. Not just Tronstad being brutalised, but a fight. Involving quite a few people. I find Lindstrom dead, across the road, and I find you holed up here with every other man in Blodstein.'

Wold looked around now, as though he knew exactly which men were out there, and exactly where they were stationed.

'I've also got one of my own missing, uncontactable.'

He let that one sit. Who? And what did that have to do with anything?

'So please, Sigurd, I've had enough of this night already. I'm not having these outsiders turn my town into a horror show. Just tell me what's happening. Tell me how I can help.'

Well, this was a surprise. Berg and Erling flicked a look to one another, as though both were as shocked as the other. But then Wold had come alone, and not with a hoard of police officers from near and far. Even that, though, didn't mean much, and possibly only that Wold wanted to get more for himself from this situation.

'The Russians attacked Tronstad and my wife,' Berg said. 'They attacked me too. Took me to that house. Tronstad was already dead when I got there. They would have done the same to me and Isabell. If it wasn't for Erling.'

'And Lindstrom was caught in the crossfire, I assume,' Wold said, turning his attention to Erling.

Erling simply nodded.

'There's three of them now,' Berg said. 'The one who butchered Tronstad... I've not seen him before. There's three of them and they have Henrik too. We need to find them and deal with them and get him back.'

'*Deal* with them?'

'Whatever we have to do.'

'You're asking my permission to allow you to cause more mayhem, more bloodshed, on the streets of my town?'

'I'm not asking. And it's not your town.'

The look on Wold's face... like he'd chewed on a wasp.

'Any man who helps me–'

'You think I want your money?' Wold spat.

As if he hadn't taken backhanders before. As if the entire relationship between the two of them wasn't based off and borne from that fact.

'What choice do you have?' Erling said, unprompted. Did his

opinion really matter? 'This is us versus them. And you're one of us.'

Actually, not a bad choice of words, and the slight nod from Wold suggested those words had hit home.

'We're going to finish this,' Berg said. 'If you see or hear anything from the Russians, you tell me.'

'And if I don't hear or see anything? What? Are you going to stay out here forever, hiding?'

'I'm not hiding,' Berg said, realising that he sounded a little offended by the implication.

'I'll do what I can,' Wold said. 'Mainly because I don't want anyone else from this town hurt. Who do you think has to tell their families, has to help them pick up the pieces? But when this is over... you and me–'

'When this is over? Let's worry about getting there first.'

Wold glared but said nothing more. The next moment he turned, and with the guard by his side, walked away.

41

Ryker and Pettersen barely spoke a word to one another for the last hour of the journey. Ryker felt weary, Pettersen – driving – likely even more so. She'd received several calls from Wold during the drive. She hadn't answered once. Hadn't listened to his voicemails either. She truly had placed herself on the outside, though even in their silence, Ryker sensed that in shunning her boss, she'd only increased her sense of isolation and vulnerability, and her demeanour had become more and more downbeat as a result.

'Take the turn here,' Ryker said.

Pettersen sighed and followed his instruction. The road ahead had no lights. The beams of the patrol car's headlamps bounced and jostled through the trees surrounding them.

'What are you expecting to find here?' Pettersen asked. 'Do you really think they'd have simply brought Henrik back to the same house again?'

'It would be stupid not to at least look here.'

Though the truth was he had been torn as to what approach to take; the direct route, simply driving up to the house, or the indirect route through the forest as he had done the day he'd rescued Henrik. A rescue which now seemed pointless.

He hadn't explained or discussed those two approaches with Pettersen, simply opting for the former choice. Direct. They'd face whatever threat lay beyond them head-on.

'Should we not at least turn the lights off,' Pettersen said, slowing the car as she spoke. 'So we don't spook whoever is here?'

'No,' Ryker said. He thought about trying to explain why, but then he saw the men up ahead, holding their position in the middle of the road. 'It's too late now.'

Pettersen sighed. The car crawled forward to the two men. Both were big and bulky, though it was hard to tell how much of the bulk was due to their winter gear to keep them warm in the frigid night. One had a meaty-looking wrench that he held in both hands. The other had a bat in one hand, a radio in the other.

'Do you know these two?' Ryker asked.

'Shit,' Pettersen said, not in answer, but Ryker assumed because the guy brought the radio to his mouth.

'I knew this was a bad idea,' Pettersen added. 'They're calling for backup.'

'Just stay calm. You're the police. You're in charge here.'

Pettersen shot him a dubious look but said nothing.

She rolled the car to a stop by the men. One went to her side of the car, one to Ryker, who stared out of his window to the man by his door – the one with the wrench. He glared back at Ryker, face full of suspicion.

Pettersen rolled down her window. As Ryker had become used to now, she began a fast-paced conversation in Norwegian. Calm but strong, as ever. The man with the bat, shivering as he spoke, appeared agitated and suspicious, but after a while it became clear he was losing whatever argument they were having.

A couple of times Pettersen looked and indicated over to Ryker. He said nothing. Tried his best to catch any familiar words from the conversation. Police. Wold. Night. Henrik. Those were about the only ones.

With a sigh Pettersen turned away from the man and closed her window.

'He won't let us past.'

'Because?'

'Because he's been told not to let anyone past. He's already informed whoever is on the other end of that radio that we're here.'

'We?'

'I told him Wold sent me. That I've arrested Carl Logan and I'm not sure what I'm supposed to do with him.'

'Did he buy that?'

'Not exactly. He said they'll contact Wold to ask him.'

Was that good or bad? Ryker didn't know. The look on Pettersen's face suggested she wasn't happy about the situation at all, though was that more of the prospect of the involvement of Wold than anything else?

A tap on Pettersen's window. She opened it again. A more brief conversation this time before she closed it once more and shut the engine down.

'We can go through,' she said. 'But on foot.'

'Do we even know who's in the house?' Ryker asked. 'Berg? Wold? The Russians? Henrik?'

'Now you worry about that?' she said with an eye-roll – a playful gesture? 'I know as much as you do.'

'Then let's go and find out.'

Ryker and Pettersen stepped out in unison. No sooner had Ryker closed his door as the meathead with the wrench grabbed him, spun him around and pushed him up against the side of the police car. Pettersen shouted out in protest – about the mistreatment of her car, or her 'prisoner', Ryker wasn't sure. It didn't even matter. The next second she, too, was up against the metalwork, the radio guy patting her down.

The man behind Ryker forcefully spread his legs. Felt from his groin to his ankles, back up to his hips. Then he used his forearm on Ryker's neck to crush Ryker's head into the car, pinning him. Ryker gritted his teeth and sucked it up. A few seconds later and the pressure was released before the guy hauled him back straight.

'Walk.'

Ryker looked over at Pettersen. In the thin moonlight he couldn't quite read the look on her face. They were lined up next to each other at the front of the car. Wrench Guy stood in front, while the other guy spoke into his radio one more time. Then he came up to his friend and barked an instruction at Ryker and Pettersen. The two of them exchanged a glance before they stepped forward – the two men by their sides to chaperone.

The men really should have thought their plan through more thoroughly.

Ryker swung around. He grabbed Wrench Guy by the throat with one hand. He squeezed hard and hauled his knee up and smashed it into the guy's privates.

'Shit, no!' Pettersen shouted. Ryker thought he'd given her the look. Thought she'd understood. Perhaps not. Either way, she was in this fight now too.

Not worrying about her, yet, Ryker hit the guy again and the wrench came free. He let go and the man collapsed to the ground, gasping for breath as he clutched his groin. Ryker grabbed the wrench. Glanced to his side to see Pettersen wrestling upright with the other guy, trying to get him into a submission hold.

Ryker lifted the wrench up to finish off the guy below him...

'No!'

Another shout from Pettersen. If the instruction had been to him, Ryker didn't heed it. He smacked the wrench down onto the guy's back, sending him sprawling, face down with an oomph.

Ryker turned. Ready to strike again. No need. Pettersen had him. A hammerlock. She kicked him in the back of the leg to send him down to his knees.

'Get the cuffs!' she shouted to Ryker. He grabbed them from her belt. Clasped one before she took over. She kicked the cuffed man down into the dirt. Turned to Ryker. Yeah, it was dark, but the pissed off look was clear enough.

'What is wrong with you!' she said.

'Me? I'm just evening the odds a little.'

'You don't even know who they are. Why they're here. Who else is in that house.'

'That's why I only hurt him a little.'

He glanced to Wrench Guy who squirmed and groaned on the ground.

'Do you have any more cuffs?' Ryker asked.

'Yeah.'

'Maybe you should get your shotgun too.'

She glared at him. Said nothing before she moved for her car.

Ryker grabbed the radio from the ground. Gave it a quick once-over before he dropped it again and crushed it under his heel.

Together with Pettersen they cuffed the second guy then put both men – grumbling and fighting, just a little – in the back of the police car. Not that they were under arrest, but at least in there they were secure enough. For now.

'Ask them who's at the house,' Ryker said when Pettersen grabbed the door to lock them in.

'I already did,' she said.

'And?'

'And I was told to stick my fist up my asshole.'

'You'll have to teach me the Norwegian for that one.'

She didn't look impressed by his quip.

'Are you ready?' he asked.

She moved to the back of the car. Opened the boot. Took out the shotgun.

'Ready.'

They set off along the track, through the dark. No headlights now, no torch, just the light of the moon and the silence of the night.

'This is a really bad idea,' Pettersen whispered.

Ryker didn't say anything.

'They already know we're coming,' she added.

'They're expecting us to arrive with their guards by our sides.'

'It's not going to take them long to realise that isn't the case.'

'No,' Ryker said.

Pettersen stopped and turned to him. 'No? Is that all you have to say? No?'

'What else should I say?'

'How about explaining to me what your plan is? What do we do when we get there?'

'We can't possibly know, as we don't even know who *is* there.'

Silence as she glared at him. 'Really? Is that it?'

Ryker shrugged. He knew his calmness and nonchalance wasn't winning her over, but he also thought her agitation and rumination had more to do with her nerves than anything else.

'All I know is I'm doing this, here, tonight. I'm going to that house. I'll fight every man and woman there if I have to. If

Henrik's there we'll take him away to safety. If he's not, we'll find where he is and go there next. I'm sorry, but that's the plan.'

'And what if we take one step closer and they put a bullet in your brain with a hunting rifle from fifty yards away?'

'On balance, I'm not sure that's likely.'

'Have you always been like this?'

'Like what?'

'So...' She huffed and then rattled off something in Norwegian. An insult of some kind. Or just verbal diarrhoea in exasperation.

'I've been in plenty of situations like this before,' Ryker said. 'And getting the job done is more important than worrying about possible outcomes.'

Pettersen sighed and Ryker sensed another protest brewing until he moved off.

'We could at least go into the forest,' she said. 'Try to surprise them.'

'Why? Like you said, they already know we're coming.'

Pettersen didn't respond again, except to show her continued dissatisfaction with a renewed grumble under her breath. She held the shotgun in both hands as they walked, the barrel pointed to the ground in front of her. Ryker really hoped they didn't need to use it. In many ways having the gun made him all the more nervous. He'd fired plenty of guns in his life. Had killed plenty of people with such weapons. Yes, they made him feel more safe. But bringing a gun to any situation also changed the dynamic. Once that first shot was fired... all bets were off.

Before long the house came into view. Who could miss it, with the security lights blaring as they were. Ryker and Pettersen remained in darkness a few more steps, but it became apparent when they were finally visible because of the increased action in front of them.

'Berg's here,' Pettersen said.

Ryker thought he'd spotted him too. He'd never met Sigurd Berg before now, but his demeanour – standing tall by the house, staring straight ahead at the new arrivals, while others moved into action around him – gave him away.

Ryker spotted Erling too. By Berg's side. Sonja as well. Movement in the forest to the left and right. Two other men peeled away from the house, walking a few yards apart from each other, half-crouching as though not sure what to expect as they closed the distance to Ryker and Pettersen.

One of them shouted over. The one with the shotgun in his hand. The shotgun that was up to his shoulder, the barrel pointed at Pettersen. Ryker could only guess he'd told her to toss her weapon.

She glanced at him, a questioning look on her face.

Then, as if for Ryker's benefit, 'Drop the weapons!'

English this time.

Ryker tossed the wrench. It clattered a couple of feet in front of the guy holding the shotgun. Ryker kept moving toward the other guy who, crowbar in his grip, held up like a baseball bat.

'Ryker?' Pettersen said.

'Put it down,' he said.

She did so.

'Hands in the air,' the shotgun guy said, waving the barrel back and forth between Ryker and Pettersen.

Pettersen stopped moving. Ryker wished she hadn't. He'd been about to make a break for the guy with the crowbar, but he wouldn't leave her behind with that shotgun in range. He stopped with her. Berg remained ten yards away. Not yet part of the welcoming party.

'Sigurd, what are you doing?' Pettersen shouted to him.

No reaction from Berg.

Erling and Sonja stepped forward, as if to protect their boss.

'Where's Henrik?' Ryker shouted. 'We only want him. Give us the boy and we'll go.'

A few questioning glances. The two men in front of Ryker came to a stop. Not quite reaching distance.

Ryker took another step forward. Doing so drew an angry shout from the man with the gun as he fixed the barrel firmly in Ryker's direction.

Until... 'Please, Sigurd, I don't know what's happening here...' Now Pettersen moved forward. One step, two, three. She went past Ryker. Then stopped and opened up in Norwegian. Ryker didn't concentrate on her words. Only on the two men directly in front of him. Pettersen moved again and the guy with the crowbar edged closer still. The guy with the gun went back. Okay, so that told a lot. He didn't want that gun in his hands. He was scared. He didn't want to shoot. Especially not at a police officer.

With Pettersen distracting everyone, Ryker made the move first. He darted forward. The guy with the crowbar sprang into action, rushed forward too. He coiled the crowbar behind his head, ready to swing in a vicious arc. Solid contact on Ryker's skull with a weapon like that could prove fatal. Maybe the guy knew that. Maybe he didn't.

The bar came forward with a growl of determination from the man's lips. Ryker pushed his weight back, kicked his feet forward to slide across the dirt in a two-footed tackle. The crowbar swung uselessly through the air, connected with nothing. The momentum sent the guy off balance just as Ryker made contact. He took both legs with him. The guy collapsed on top. Ryker grabbed the crowbar from him, pulled himself out from underneath and smashed the metal down onto the man's ankle.

Crack.

A howl of pain. Probably a broken bone or two, but much kinder than the broken skull the man had intended for Ryker.

Another swipe arcing Ryker's way. The butt of the shotgun. Not the weapon's intended purpose, but still a nasty blow if the wood made contact. Ryker ducked and the butt smacked into his back. Painful, but not serious. He sprang back up. His feet lifted off the ground. He balled his fist and it crashed into the underside of the man's chin with ferocious force, sending him to the ground two yards further back. The gun clattered away.

Ryker looked over. Pettersen groaned, pulling herself to her feet. A dribble of blood wormed down the side of her head. Hit with the shotgun too?

'Behind you!' Ryker shouted.

Sonja. Not just her in fact, but bodies everywhere all of a sudden, as if an army had sprouted from the trees around them. Ryker spun. Swung the crowbar. Solid contact on the hips of a man charging him. He spun again, deflected a bat with his forearm, though the strike sent a painful judder up his arm into his neck. He swiped with his leg, unbalancing the attacker before sending his elbow into their ribs.

He took a blow to the back of his head which sent him stumbling. Stumbling forward. Toward the house. Right into the path of Erling. The big man reached out and grabbed Ryker by the throat. Lifted him off his feet. No mean feat considering Ryker's own height and weight. A headbutt sent Ryker's vision spinning. Erling tossed him to the ground. A boot came down for Ryker's face... Not Erling's. The boot belonged to the guy who'd moments ago hit Ryker in the head. Ryker caught the boot. Somehow found the strength to hold it at bay. Summoned a deeper reserve to bounce back to his feet, still holding the boot. The man stumbled. Ryker tossed him and let go and the guy landed on the ground, the back of his head first. He wasn't getting up for a while.

Erling. Where was he?

Too late.

A thick arm laced around Ryker's neck from behind. Pressure to the back of his legs sent him down, much like Pettersen had done earlier to the man with the radio.

Ryker fought against the arm that choked him, but Erling was simply stronger. Ryker dug his nails into flesh, clawed, but got a fist to the kidney in return. Another made his eyes water. Powerful shots. Enough to do serious damage if Ryker allowed himself to be pummelled over and over.

'Okay, okay,' Ryker choked out, relaxing his body a second, bringing his arms down, hoping Erling would give him some slack. He didn't.

'Let him go.'

Ryker flicked his gaze as his face contorted and he tried in vain to breathe. Pettersen. On her feet. Sonja wasn't. Sonja was lying, belly on the ground, angry eyes staring to Ryker. Pettersen's boot on Sonja's back helped to hold her own, but the shotgun in Pettersen's hands, the barrel inches from Sonja's head, likely proved even more persuasive.

As Ryker coughed and spluttered he looked around at the writhing, groaning bodies. No serious injuries, but certainly a lot of people wouldn't be up for fighting again tonight. Ryker's main concern, though, remained Erling, and his vice grip around Ryker's neck.

'I said, let him go,' Pettersen repeated, before prodding the shotgun barrel into the back of Sonja's head.

Doing so only made Erling squeeze with all the more vigour and Ryker wheezed and rasped for breath. He raked at Erling's arm once more, hoping it would cause him to ease the grip.

Nothing.

'You two,' Berg said as he moved closer, a sneer on his face, a honcho by his side.

Berg still had the numbers, but he looked a little rattled, even if the shotgun that the man with him held on to was pointed at Pettersen. 'Who do you think you are?'

'I told you,' Ryker choked out. 'We just want the boy.'

Berg didn't even look at Ryker, never mind respond.

'Put the gun down, Inspector,' he said to Pettersen.

'Let him go first. I *will* shoot her.'

'I wouldn't doubt you keeping your word,' Berg said. 'But you know as soon as you pull the trigger you're dead too?'

Pettersen seemed to consider this, as if weighing up whether it was worth it.

'We both throw the guns,' Pettersen said. 'Erling lets Ryker go.'

Berg raised an eyebrow as he flicked his gaze to Ryker. Likely because he'd not heard that name before, but only knew Ryker as Carl Logan, the name he'd first used in front of Wold.

'When Wold finds out about this–'

Berg sniggered at Pettersen's words. A childish move that clearly irritated her.

'I'm sure you two will have lots to talk about after tonight,' Berg said.

Ryker wrestled with Erling's arm again, and Berg nodded to his man. 'Let him speak.'

The grip loosened just enough.

'Henrik,' Ryker said. 'No one else... needs to get hurt tonight. Just... let him go.'

'Let him go? You think he was my prisoner here?'

Berg took a step forward. He crouched down, his eyes fixed on Ryker now.

'You've caused me a lot of problems. A lot of heartache. What did I ever do to you?'

Ryker said nothing.

'You came here once before. Attacked my friends. Took

Henrik from me. And look what has happened since. There are people dead now because of *you*.'

Ryker still kept his mouth shut.

'Didn't you ever think to ask yourself why him? Why Henrik?'

'I know more than you think,' Ryker said.

Ryker's decision to speak up drew another fist to the kidney from Erling.

'Hey, it's okay,' Berg said, calling his man off. 'Let him talk.'

'I know you went to see the Johansens,' Ryker said through laboured breaths. 'They're dead now, aren't they?'

Nothing from Berg. Confirmation?

'I also know someone took Henrik again tonight. In Trondheim. Killed four of his friends. That's why we're here.'

Berg shook his head. 'You really know nothing at all.' He let that unfinished statement hang. 'Look around you. What is this place?'

Ryker didn't really understand the question.

'Does this look like a prison to you?' Pause. No answer. 'Henrik was never my prisoner here. How do you not understand that?'

Ryker's brain whirred.

'I would never harm that boy,' Berg said. 'He's my son.'

Ryker looked to Pettersen. No reaction on her face, but he could imagine the same doubts firing in his mind, also fired in hers. The last time he'd been here, Erling had said the same as Berg. Like some bad soap opera where every guy thought he was the boy's father.

But... did it make sense this time?

'I didn't know until recently,' Berg said. 'I brought him here to keep him safe. I have many enemies. I think you may even have met them already. They want to harm me, *and* my family.'

The Russians?

'And he *was* safe here.' Berg spoke those last words with what appeared to be genuine bitterness. He rose to his feet once again. 'He was safe here. Until you arrived. Now he's gone.'

Ryker didn't know what to say. Had he really read the situation so wrong? Had he inadvertently placed Henrik in danger? Caused the deaths of those youngsters in Trondheim?

In a way, it didn't even matter if it was the truth or not. What mattered was making sure he was safe.

'He's not here,' Ryker said. 'But you know who has him.'

Berg said nothing. He turned away. Whispered something to the man with the shotgun. Ryker couldn't hear the words. Perhaps Pettersen could, because the next moment, she lifted the barrel of her shotgun up, away from Sonja, and fired.

42

The shotgun pellets splatted into the gunman's leg and the dirt around him. He collapsed in a heap, screaming in agony. Ryker had no idea what had caused Pettersen to fire. Had she expected the man was about to shoot her? Had she simply taken the chance?

Either way, Ryker wouldn't let the moment slip by.

He grabbed Erling's arm and wrenched forward. Tumbled to the side. If he'd been standing, the aim would have been to take Erling off his feet and toss him over Ryker's shoulder. A perhaps impossible task really, given Erling's size and weight. But Ryker was no slouch, and he had enough strength, enough momentum and determination and know-how, to pull Erling's body mass with him. Erling, so intent on maintaining the hold rather than anything else, ended up on the ground, on his side, Ryker next to him, the choking grip still tight... but not as tight as before.

Erling growled in anger, went to renew the hold. He should have considered Ryker's intentions instead. Ryker lifted his elbow and sent a stinging blow into Erling's ribs. The grip on his neck weakened. Another hit. Another. A crack accompanied the third one. Perhaps a broken rib. Perhaps not.

Ryker finally pulled the arm off and jumped back to his feet, his vision blurred from effort. His lungs ached. His head throbbed... He battled through it.

Erling went to get up. A kick to his chin kept him down.

'Ryker, here.'

He looked up and caught the flying shotgun and pointed it straight at Erling to halt any further attempt by the big man. Ryker looked across. Pettersen renewed her position, her own shotgun pointed at Berg. Berg, who didn't look in the least bit concerned.

Just really, really mad.

'You...'

He seemed to lose whatever insult he'd planned and ending up shaking his head despondently.

'Henrik,' Ryker said. 'Where is he?'

'I already told you. He's not here.'

'You also told me he was your son. So it's not as though shit doesn't come out of your mouth.'

Nothing from Berg. Ryker took that as confirmation of the lie.

'He's not here,' Berg said after a few moments of silence.

'Then you won't mind showing me around the house.'

Berg glowered.

'Well, go on then,' Pettersen snapped, though it wasn't clear who she was speaking to. 'I'll keep an eye out here.'

Did Ryker really want to leave her alone with Erling and crew? Not that they had much fight left in them... but it would only take one to make a move...

'Come on then,' Berg said before calmly turning and walking away. As though he remained in charge. The man certainly had gall.

Ryker kept his eyes busy as they walked, Berg two steps ahead. He saw no movement in the trees or within the clearing. He was almost certain everyone with Berg had already been involved in the fight. Almost certain, but he still needed caution. They reached the front entrance. Berg didn't pause. He opened the door and stepped inside. Ryker moved in behind him. A quick glance over his shoulder. Pettersen remained in place, in control.

Berg stopped and turned.

'So?'

'Room by room,' Ryker said. 'Keep it slow. Keep your hands where I can see them.'

Berg turned and got to it. Ryker followed his every step. Berg remained calm and somewhat nonchalant, but as the seconds passed Ryker also realised Berg had no secret plan. No ambush.

The second-to-last room they came to was a bedroom. Ryker jumped in surprise when he realised someone was in there already. His finger twitched on the trigger before he processed the woman, slumped in the corner. Handcuffed to a radiator.

'My wife,' Berg said without apology. 'It's a long story.'

'You might need to try harder than that,' Ryker said.

'I haven't laid a finger on her,' Berg said. 'The Russians attacked us both tonight. We were lucky to get away from them alive. Now they have my son. I *will* get him back.'

Ryker ignored that comment. Was Berg really intent on holding that line?

'None of that explains why she's handcuffed in here,' Ryker said.

Berg sighed. 'Darling, will you please tell this man what happened?'

She lifted her head. Her eyes were bloodshot. Her hatred clear. She said nothing.

'Release her,' Ryker said. 'Release her now.'

Berg glared. 'And then what?'

'I don't give a crap. She can put the kettle on. She can run through the forest to wherever. But I'm not leaving her like that.'

'You don't even know her.'

'Do it now.'

Berg sighed. 'The key is in the lounge.'

The only room they hadn't been to.

'After you,' Ryker said.

They moved on through. Ryker became aware of increased chatter outside. He moved to the window and pulled aside the sheet that acted as a curtain and peeked out. No problem. Pettersen had the crew lined up on the floor, on their knees, hands above their heads. She wouldn't be able to watch over them indefinitely, alone, but she wouldn't need to. Ryker was almost done.

'Here's the key,' Berg said.

He tossed it over. Ryker didn't make an attempt to catch it. The key clattered off him and to the ground.

'You do it,' Ryker said, intent on keeping both hands on the gun as long as he could.

Berg grumbled but didn't move. Then, 'I told you he wasn't here.'

'Where's Wold?' Ryker asked.

'Why would I know?'

Berg's phone vibrated in his pocket. Ryker wondered if it was the very man himself.

'Can I take that?'

Ryker thought for a second.

'If anything other than a phone comes out of your pocket, the shot will be to your balls. Got it?'

Berg paused. Then pushed his hand into his pocket. Drew out his phone. His face turned. Disgust.

'Who is it?' Ryker asked.

'Who do you think? The Russians.'

'Answer it. Put it on speaker.'

Berg hesitated, but then did so.

'We have him,' came the drawl through the tinny speaker. 'We have the boy.'

'Where?' Berg said.

'At your factory. You have one hour or he's dead. And then we'll come back for you and your wife and finish what we started.'

The line clicked off.

Berg looked to Ryker. They held each other's eye.

'So?' Berg said.

'So get the key. Free your wife. Then we go and get Henrik back.'

'We?'

'Unless you want to go alone?'

Berg shook his head and scoffed. 'This is a crazy fucking night.'

'You got that right,' Ryker said.

43

Three cars made up the convoy. Erling, Sonja and one other man were up front in the Nissan pickup. Three more men were in the older, more battered Toyota pickup behind. Pettersen's patrol vehicle took up the middle spot. She drove, once more. Next to her up front was Berg, with Ryker sitting behind Pettersen, his eyes on Berg and only Berg. He didn't trust him, but he did trust that at least he wasn't working with the Russians, even if he still didn't fully understand what was at play between the parties, nor who Henrik really was.

'What happened to you and your wife?' Ryker asked.

She remained at the house. Uncuffed now, though with the remaining contingent of Berg's gang watching over her. For her protection, or to keep her captive? Ryker really didn't know. Would those guys even put up much of a fight if this entire trip was a ruse by the Russians so they could go back to the house and annihilate anyone left there?

No, those men were battered already, it wouldn't be much of a fight, but why would the Russians – if they had Henrik, the asset – want to do that in any case?

'I asked you a question,' Ryker said.

'It's a long story.'

'Then give me the short version.'

Berg sighed. Because he was building up to it, or because he was thinking of how to lie?

'We haven't been good for a long time. I thought she was having an affair. But the man she was with was actually a lawyer.'

'You hired a private investigator,' Ryker said.

'And the Russians killed him.'

'Why would they do that?'

'To put pressure on me. They found out about Henrik. They also found out that my wife and Tronstad – the lawyer – were trying to find dirt on me. They figured out about Henrik too. My wife wanted any dirt she could find about me. My personal life, my business life. The Russians cut Tronstad apart getting him to talk. Skinned him to find out what he knew.'

The last words were slightly choked, with what Ryker felt was genuine emotion, even if he didn't fully understand the Russians' actions based on Berg's explanation. Tronstad, if he was nothing but an everyday guy, a lawyer, likely would have spilled whatever he knew with the lightest pressure. He didn't need to be skinned to talk. So had Berg lied about something, or were the Russians – or at least one of them – basic sociopaths?

'They would have killed my wife too...' Berg said. 'I'm not sure about me. They need me. They need my business. That's why they're here. But they don't have to kill me to hurt me.'

'They're blackmailing you?'

'It's a bit more complicated than that.'

'No. Not really. If what you're saying is true–'

'Of course it's true!' Berg blasted, turning around in his chair to glare at Ryker. 'This isn't the sort of thing anyone would make up. I *saw* what they did to Tronstad. That would have been Isabell. If Erling and the others hadn't saved me then I'm sure the Russians would have tortured me, too, even if they wouldn't have killed me. You said there were dead bodies in Trondheim? Tell me about that. That's why you're here now, isn't it? You saw what they do, and you want revenge.'

Were Ryker's intentions that obvious? Images flashed in his mind of the bloodbath in Trondheim. Berg smiled, apparently pleased with his own deduction.

'Those Russians are everyone's enemies here,' Berg said. 'We can stop them.'

'And then what?'

No response from Berg.

'And then what?' Ryker asked again.

'I don't understand what you mean.'

'We deal with the Russians tonight. Get Henrik back. And then what? The Russians here, they're it? Just three of them, their own little empire?'

'No. It's not the three of them. Of course it isn't.'

'So what happens next? Their boss sends more people over. Another wave. Another after that if needed.'

'Let's worry about the future another time,' Pettersen said. 'We're here.'

Ryker hadn't been looking out of the windows at the darkened scenery at all. For all he knew they could have travelled in any direction, could have been anywhere. What he saw as they came over a rise in the road was a large, mainly corrugated steel structure looming in the near distance, sitting behind a high security fence. A series of lights provided illumination across the building's grounds, but he saw nothing but blackness beyond – the sea?

'You know this place?' Ryker asked Pettersen.

'Of course.'

'It looks quiet.'

'It's the middle of the night,' Berg said, as though Ryker was an idiot.

'Just two cars, I see.'

Two cars. Three Russians. And Henrik. Hopefully.

'You don't have night shifts?' Ryker said. 'No night-time security staff?'

'No,' Berg said. 'Anyone here already is with them.'

'How would they even get access?'

'I don't know.'

Ryker wasn't sure he believed that, but he also didn't know why Berg would withhold on him now.

The car in front rolled to a stop by the closed gates.

'So come on, Ryker, what's the plan this time?' Pettersen said, pulling up too.

Ryker thought, but said nothing.

'Let me guess, we walk right in and get the job done?'

Without seeing her face he really couldn't be sure whether she was mocking him or not.

'Three men wait on the outside,' Ryker said. 'In case anyone else shows up. The rest of us go inside. Two up front, two at the back. Me and Berg in the middle.'

'And the guns?' Pettersen asked.

'Not for me. One up front, one at the back.'

No one said anything.

'Agreed?' Ryker asked.

'Why not,' Berg said.

Up ahead, Sonja opened the gates and once her car was moving again, Pettersen followed them in. The three cars parked in a row, the opposite side of the forecourt to the two cars already there.

Everyone stepped out. Ryker took a deep inhale of fresh, sea air. Cold, but it helped to clear his head a little. Not for the first time tonight the unknown lay ahead, but for once he at least had numbers on his side. Unless he'd read the whole situation backward.

He looked about the place. Certainly the darkened grounds had plenty of places for people to hide out, though Ryker spotted nothing to worry him. He saw it as unlikely that the Russians had an entire other army of men, loyal to them, disloyal to Berg.

Ryker remained silent as Berg and Pettersen quietly corralled the troops. Soon Pettersen came up to him.

'We're ready,' she said.

Ryker nodded. 'Let's go.'

He looked over to Erling. The big man glared at him. Anger and venom. Clearly he didn't like that Ryker had bettered him earlier – kind of, anyway. But for now they were on the same side. Ryker would remain wary. Of all of them. The only person in the group he truly believed to be on his side was Pettersen, and even with her he wouldn't trust her one hundred per cent. She was still one of them. A local. He was the outsider.

As were the Russians.

They moved off in formation. Sonja – gun in hand – at the front with Erling. Pettersen – gun in hand – and some other guy at the back. Ryker walked next to Berg.

'The side entrance,' Berg said.

He didn't say which side, but they all veered off to the left. Clearly the others all knew this place a lot better than Ryker did.

The side door – closed – came into sight and Sonja stopped and swung around, stooping low to point the barrel of her shotgun into the darkness.

Everyone else paused. A few murmurs of disquiet.

'There's nothing there,' Ryker said.

That received a glower and a mumbling rebuke from Sonja and Erling though Ryker didn't understand the Norwegian.

They carried on to the door. Erling opened it. Light spilled out from within. Sonja, gun held out, stepped in first. Everyone else paused. As though waiting for the sound of gunfire or some other indication of what lay beyond. Nothing. Erling moved in next. Ryker grabbed Berg, holding on to the back of his coat to push him forward and keep him close. Insurance. A human shield. Whichever, Ryker didn't care for Berg, even if they were on the same side right now. Kind of.

He pushed Berg over the threshold. Took in the space in front of him. A big space. Warehouse, factory, offices, all in one. The area directly in front of them was cleared and well lit. Polished concrete floor. Two men on their feet: the Russians. Henrik was on his knees in front of them. A cloth gag in his mouth. Hands behind his back. The shorter of the Russians – Bulldog – had a gleaming knife in his hand, a few inches from Henrik.

'Good evening,' the taller man said with a callous smile as he took in the new arrivals. His smile faltered a little when he looked at Ryker, then again when he clocked Pettersen, still in her police uniform.

'Quite a party now,' he said.

His little bulldog grinned. Or was it a grimace?

The last man in closed the door. Ryker and the others all stood in a line looking to the enemy.

'I don't believe we've been properly introduced,' the tall man said, fixing his gaze on Ryker.

'Not yet,' Ryker said.

'My name is Valeri Sychev. This is my associate, Andrey.'

'Nice to put a name to a face.'

'And you are?'

'James Ryker. Or Carl Logan. Call me whatever you want.'

A raised eyebrow from Sychev.

'Where's the other one?' Berg asked.

Sychev's smile broadened. 'Konstantin?' Then a shake of the head. 'I've really tried very hard, but it's so difficult to get him to do what I ask. He's so.... primal.'

Sychev turned and called out to the darkened area behind him.

A scrape and a scratch echoed and then came squeaking. Old wheels turning. Ryker remained rooted, at the ready, but to his left and right he sensed growing nerves, shuffling of feet.

Out of the dark... Ryker sucked in a breath. A trolley. Pushed by a man. On the trolley... It took Ryker several beats to understand what he saw.

A big, bloody, pulpy mess. Raw, lacerated flesh.

A person. Definitely a person, though almost unidentifiable. The madman pushing the trolley wore nothing but a pair of jeans. The skin of his muscular torso was lined with scars and streaked with blood.

His eyes...

Ryker shivered.

Konstantin stopped. He tipped the trolley up and the heap of flesh slid off and plopped to the floor where it lay unmoving. Ryker flinched at the horrific sight and sound. Whoever the lump was, they were dead. But they'd suffered horribly before their final breath. Death, most likely, had come as a welcome relief.

'What have you done?' Berg gasped.

Sychev and Andrey didn't look in the least bit moved. Konstantin... he didn't look anything. He had nothing there, no emotion at all.

'You should be thanking me, Sigurd,' Sychev said. 'This man was working against you. Trying to ruin everything for you.'

Another gasp from Berg, as though he'd just figured out who it was, then, 'Marius?'

'A worm of a man. Not like you. Not like me. Do you know he even let us in here tonight? He knew what we were planning for you, but he let us in here anyway. How could you ever have trusted a man like that?'

No one said anything. Ryker looked to Pettersen. To Erling. Shock. That was the main reaction he saw. Shock, and fear. Yet Ryker and the others had the numbers. Had guns too. They couldn't let the advantage slip.

'Give us the boy,' Ryker said. 'That's all we came here for.'

Sychev scoffed. 'That might be why you're here, but I'm sure you don't speak for everyone.'

'Give us the boy,' Pettersen said, pointing her gun to Sychev.

No reaction at all from the Russians to the threat.

'You can have him when our business is concluded,' Sychev said.

'You know who he is, right?' Ryker said.

'Henrik? Yes, we've been told.'

'Then give this man his son back. Whatever business you have, it doesn't involve Henrik.'

Doubt now in Sychev's eyes. Doubt, and confusion.

'His son?'

Berg shuffled. 'Just give us the boy. Then we can talk.'

Then Sychev laughed. Loud, and long. Ryker had doubted Berg's claim. Now he was certain Henrik wasn't Berg's son. So who was he?

'Go and get him,' Sychev said, turning to Konstantin, then back to Berg. 'You're even more sneaky than I imagined.'

Konstantin went to move away. 'Don't move!' Pettersen shouted.

'I'm sorry, lady,' Sychev said, 'but this is important.'

Pettersen looked to Ryker. He looked to Sychev.

'Go and get who?' Ryker said.

'You'll see.'

Ryker nodded to Pettersen. She pulled the gun down, just enough to make it clear Konstantin could move. He disappeared into the dark once more.

Sychev focused on Berg. 'Have you lied to everyone here, or only to your new friend?'

Ryker turned to Berg. The guy looked like... well, he looked like he'd been found out. Ryker clenched his teeth in anger, even though he'd suspected as much.

'Henrik isn't his son,' Sychev said. 'He's the son of Erik Rosen.'

'Who the fuck is Erik Rosen?' Ryker asked, not bothered about hiding his irritation.

Sychev tutted. 'You really should have done your homework before befriending this man. Rosen is his competitor. It's that simple. Your good friend here is nothing but a... a megalomaniac. I love that word! He kidnapped the poor boy to blackmail his competitor. This is about money, pure and simple.'

'No,' Berg said, shaking his head in defiance.

'No? We could always ask the man himself.' Sychev looked behind him. 'He's here too. In a little better shape than poor Marius, I should say. After all, Erik still has value–'

'No,' Berg said, managing a manic cackle.

Everyone in the room stood in silence. A turning point? Sychev certainly looked a little less certain of himself given the conviction in Berg's taunt.

'He's not my son,' Berg said looking at Ryker. 'I told you what you needed to hear.' He faced Sychev. 'And I'm sorry but he's not Rosen's son either.'

'Then who the fuck is he?' Erling said, sounding impatient. A little bit angry. Ryker understood the sentiment. What the hell was going on?

'He's Jesper's son, you piece of shit,' Berg said. He stepped back, his face screwed in anger. 'Kill them!'

He looked to Pettersen, then to Sonja. Both were hesitant...

But then both lifted their weapons...

'Now,' Sychev said, absolute calm, despite his predicament.

The lights flicked off and the room plunged into darkness.

44

A shotgun blast to Ryker's left – Pettersen. Then another to his right from Sonja. A flash of fire erupted with each shot, lighting up the space in front of him in strobe for a fraction of a second each time.

Then blackness. Shouting, screaming. Thuds. Cracks.

Carnage.

Ryker stepped back. Air whirled around him. A cry of pain nearby. He swivelled left, then right. Reached out, thinking someone was right by him. Thin air. Where was Berg?

Thud.

Someone on the floor right next to him.

Then another shout of pain a little further away. Ryker moved that way. Why? Why not keep going back until he hit something solid? The wall?

Because he wasn't there to cower. He was there to help.

Something, someone brushed against his side. He spun, reached out... Nothing.

Another blast of a shotgun. Another flash as the room lit up momentarily. People... bodies.

Darkness once more.

A blood-curdling cry.

Thudding.

'Get the lights!' Ryker shouted out. 'Pettersen, get the damn lights back on.'

Before we're all dead, he thought, but didn't add.

A few seconds later...

The lights flicked back on, just as a blur of movement raced right in front of Ryker. Andrey, the little bulldog. Ryker bent at his knees, pushed his weight to his toes, ready to move.

Click.

The lights went off again.

Andrey smashed into Ryker. They ended up on the deck. Ryker could see nothing, but felt and heard Andrey. Breathing. Snarling. Ryker took a blow to the side. Used his fists and his elbows to try and retaliate and try to find the space to get the man off him.

A blow to Ryker's face burst his lip open and he swallowed blood. He heaved and groaned and lifted Andrey and slid out from underneath. He winced when a shock of pain pulsed across his chest. A slash from a knife?

Click.

The lights were on again. Blaring. Ryker squinted, trying to get his focus. He and Andrey were both on their feet. Andrey rushed forward again. The edge of the knife swung for Ryker's throat. He craned his neck back. The blade nicked him. He grabbed Andrey's forearm, used the natural momentum of the deflected blow, pivoted the arm at the elbow and pushed hard and fast... he heard – felt – a suck and squelch and Andrey inhaled sharply as the blade sank into his neck, just below his ear. Three, four inches of metal disappeared.

Ryker let go. Andrey, eyes bulging, dropped to his knees as he clutched the knife handle with both hands. He yanked it out and a spurt of blood erupted.

He collapsed to the ground.

Ryker went to grab for the discarded weapon, but found himself momentarily distracted, looking around.

Bodies and blood everywhere. Pettersen remained standing. Gun in hand, backed up in a corner by the light switches. Erling was down, badly injured, blood all over him, but breathing. Sonja was down and wouldn't ever get up given the blood-spilling hole in her neck. Berg... where the hell was Berg?

Sychev remained in place. Henrik was there, too, on his feet, Sychev behind him, knife to his throat.

No Berg. No Konstantin. Konstantin, who Ryker was sure was responsible for the majority of the carnage he saw.

Ryker glanced to Pettersen.

'You loaded?' he asked her.

She shook her head. Couldn't she have lied?

The other shotgun remained in Sonja's death grip.

'Let Henrik go,' Ryker said, taking a step toward Sychev who shook his head.

'Move again and I'll slit his throat.'

'No. You won't,' Ryker said, defying the order.

Sychev stepped back, dragging Henrik with him. Ryker saw, out of the corner of his eye, Pettersen moving too.

'Jesper's your boss, isn't he?' Ryker said, putting the pieces together.

No answer.

'I bet he didn't know he had a son here, in Blodstein.'

'No closer. I'm serious.'

'You're going to slit the throat of your boss's son? I've never met Jesper, but given the types who work for him, I'm imagining he might not like it if his son gets hurt.'

'Hey.'

The voice came from behind Ryker. He twisted.

Coming in through the open door... Berg, knife at his neck. Konstantin held the blade.

'He tried to run,' Konstantin said.

Ryker was sure he saw Pettersen roll her eyes. Konstantin pushed Berg forward, moving further into the room. Pettersen shifted around them, giving them a wide berth, herself edging back closer to the door now, to block it?

'So what now, smart guy?' Sychev said to Ryker.

'Let Henrik go. Whatever is happening here, you don't have to hurt him.'

'I'm sorry, but you see, the problem is, no one outside of this room even knows who this boy is.'

Ryker hadn't thought of it like that.

'Jesper doesn't know he has a son,' Sychev said. Confident, but angry too. Angry at Berg, Pettersen, Ryker, all of them. He wanted to punish them. 'If all of you die here tonight, Jesper doesn't ever have to know.'

Was he bluffing?

'Ryker, now!' Pettersen shouted.

Click. Darkness again. Not the greatest plan, but Ryker took the opportunity. He darted forward. Collided with a body. Too hefty to be Henrik. They collapsed to the ground. Ryker grabbed the head and smashed it into the concrete. Did it again.

A shout of pain, from behind him, before the lights came back on.

Beneath Ryker, Sychev's body was limp. Still breathing, but he wasn't getting up in a hurry. Ryker jumped up. Spun around. Berg, on the floor across the other side, held his hands to a bloody wound in his gut.

Henrik was on the floor next to Ryker, grimacing as he tried to prop himself up. Pettersen was by the door, hunched over, shotgun on the floor, she clutched at her arm. Knife wound?

'I'm fine,' she said. 'He went out.'

Konstantin. Ryker wouldn't let him get away. Not after what he'd done.

Ryker went to take a step forward.

'Aaaahhh!'

He jumped back around.

Henrik dove forward, on top of Sychev, his bound hands clutching the handle of the knife which he plunged into Sychev's chest. He pulled it out and stabbed again.

Ryker was lost for a moment. He hadn't expected that... viciousness. Anger, hatred, and violence in Henrik's eyes...

'Don't let him get away,' Henrik said to Ryker, his words an angry sneer.

Ryker said nothing. He glanced once to Sychev's corpse, then rushed for the door.

Berg was in a bad way, but still alive. Did Ryker trust Henrik in the same room as the man who'd kidnapped him?

No.

'Watch Henrik,' Ryker said to Pettersen.

He noticed the slash on the sleeve of her coat. Long, probably a deep cut given the pain she was clearly in, but she wasn't in serious trouble. Could she stop Henrik if he went to attack Berg?

Ryker pushed the thought away.

He rushed outside then stopped. Darkness. He waited for a couple of seconds to let his eyes adjust. Not as dark as the warehouse had been. To his left the lights remained on in the forecourt, and the moon was visible through the thin clouds in the night sky. Ryker scanned. He saw no movement by the parked cars. All five remained in place. But he spotted three bodies there. The guys from Berg's crew who were supposed to have kept watch. Not their fault. They hadn't been ready for someone like Konstantin.

The faintest of noises from behind Ryker.

He spun. Nothing he could see. He edged forward. Forklift truck. A sea crate. Wooden pallets.

A flash of movement. Between two piles of pallets.

Ryker stopped and listened and watched.

Engine noise behind him now. He glanced. Two headlights pointed his way, from the other side of the security fence. What the hell? Someone joining the party?

Noise again.

Ryker spun. Saw the outline of the figure five yards in front.

He wasn't expecting the flying dagger. Ryker winced as the blade thudded into his thigh. He shouted with equal anger and pain as he yanked the knife out.

There he was, rushing forward.

'Now I have your knife,' Ryker said, ready to tackle the onrushing beast. Except at the last second the shape shifted across and disappeared into the blackness.

An illusion? Ryker was sure Konstantin had been rushing toward him.

He spun left, right. No Konstantin. He looked behind him. No headlights now either. Where had they gone? Whoever *they* were...

He moved forward, further away from the light. Further toward the gentle lapping of water – the only sound he could make out above his own breathing, and the slap of blood on concrete as the liquid dripped off the end of the knife.

Ryker moved between two piles of pallets. A corridor, several yards long. He reached the end. The edge of the dock gave way to water.

A rush of air behind him. Or so he'd thought. But when Ryker spun he could see nothing there.

Just the wind? He carefully retraced his steps toward the factory. Reached the end of the pallets again.

Behind him. This time he was certain. He spun around.

Except Konstantin wasn't on the ground, but flying through the air, off the top of the pallets. He clattered into Ryker. They both tumbled. Ryker had the focus to swipe with the knife as they fell and he caught the Russian on his side. Enough to knock the guy's focus, and causing them to land on the ground apart from each other.

They were soon both back to their feet, but even despite the blow, the Russian was quicker than Ryker. He stooped low and slashed with another knife that caught Ryker on his lower leg.

Ryker turned. Where had he gone?

Another stab of pain on the back of his other leg. Ryker had to fight to stay on his feet. He turned the other way. Nothing. Konstantin was everywhere and nowhere. A scrape across Ryker's back this time and he imagined the skin and flesh parting. He reeled forward in shock, his body tense as pain shot through him.

Finally he saw him. Knife twisting forward. Ryker only partly deflected the blow. The blade scraped his arm but he concentrated on getting his man once and for all. He drove forward and plunged the knife into Konstantin's side. Took the Russian by the throat. Plunged the knife again and they collapsed to the floor, Ryker on top.

He straddled the stricken man. Ryker trusted his aim. The damage he'd caused to Konstantin's kidneys... survival was unlikely. But he wasn't dead yet. With his face cast in the light coming from the open factory door, Ryker saw no defeat in his eyes. He still looked calm, in control.

Doubt flashed in Ryker's mind...

Boom.

He jumped in shock. Not just at the noise but at the spatter that covered his face. He wiped his eyes. His mouth. Blood and sinew and brain and bone. He looked down at the mess which a second ago had been Konstantin's head.

'Get up,' came the call from his right.

Ryker looked over. Wold, shotgun in hand.

'Drop the knife, then get off him, or you'll end up just the same.'

Ryker did as he was told.

His body ached. The wounds he'd taken throbbed and ached. He was losing blood too, light-headedness worsening with each beat of his heart.

'I knew you were bad news,' Wold said, stepping toward Ryker.

'No, don't.'

Pettersen. Still clutching her arm, she stumbled out of the factory. Wold glanced to her but didn't move the gun from Ryker.

'Please,' she said. 'He's not one of them.'

But Wold was one of *them*. In bed with Berg.

'Where's Sigurd?' Wold asked, looking at Ryker.

'Sigurd's dead,' Pettersen said.

Ryker slumped a little.

'They're all dead,' Pettersen said. 'Except for us, and Henrik.'

On cue, Henrik stepped out at Pettersen's side. No knife now, his hands were unbound and by his sides. Had Berg succumbed to his injuries or had Henrik finished him off too?

'It's done here, Wold,' Ryker said. 'Whatever hold Berg had over you, it's finished now.'

Wold's eyes narrowed – anger. Clearly he didn't like Ryker's insinuation of his corruption, but the fact he didn't try to argue against it suggested Ryker was spot on.

'He's right,' Pettersen said. 'It's okay now. Everything's going to be okay.'

Wold looked like he really didn't believe that at all, but after a few seconds of tense stand-off, he finally lowered the gun, as Ryker collapsed to his knees.

45

Despite his injuries, Ryker stayed on the scene for several hours, though kept well back from the action, well back from the growing crowd of police and paramedics that grew as night wore on to morning, and as the sun rose low in the east. By that point Ryker, wounds dressed and body full of drugs, had taken a position alone, by the edge of the water, watching Pettersen. About thirty yards away, she spoke with two plain-clothed men who Ryker presumed were police, given their looks and their stiff manners and the way Pettersen held herself with them – though Ryker was sure they, and most of the others who had arrived, weren't local, but from a central command further afield. The fact alone that they'd taken nearly two hours to get to the factory was a giveaway.

Pettersen glanced over and in doing so drew the attention of the two men. Ryker carried on staring. Eventually the men turned and headed for the warehouse, and Pettersen slowly walked over.

'You're shivering,' she said to Ryker.

'A warm shower would be nice.'

'I can't believe you're still here. I can't believe you're still awake and not in a hospital bed.'

'I'm kind of used to it.'

She looked curious but didn't say anything more to that.

'You should go. There's nothing more you can do tonight. This morning, whatever it is now.'

'I'm free to go?'

Her eyes narrowed. 'You don't think you should be?'

'Those bigwigs don't want to talk to me?'

'Bigwigs?'

'The out-of-town police.'

She looked over her shoulder, as though expecting them to be there.

'I'm sure they will. But you're not under arrest, and there's no reason to keep you here. Why don't you go to town. Back to the guest house and get a few hours' sleep.'

'I don't have a car. I came here with you, remember.'

She sighed, but then her face relaxed. Not a smile, but not far from it.

'Come on,' she said. 'I'll give you a ride.'

They didn't go to the guest house. Despite their tiredness, Ryker knew they were both also hungry. The café was open with a small number of punters enjoying breakfast and coffee.

Ryker and Pettersen received suspicious glances from all around. Perhaps because of the bandages and the state of their clothes, all bloodied and dirtied and mussy. Perhaps because Ryker, the outsider, sat down to eat with a local police officer, or, most likely, Ryker decided, because everyone in the close-knit town already knew most of what had happened at the factory, even if Ryker still struggled to get his head around it all.

'We wouldn't have this outcome if not for you,' Pettersen said.

Ryker didn't know how to take that. The three Russians were dead. So, too, was Berg and a number of other locals. Was that in any way a good achievement?

'Do you know who Jesper is?' Ryker asked.

Pettersen shook her head. 'I've never heard that name until now.'

'He clearly has a connection to this town.'

'You really believe he's Henrik's father?'

'I believe he's the kind of man who has assassins and gangsters working for him. Who sends people overseas to extort and torture and kill. And you said yourself the Russians have a long history here.'

A little bit of colour drained from Pettersen's cheeks.

'You think he'll send more people here now?' she asked.

'I think he's not going to be very happy with how tonight went.'

'But he won't know anything about Henrik.'

Fair point. Berg had – probably very deliberately – kept the truth of Henrik's parentage to himself. His plan of extortion hadn't gone to plan, far from it, and in his death, and the deaths of Jesper's henchmen, the secret remained a secret, at least to Jesper.

'Not yet, he doesn't. But, in my experience, secrets like that have a habit of coming out one way or another.'

Pettersen didn't say anything. Their food arrived. Both tucked in, the silence extended and grew more awkward.

'What will you do now?' Pettersen asked after a while, a certain sadness, apprehension in her question.

'Shower and sleep.'

She smiled but it didn't last long. 'You know what I mean.'

'I don't know yet.'

'You saved Henrik. You brought down the bad guys. Nothing for you here anymore, I guess.'

She held his eye as she spoke. He wasn't sure if there was a hidden insinuation to her words or not, whether she hoped for a correction. Was there anything in Blodstein for him? Well, there was *her*.

They carried on eating. Ryker finished his plate without another word spoken. Pettersen still had more than half of hers left when she put her knife and fork down. Nothing like a night of bloodshed and near death to spoil an appetite.

'It'll be me to tell the families,' she said, even more stoic than before. She shook her head. 'So much pain.'

Ryker had no answer to that. He hadn't known Erling, Sonja, the others, except in a combative sense, but, of course, they'd each have loved ones. The unseen innocents always suffered.

'I can sense you're going to beat yourself up about this,' Ryker said. 'But you shouldn't. None of this, none of the pain or the death, was caused by you or me. Berg, the Russians, Erling, Sonja, they all made choices. Bad choices, if you ask me.'

'You're saying they all deserved to die?'

Anger now.

'No,' Ryker said. 'Not all of them. But their deaths aren't on you. You were fighting for the right side. Just remember that.'

She looked out of the window but said nothing.

'Have you heard the one about the bank robber and the Norwegian?' she said, turning back to him, her face still downcast.

'I don't think so.'

'It's the Wild West. A hooded robber bursts into a bank and forces the tellers to load a sack full of cash. On his way out the door, a brave customer grabs the hood and pulls it off, revealing the robber's face. The robber shoots the customer in a flash. He looks around and notices one of the tellers looking straight at him. The robber instantly shoots him also. Everyone in the bank, by now very scared, looks intently down at the floor in silence. The robber yells, *Well, did anyone else see my face?* Silence. Everyone is too afraid to speak. Then, an old Norwegian lady tentatively raises her hand and says, *My husband got a pretty good look at you*.'

She tried not to smile but it didn't work, especially as Ryker grinned back at her.

'Good one,' he said, though he wondered whether the joke had come to her mind due to some sort of corollary with the Bergs' rocky marriage, which had hardly helped the situation come to a happy end, even if Isabell had survived.

Pettersen's phone blipped. She picked it up and stared at the screen.

'I need to go,' she said.

She got to her feet.

'Don't worry,' Ryker said. 'I'll pay.'

'No need. We always eat here for free.'

She nodded over to the waitress in acknowledgement, then glanced back down to Ryker.

'You'll still be here later?' she said.

'In the café?'

'No. In Blodstein.'

A pleading look in her eyes.

Ryker nodded.

She turned and headed for the door.

———

An hour later Ryker was sitting on the wall by the crossroads, hands in his coat pockets, his head huddled down. With a grey sky above letting no sunlight through, the morning felt colder than any other he'd experienced in Blodstein, and that was saying something. Perhaps his tiredness and his injuries had sapped his resistance.

Across the road a figure turned onto the pavement from a side street. Slight, not very tall, hood over the head, Ryker thought it was a young woman at first, but as the figure neared he realised who it was. Henrik. Without properly looking up, he found his way to Ryker's side where he turned and propped himself up against the wall.

'You're waiting for the bus,' Henrik said.

'Yeah,' Ryker said.

'A long wait. It only comes three times a day.'

'Not long to go now.'

'Do they know you're leaving?'

Ryker presumed 'they' meant police. Either way, he didn't answer.

'Where are you going to?'

'South.'

'Out of Norway?'

'Eventually.'

Silence for a few moments. An old man and woman approached further down the street. They were a few yards away when they stopped, pondered, then crossed the road to the other side. Deliberate?

'This all happened because of who my dad is,' Henrik said.

'I think so.'

'Do you know him? Jesper?'

'Never met him. But I can imagine the type.'

Ryker glanced to his side. Henrik stared with curiosity but didn't ask what Ryker had meant.

'He's not a good man, is he?'

'Hard to imagine he is, given what happened here.'

'Will you try to find him?'

Ryker held his eye until the boy looked away. He could only

imagine the conflicting thoughts going through his head. His whole world had been turned upside down, but he'd also been involved in carnage and death and... had himself killed. A turning point for sure. Which direction would his life take now? A long, dark path lay in front of him. But it wasn't the only path.

'Sorry,' Henrik said. 'I just thought... that's maybe what you do. Track down the bad guys wherever you go. Make them pay.'

Ryker sighed. He closed his eyes for a couple of beats. Willing his mind not to take him where he thought Henrik wanted him to go. He knew the more he thought about it, thought about Jesper and the devastation his actions and commands had caused, the more he'd want to make amends.

'Would you come with me?' Henrik asked.

Ryker didn't answer.

'If I told you now, I'm leaving here. I'm going to Russia. I'm going to find Jesper, my father, and kill him for what he's done. Would you come with me? Help me? Protect me?'

Ryker looked back to him. 'You don't want to do that.'

Henrik glowered. 'Don't I? Look at what he's done.'

'By all means, leave this place,' Ryker said. 'Perhaps it's best if you do. You have nothing here. But if you go after Jesper now, most likely you'll end up hurt. Dead. Even if you don't, even if you do somehow manage to find him, take your revenge, the story doesn't end there. It never does.'

'But if I had you to help me–'

'If you had me... you'd only be drawn to even more bad shit. That's the way it is.'

'That's why you're running?'

'I'm not running.'

'Going from place to place. No home. No friends.'

Ryker said nothing.

'So not Jesper. Not yet. But I could still come with you. Wherever it is you're going.'

Ryker had to admire his tenacity. And resilience. Bravery. And even though he was sure that he had so much he could teach someone young like Henrik about the world, about life, he was also sure... no, Ryker really didn't know what he was sure of. He just knew a fourteen-year-old boy had no place by his side.

'Sorry, kid.'

Ryker looked off to the left. Movement. A car. A police car. It pulled to a stop by the side of the road across the other side of the junction. No one got out. Ryker kept his eyes focused on the windscreen. Pettersen?

'You like her,' Henrik said.

Ryker didn't answer. The sound of a chugging diesel engine filled the air. Ryker looked the other way and spotted the bus coming toward them. He got to his feet. Henrik moved alongside him. The bus pulled to a stop and the doors opened. Ryker looked to Henrik and simply shook his head.

'Sorry,' he said.

The boy sank a little and shuffled back. Ryker glanced the other way. Pettersen stepped out of her car, but she didn't come toward him. She hung off the open door as Ryker moved onto the bus.

He paid and took a seat in the near empty space.

When he looked out, Henrik had already gone. Where to Ryker had no clue. Would Henrik be safe now? Ryker really didn't know, but whatever Jesper did or didn't know about his biological son, Henrik surely wasn't the kingpin's enemy.

A hiss as the doors clanked shut, and a plume of diesel smoke wrapped around the back of the bus as it shuffled forward.

Ryker caught Pettersen's eye. She stared right at him. Disappointment, more than anything, etched on her face. He felt bad. Guilty. A little sad for them both. He lifted his hand in a sort of a wave. She hesitated but did the same.

Moments later she was out of sight behind him.

———

The grey sky above remained as Ryker walked along the harbour front in Trondheim, though the air was filled with sleet which blasted into Ryker's face from the sea. The ferry had arrived. Ten more minutes until departure. He had a ticket in his pocket but remained torn as to whether he'd made the right decision.

He stopped a few steps from the foot entrance. Cars and lorries slowly crept along toward the hull that was wide open like a whale swallowing shoals of fish.

He took out his phone. Went to the call option. Only Pettersen's number in this handset. But what would he say if he called? Only hours ago he'd walked away from her. For good. Was he about to turn around now and head back?

As much as part of him wanted to, no, he wasn't.

Then there was Heidi, the happy chatty redhead he'd encountered on the ferry over here. He still remembered her number. Certainly her company, if he stayed here any longer, would make a refreshing change to the last few days of carnage...

No. Not her either.

Simona, back in Prague. No. He was done there too.

Despite everything, it was Pettersen's number his finger slowly typed out. Then promptly deleted. No. He liked her. He liked so much about her in fact, but the long, quiet, boring drive from Blodstein to here had made him realise one thing; everything he liked about Pettersen was because she reminded him so much of someone else. Not Angela, no one would ever match her and how she'd changed him. Pettersen reminded him of Sam Moreno.

Should Ryker have left her? Was he really protecting her by being away from her?

He subconsciously typed out her number as his brain rumbled. His fingertip hovered over the green button, waiting.

A man called out to him. Norwegian. He didn't understand the words. He looked across. An orange-jacketed man standing by the ferry beckoned to him.

'Are you coming?' he shouted out, English now. 'Last chance.'

Ryker sighed as he cleared the number, then stuffed the phone back in his pocket.

With one last look over his shoulder, one last thought of what, and who, he was leaving behind, he stepped on board.

THE END

ABOUT THE AUTHOR

Rob specialised in forensic fraud investigations at a global accounting firm for thirteen years. He began writing in 2009 following a promise to his wife, an avid reader, that he could pen an 'unputdownable' thriller. Since then, Rob has sold over a million copies of his critically acclaimed and bestselling thrillers in the Enemy, James Ryker and Sleeper series. His work has received widespread critical acclaim, with many reviewers and readers likening Rob's work to authors at the very top of the genre, including Lee Child and Vince Flynn.

Originally from the North East of England, Rob has lived and worked in a number of fast-paced cities, including New York, and is now settled in the West Midlands with his wife and young sons.

Rob's website is www.robsinclairauthor.com and he can be followed on twitter at @rsinclairauthor and facebook at www.facebook.com/robsinclairauthor

A NOTE FROM THE PUBLISHER

Thank you for reading this book. If you enjoyed it please do consider leaving a review on Amazon to help others find it too.

We hate typos. All of our books have been rigorously edited and proofread, but sometimes mistakes do slip through. If you have spotted a typo, please do let us know and we can get it amended within hours.

info@bloodhoundbooks.com

Printed in Great Britain
by Amazon

10545719R00195